Praise for James

BIRMINGHAM, 35 MILES

"Poetic, grim and hallucinatory, this harrowing work is not for the faint of heart, though it will appeal strongly to anyone who loved Cormac McCarthy's *The Road*."

—*Publishers Weekly*

"*Birmingham, 35 Miles* is just the novel we need in these scary times. Devastating, full of hard truths, but also beautifully written, deeply felt, and full of hope. I couldn't put it down."

—Brock Clarke, author of *An Arsonist's Guide to Writers' Homes in New England*

"*Birmingham, 35 Miles* is part tender and gritty blue-collar family drama, part environmental dystopia novel. Braziel provides an allusive catalog of the last century of Southern literature, invoking everything from Faulkner's *As I Lay Dying* to Walker Percy in his postapocalyptic mode to—most powerfully—a terrifying literalization of the old Agrarian ideals of home and soil. Braziel's characters are so attached to the land and each other that they're willing to stay even as prisoners, miners who literally scrape a living out of the clay by night and hide from the brutal sun by day. Smart and subtle—this is a chilling, promising debut."

—Michael Griffith, author of *Spikes: A Novel* and *Bibliophilia: A Novella and Stories*

"I welcome James Braziel's debut novel as an extraordinarily lyrical and innovative work. It is both a speculative novel about the brutal consequences of global warming and a traditional work that memorializes the landscapes and relationships of the rural South. Most of all, it is a rumination on love and survival that is visionary and inspiring."

—Anthony Grooms, author of *Trouble No More: Stories* and *Bombingham: A Novel*

BIRMINGHAM, 35 MILES

JAMES BRAZIEL

BANTAM BOOKS

BIRMINGHAM, 35 MILES
A Bantam Book / March 2008

Published by
Bantam Dell
A Division of Random House, Inc.
New York, New York

Book design by Donna Mugavero

Pages 291–92 serve as an extension of this copyright page.

Bantam Books and the rooster colophon are registered trademarks of Random House, Inc.

Library of Congress Cataloging-in-Publication Data
Braziel, James.
Birmingham, 35 miles / James Braziel.
p. cm.
ISBN-13: 978-0-553-38502-1 (trade pbk.)
1. Climatic changes—Fiction. 2. Desertification—Fiction.
3. Regression (Civilization)—Fiction. 4. Place attachment—
Fiction. 5. Alabama—Fiction.
I. Title: Birmingham, thirty-five miles. II. Title.
PS3602.R398B57 2008
813'.6—dc22
2007036280

Printed in the United States of America
Published simultaneously in Canada

www.bantamdell.com

BVG   10 9 8 7 6 5 4 3 2 1

For Ray

Acknowledgments

Thank you, Jana, for your caring, your persistence, and your enduring love. Thank you, Jessi, Maddie, and Dylan, who inspire me every day. My parents, Barbara Braziel and Dr. Delano Braziel—you are wonderful. Ron and Judy Evans for your caring. Tony Grooms—the best teacher, a great friend. Richard Messer, Larry Brown, Phil O'Connor, Michael Mott, Coleman Barks, Howard McCord, and Robert Early for your guidance. Amy Stout—no author could ask for a better advocate. My editor, Joshua Pasternak, who steered this project with great ideas and enthusiasm. Jay Twomey, Michael Griffith, and Brock Clarke for your friendship. My siblings Marti, Leslie, and Del, who still manage to put up with me. I come from a family of wonderful aunts: Auerila, Lorraine, Essie Mae, Anna, Lenoire, and, of course, Ruby. The staff at the Clifton branch of the Cincinnati Public Library: Jenny Gomien, Don Baker, Eric Davis, and Betsy Black, who have answered every query. Charlene Thompson, Stan Corkin, and Amanda Smith for your help. Raymond Wiggins, Raymond Andrews, and Lisa Lentile—you are still missed.

BIRMINGHAM, 35 MILES

June 21, 2044

Dear Mat,

I dream more now—all night, the sand and wind. It tears, gnaws slowly at my arms and ankles, my neck, whatever I can't bury under clothes and sheets. I'm never certain if I'm simply dreaming. When I wake up there's still that sound as if the hollowness in my stomach has been turned inside out; that grit on my tongue as if all day the sand tried to choke me. Of course, I'm not telling you anything you don't know or haven't felt yourself, Mathew. The desert has a way of making all of us parched and empty, less and less of who we are.

Remember when we married and you said you would go with me anywhere? I've tried to get you to leave Alabama like your father tried to get you to leave. But you won't. And since you've stopped talking, I feel myself being pulled into the desert, its senselessness, where I find you and can't pull you out.

I want you to know that I've stayed here as long as I have because I love you. But love can't heal everything, can it? Love doesn't make you secure, make you any less empty. Love doesn't make people move. Not your love. Since your father's death, you've become as lost as the desert sands blowing through my dreams. I wonder, when will you come home to me? When will you come to me?

I want you to come to Chicago, and if I could, I would force you to. I would put you on the bus, force you to turn and turn until I had made you responsive again, so you could make me whole again. Maybe my wanting, my wishing, is selfish, but it's real.

Last week after your birthday when I asked you to dance, when I grabbed your hand and we started into step like your father did with your mother—the two of us in the kitchen where I always dance alone after sup-per—we stepped but only a small distance, not even a full circle before you let go. And you wouldn't tell, you didn't explain why, as if the wind had taken your voice finally, completely.

Mat, each time I've tried to get you to talk, you've closed yourself off, and I can't wander outside of you, your body, your thoughts anymore. Right now, the only thing left to me is the desert and all of its ghosts, the ones that are yours mixed with my own two fathers who died mining—I've tried to tell you these things, I've tried to bring you closer.

Abandoning someone you love is too full a sadness. The body crumbles as if you've abandoned the most important part of yourself. My mother wrote that in one of her letters after Terry's death, after she left for Chicago. *But I don't want to die, Mathew. Which also makes me selfish, I know. I don't want you to be alone either, but I can't keep going in this nothingness.*

Every moment now I ask myself, and when I'm finally on the bus, even when I'm in Chicago, I'll still ask, why couldn't I convince you, Mat? Why couldn't I pull you away? There are too many ghosts here already. So why won't you come along with me? When will you come along?

CHAPTER 1

Fatama, Alabama, June 2044

Working on fence posts was my grandfather's work, my father's work for some time, until the winds and sand came in from the coast, and the sky opened up a wound over southern Alabama, Georgia, and Florida, a blinding eye swirling, burning until everything in the Deep South became too dry. No crops would take, and then my father became a clay miner who told me, "Clay rocks are good for nothing but the money. And there's not much of that, Mathew, except for the government, what they're willing to give to keep us here." But money or no money, my father would have stayed and died just as he did.

When I think of him, I see him standing, the stance of an old dancer, his chubby hands positioned as if ready to go into step—one, two, swirl and swirl. My Uncle Wayne called him a graceful pig because my father was not so tall, though he learned the routines perfect. When I think of him, he spins me across a field he's talked about—green with a ceiling of blue and thick-shouldered clouds I've never known. All I've held is this desert Alabama wasteland. My father takes me round and round, lets me go, lets me fly.

Working on fence posts was my grandfather's work. He put up fences for anybody in Coffee County and counties around. "Ten dollars for every six feet of post," my father told me, some still hanging on, the barbed wire torn and twisted on itself, snapping in the wind like lion tamer whips that come howling. It was my father's work, my uncle's work for some time.

But then the earth turned crazy, and the ozone opened up like a wound, giving the sun permission to burn off every field, devour even the trees—oaks, swamp cypress, and pines that had survived for years with roots clear to the ocean, down to the red-hot core—the sun scorched out that preserved life, splintered branches and trunks into bone, "And it was finished," my father said. "Every town in a panic after years of drought and heat, the government saying to stay calm. The earth let go of itself. The wind pushed the black grit on top of us and pushed, and when it stopped, people fled to Birmingham, Atlanta, and further north—" The Saved World, we call it, too crowded even before we arrived, so the government sent in the national guard to keep us back. What followed—heavy rains in winter, parching droughts in summer. Nothing will germinate, will take root, all of our food brought in from the Saved World so we won't starve.

A string of checkpoints now stands north of the desert, just south of Birmingham and Atlanta, stretching to the Mississippi. This is a marshaled land, a separate land, disappearing as quick as my father's dance steps in the kitchen. But with enough money you can purchase a visa, emigrate, ask for asylum at least and hope the government will grant it. We just choose to stay, they tell us—our community of miners pocketed along the rivers, our existence a contradiction of mud and snakish water engulfed in all this blowing sand. I work the Tensaw and Alabama and Coosa like my father, my uncle. River people, river trash, clay miners, no one's people. We start in Mobile after the spring floods and chase the dwindling channels north, pumping water to the sites where we dig and dig for clay rocks, "For nothing," my father assured me.

There is other mining in the Deep South—mining for real things like limestone and kaolin, granite, coal—what the Saved World can't afford to lose. But us, we dig to keep ourselves here, to keep busy until death, living in a time warp of old things—trucks from the turn of the century; fire hoses bursting along the skin; scratched-up tools, clothes, and dishware that have already seen one life. We string all of it together, packing and unpacking each item as we move along the river to keep us human.

It was thirty years ago, 2014, 15, when the winds changed direction for good, the sky opened up and killed out the life here. Thirty years since everyone tried to escape the dust storms and couldn't. Thirty years since I was born and my mother hemorrhaged. Thirty years of emptying ponds and lakes for clay rocks at Dothan and Sumner's Hill, then following the shrinking and swelling of the Alabama and Coosa until the dust and dirt now live in our beds when we sleep. There is no escaping, no damming the sky. Scientists have tried tricks. Politicians have made promises, all of them afraid that the wound will eventually open more. I've uncovered their fear in my dreams—the belly of the sun growing hungry, fire coming down as I take a mining rope tight, climb and climb, clinch the rope with one hand, trying to seal the sky with the other, slip its skin back together until the sun has had enough and burns through me, through us all. "And what will matter then?" I had asked my father. "What will happen to us then?" But he wouldn't answer.

Four months ago, in February, the very center of our winter, we came to a sign that read *Birmingham, 35 Miles*. A little further stood the junk and waste of a landfill, its red crossbones posted in sand with the Saved World's beautiful green just beyond, just out of range in those ridges of chert and sandstone.

Birmingham burned into that rusted sign—all we had read about in school, had talked about on our work breaks—the Saved World was now tangible. We felt it most in the cool shafts, our hands mudded with rocks and water, tearing out clay, thinking we could dig that 35 miles under the checkpoints on our own. We could taste it in our food, and dream it so clearly in our dreams: blue sky, full, wet grass, running and breathing, an authentic life.

Some miners defected by the second evening. The rest of us counted bodies, wondering who would be missing tomorrow. We wondered if they would make it or be caught by the patrol squads, labeled deserters, brought back, and imprisoned. And after hours of digging closer to Birmingham, I pulled myself from a mining shaft and found my father plunked down on a bucket, all the grace of his dancing subdued under layers of red clay.

I told him, "Maybe now, maybe now I'll go. Take Jennifer. But will you come with us?" For years my father had tried to convince me to leave the desert.

"I want you to," he said, his voice fading, his body hunched over. "But I can't leave where your mother is, my father, Wayne, the farm—"

"All dead," I tried to convince him. "All swallowed up in sand."

"I know," he said quietly, and his eyes, those flecks of blue I had watched and watched and waited on, those eyes focused on a hung lantern behind me, black smoke swaying up, splitting the curl and fall of wind as if this was the place to travel, this was where you became the pure black nothingness over the light, escaped the desert, or at least yourself.

My father tangled his fingers through his silver beard, short like the end of a barber's brush, then roughed the wet clay deeper into his swollen face. He kept silent, and I left him, went home to Jennifer, telling her nothing of what my father and I had said.

That morning he didn't come home. He stayed at someone else's house, someone else's trailer—surely that's what he did. But in the evening, I found him asleep in his truck, his body crumpled and dirty. "Get up," I told him. "Get up."

We had made it to the gates of Birmingham like Moses overlooking his promised land after years of wandering and searching, like an army ready to enter. Then spring came in March and the rivers flooded; we were forced back to Mobile to begin again, the roads we had dwindled along— Highways 32, 28—washed and broken, the holes we had dug from the year before already full with sand and mud, disappeared. And on the way to Mobile, my father died.

I keep thinking of that sign and the landfill as I pull my rubber trousers up—waders, fly fishermen call them up north. Here, they're for survival, protection in the mining holes. The trousers are flexible like a fish body, a mer- maid's fin slipping from my hands, slapping coolly at my legs. The June sun has been down since 9:00. It's almost 11:00. I have to be at work by 11:00, but I can't get myself going, and I don't care about the hurry of minutes, the rou- tine, the constant fall and push of wind beating on the trailer's body.

Tonight it's the landfill outside Birmingham I keep

thinking of, the steel beams that pointed fingers at us when we first arrived. Someone spotted a yellow-white dog, its carcass hung on a beam, spinning round and round until its yanked arm tightened and the animal spun in reverse, only to coil tighter. The skin and hair on its muzzle were singed black, exposing a flash of white teeth. The ribs had bowled out, a long tunnel, bottomless where the guts had fallen. And when I first saw it, I wondered whose mutt it was, who brought it here? Had the dog always been fierce and angry? Leathered and broken? Surely someone had once fed it and offered kindness.

The longer we watched, the more the junk seemed to rise and twist into something useless, waiting until dusk to be remade into something else. That's when the plastic bags and wires breathed like a single body, a dragon's head with the yellow dog's muzzle ready to lurch forward into our camp and gobble us into its rust.

In front stood the Birmingham sign—35 *miles*—and I had asked my father, "Will you come?"

He didn't answer. He just stared at the lantern's flame shooting up through the black behind me, the wind driving north dusting our mudded clothes with sand.

As I reach over to smother the flame, the lantern isn't here anymore—it's just another dream.

"Focus on your work," I tell myself, and loop the heavy suspenders across my shoulders. I grab my hard hat, check the switch. The light flickers and fails, red clay shimmering on metal like diamonds.

When my father came home from work, that same clay used to glitter on his skin, his body half-asleep, but his hands, his face alive with mica. And later when he danced in the kitchen, I stood at my bedroom door with a sliver of light, enough to watch him step around the table, hold the air as if it were my mother.

I've already had breakfast. There's only one thing left

to do, and still I'm hesitating. I glance at my watch again, the pointer clicks one-two, one-two like Father's steps, their slide across a kitchen floor when I was ten and eleven and supposed to be sleeping. In the watch's face, I notice my reflection: high cheekbones from Mamma's side, our brown summer skin, my forehead broken at the center, two broad plates descended from my father, his eyes and my eyes holding up the same ridge of eyebrow and bone. In winter, as his red skin turns pale, mine does the same, holding the same flash of sulfur. And in the reflection, his face now, the curve of his arm building and swaying where I've locked his ghost out.

Shutting my eyes doesn't help. Making fists and threats is no good either. You have to wait, so I wait until the eggs and coffee come up in my throat mixed into vinegar — a taste that is strong enough to overcome my father, his spirit.

"Get out of here," I choke, saying the words that my father used to say, an edge to his voice. I dry my lips, and the trailer's narrow hallway stares at me openmouthed, waiting.

A strong gust ambushes the tin walls, hits them so hard that surely the center of the earth has boiled up and spilled over Alabama for good.

"Out of here." The wind trails off with Father's warning, but there's one thing left to do. I put down my hat and slowly walk through the hallway.

Our trailer is tiny, just two bedrooms, a bathroom, a living room, and a kitchen, all paneled in dark wood that the heat has buckled in waves. But the trailer's roof and siding are bolted down strong, have weathered these years well in Fatama. As we follow the Alabama River northeast from Mobile, we use the houses and trailers people left behind when they fled for the Saved World thirty years ago. It's quite a spectacle to see all of us pull up in our battered

trucks and equipment—Blacksher, Eliska, Sardis, and
Fatama, those signs rusting on highway posts. We step out
like carnival workers, like thieves in a ghost town searching
for someplace decent. Because we have to use generators,
we can't take on a big house—just something small, something big enough to squeeze inside, to make meals and
light. And we have to be cautious, be ready for when a dust
storm comes on sudden, or a hurricane, or a rare lightning
storm shaking the sky loose with steaming water. It's important to inspect roofs and ceilings for damage, to push and
kick on the walls, make sure there aren't too many windows the sun can creep through, and especially take note
of how much sand has already sifted through the floors. It
took us all night to find this trailer two streets over from
Main.

"Efficient," Jennifer called it.

"Tiny," I said. I can walk the hallway in less than ten
steps, and I'm trying to walk slow, but I reach the bedroom
sooner than I want. I lean close to Jennifer, her perfume,
the smell of greasy food, noodles with mandarin sauce that
she likes, sweat that has dried into the sheets. Her shoulders sink down with my touch. My hands are freezing.
Carefully, I draw them down her back, press against the
small blades, hoping they will open like butterflies, monarchs my father told me about, yellow and black, speckled,
mustard and orange, told me how, when he was young, he
pinched the shuttered wings as they slanted in and out of
his father's purple and pink azaleas, nervously trying to
escape.

But instead of opening, Jennifer's blades tense. In one
move she turns, wrapping around my neck and pulling me
to the beige nightgown her mother sent, the perfume
mixed with sweat, the warmness of the bed, as if she knows
exactly where I am, as if she has kissed me good-bye this
way many times. Most evenings, she continues to sleep,

her shoulder blades concealing her body underneath the air conditioner barking cold and loud. And for a moment our bodies seesaw on the mattress. Maybe I will fall or she will rise enough to pin me. There is even a smile before our bodies balance into familiar shape, the stiffness in our arms returning.

"I see your father in you," she whispers. "You're thinking of him, again, just like your uncle's blue diamond." Her voice is sad, and the thick fall of black hair is tangled now. I follow the wrinkles, the long sweep under her eyes—I look harder at her face for something I knew before the sand swept in and covered us, but no matter where I turn, I see the imprint of what she's discovered and told me is true.

"It's the work," I promise. "I'm late as it is." I raise my watch as an alibi, linger over the numbers, the one hand twitching.

She shrugs. "No, it's not your work." Since my father's death, she swears she can see him in me, tells me this, her face certain for a moment—Jennifer's trust in herself has always been strong—then hazy, more and more puzzled that I can't see it, that I won't admit it.

"You don't have to go anywhere," and there's faith in her voice that she can draw me closer, that she can get me to turn. Jennifer traces the ridge above my eyebrows with her finger.

"I have to work, you know that."

"You don't have to—" she says, but stops when I pull away to rub out the sand that has fallen in my eyes.

Jennifer nods, sets her jaw firm, and rolls over, her face turned from me. Her black hair wraps around a pillow.

The wall clock reads eleven. My watch says even later. We're in the longest part of summer. In winter, work starts as early as six. One-two, one-two, my father's feet slide across the kitchen floor, and none of his timing or this time, these clocks, these hours, none of it matters. I'm aware of that.

"I'll be home," I tell her again softly, almost kiss her black hair, the grassy smell of it when it hasn't been washed for days.

"You're lying," she says into the pillow.

Get out of here. Come on now, son, my father's voice tells me, and I pull my arms loose. But when I reach the doorway, her body shifts.

"The bus leaves at 2:30, Mathew. I want you to come with me. Please, come with me to Chicago," and her voice is no longer dreamy or accusing—it builds and falls through mandarin, skin, and dust—all of it at one time something of mine, recognizable, overtaking me, sweeping to the other end of the hall out of reach.

"I want to—" But I stop there.

"Not enough," she says, and I don't return to the bed.

She is completely awake now, staring at the outside light as if it is my uncle's blue diamond, the one he searched for in the mining holes, the one he promised existed, a honeydew melon from Tina's grocery to be pulled down and opened.

She says nothing else, and I slide through the hallway, out the front door to work. I slip in the keys, crank the truck. I watch the window of the trailer. Jennifer is still sitting, all shadow, focused on the light.

CHAPTER 2

For Queen and Country, 2024

This is a weather report from WDMZ. High today 115°.
Do not go out in the sun. High levels of UV are dangerous. Ozone index at 200: CODE RED. Winds at 30 miles
per hour. Blowing sand: visibility 25 feet. Clearing some
this evening. Do not go out in the sun. Repeat: CODE
RED. Travel restricted. Listen to this station for further
updates.

—*WDMZ 1610 AM , 10:05 a.m.*

My father expected, demanded that when I graduated
high school I would leave the Southeastern Desert for the
Saved World. Though when he talked of the Saved World
it was always with skepticism, a hatred mixed with possibility. The Saved World was never easy for my father—it still
held greenness and blueness "in places," he said, rain you
could hold in your hand without it burning, a sense of his
past, but it was also kept separate from us and he blamed
the Saved World for all that had gone wrong here.

"They made choices. The same ones still, to pull everything out of the earth, use up every last mineral, every last
coal, every last reserve until nothing's left. You think the
skies in the Saved World are beautiful? Like what they tell
you in school? They're brown gunk," he insisted when I was
seven, when I was ten, twelve. Our sky is a hot white haze

fallen to the earth, dust that swells your tongue. "Nothing is fresh there."

And nothing is fresh here, I wanted to tell him.

"How do you know?" is what I said. The images of the Saved World, what was sent down to the schools, carried backdrops of blue sky and lazy, harmless clouds, plenty of air to breathe. Any pollution was managed by smoke sewers and scrubbers and the technology was building, building every day, mending, overtaking and reversing nature.

"I know," he said. "Before you were born they built domed communities. Before that they built gated communities to keep out unwanted people, and then domed communities to keep out whatever the air might bring. A cancer-free life, asthma-free, no pollution, no terrorism. You could be completely filtered if you had the money, stuck inside a dome. You call that freedom?" I shook my head and my father wiped at the clay in his beard, stared off from me. "That's what they do—lock themselves in, shut everything out like they've shut us out." But my father's vision of the Saved World remained stuck in 2014, the years before that, what he remembered and conjured must have evolved. The truth was, no one had seen the Saved World since the checkpoints and the desert border had been established soon after I was born, no one except the government workers stationed with the camp for months at a time, the patrol squads and doctors and my friend Ray when he became a liaison with Birmingham. But none of them said anything different from what the teachers had told us in school.

"They made choices," my father said. "Nothing is fresh in the cities. I know that world. I know what that world is like." He said it with absoluteness, with no possibility for contradiction. But he always added, "If you get out from the cities, you'll find blue skies in some places," and that was when his eyes shifted and managed to turn slowly the air in front of him, coil and coil the light, the walls, the whole desert itself as if he could see through the dust something possible, tangible, what could be seen shifting with what was unseen, tangling and coiling together until that turning splintered inside my body. "They have to grow food. They haven't managed to put all that under a tent or in a cave. When you get there, find those places," he said, and "Yes, sir," I answered, and nodded. But mostly when my father talked of the Saved World it was pollution and too many people stuck under domes like turtles, and only a glimmer of blue.

The North, the West, and the Newer South: that's how my father divided the Saved World. In the North, my father said, the first American Constitution had been written over four hundred years ago. It held the most people, the largest concentration of cities. The West was the frontier, and when the frontier vanished at the Pacific, they created movies in California so that new frontiers could be invented forever. Just above us was the Newer South, which at one time had been known as the New South and before that the Old South, a history that we were also a part of. As my father explained it, the Old South was about slavery and cotton plantations, and eventually tried to secede from the industrial North in the 1860s but failed. The New South was about progress and trying to distance itself from its Old South image.

"The Newer South has one goal," my father claimed, "to distance itself from us, from this wasteland," and when I asked him why they called it the Newer South, he said it was because they were running out of adjectives. "They have to be prepared for what might happen next, what else they might lose." He told me that even though the industrial revolution in this country had started in the North, industries had spread all over, and he often pointed to paper mills and rusted-out factories as we migrated along the rivers, but he never placed blame here, never admitted that possibly we had helped make ourselves into a desert. "We don't have control over our lives any longer," is what he said. "The Saved World has that now." For my father this was unforgivable. I was unsure what to believe.

Still, he wanted me to go there, to see that flawed world because he was convinced it was better than this one. "You have to understand its motives, what it expects, what to avoid. You have to be smart in how you enter." That was my father's labor, more than the mining, to make sure I was ready to emigrate. "The desert schools won't give you enough." He was convinced of that, too, so by the time I was ten and could read what my father referred to as enlightened books, his books, he mandated reading hours for us—7:30 in the morning, after school, and on week-ends from 8:00 until 11:00 in the evenings, and even some-times at 2:00 a.m., and sometimes 5:00 a.m., depending on whether my uncle came over and how tired my father was. He especially made me read about history, said it was im-portant for survival, knowing how civilizations had be-come extinct, what had been their mistakes. I liked the wars most—all that death and destruction so sudden. I skipped through the famines and blights and political wranglings, those lingering deaths, just to get to the wars.

Unlike plays and novels, the history books overflowed with pictures of armed men, their mouths open in a loud, bloodcurdling cry as they charged toward the edge of the page, toward me; I wondered if these men had made it through enemy lines, had survived countless attacks: nerve gas in World War I, blitzkrieg in World War II, lances and tomahawks, the Red Baron and spears and single-shot rifles from forts and sand dunes in northern Africa where the English had fought for Queen and Country, each uniform, each man blurring into the same man, in the same trajec-tory, the same line of fire. One day while reading, I burst out, "For Queen and Country!" my father beside me on the couch still smelling of diesel and mud—smells I liked and wanted close to me as much as I wanted my father close.

"What a joke," he said, looking up from his book on religions of the world. He ran a finger, the pinpoint of his squinting eye, along the passages in my book until he found the line I had just declared so vigorously.

I wished we had Queen and Country to die for instead of a desert to waste in, but I didn't dare tell my father this. He knew anyway because I didn't say, *Yes, sir.* I said nothing and that was the signal.

"We could have another war tomorrow," he quipped. "They might come down and draft us." He said *draft us* as if it was the most horrible thing on the planet, his head swooning close to mine, a clear warning to me. And his breath swept over me, sweet and acidic from the ice cream he always ate after breakfast. I imagined that his breath was some sort of nerve gas, and I was immune.

"I'm too young for the draft," I pointed out.

My father pulled back and rubbed more silver and red into his wiry beard. "Well, you never know what this country might do. How would you feel if you lived in north Africa, if you were the one being invaded? You never know what this country might do."

"Why do you hate it so much?" I asked him, expecting to hear about domes, again, the bruised atmosphere. I waited for the cadence of pollution and capitalism and martial law, the end of the earth to lull me into a familiar lifeless dream, but while I waited, I kept thinking of my father in a crisp marine uniform with white hat and gloves, decorated with honors, something more dignified than his mining clothes. In his hand, he brandished a sword—*brandished* was a word I had to look up—and that was all he needed to destroy his enemy.

"I don't hate this country," he said, but stopped, his jaw clenched. He rubbed his hands uncomfortably into his jeans, the fabric scrubbing against him like a washboard, and he exhaled slowly, a sound like that of air being let go from a tire. "Well, I do hate it a little bit. A little less now than when you were born."

"Because of Mamma," I said.

"Yes," he said. Maybe we wouldn't talk about domes after all.

"What happened to Mamma?"

And that was the one question that ended all of our conversations fast.

"Back to your reading," my father insisted, the fight no longer in him, and he left the couch where we had been sitting. He pretended to go into the kitchen for a glass of water and when he returned he sat in the rocking chair, an antique from his father's house that I knew was uncomfortable. He stayed put there, playing a Sarah Vaughan record, his eyes slotted open only to the book in his lap, too far for me to reach with my legs, keeping his distance for the rest of the evening.

Meanwhile at school I earned the nickname Mathew Daydreamer. I snuck in my war books to read while the teachers taught, snuck in pieces of clay from my father's face, and sat in my desk rubbing the clay into shape, reading word after word, sinking into my own world until eventually I fell asleep.

Everything around us was sand, except for the mining digs which were clay and muck and the lakes and rivers that flooded and dried. There were dead trees and sand, always sand, even the school buildings had been built dull yellow or white years ago as if the people before us knew what was coming. But in the history books, in the videos the teachers sometimes showed, in the atlases, the Internet, in every room at school, the desert was kept back with pictures of the Saved World. It was the one place where you became aware of vibrant cities, of greenery, of blue skies, of color—the places we couldn't step into, each room decorated like kaleidoscopes—what could be, if we lived somewhere, anywhere else. They were sanctuaries, even if my father said most of them no longer existed.

But the truth was, I had actually stepped into some of these places—I had walked through green grass, my feet cold and damp. I had touched crops of peanuts and corn, the scent of shucked corn silk on my hands, had seen the blue sky for real, though I could tell no one this. Who would believe me? Daydreamer, Daydreamer, Mathew.

One day, I slipped up.

Ms. Jones was talking about the Great Plains and how the farmers produced wheat and corn.

"Can someone tell me about corn?" Ms. Jones asked.

"Mathew," she said, calling loud enough that the boy one desk behind, a skinny boy with too many bones in his hands, slugged me in the back to wake me.

"Yes, ma'am?" I responded with as much obliging respect as I could muster, my head still dizzy, the room smelling of glue and pens, which didn't help.

"Tell us about corn."

"It's sweet," I said, "with butter."

Some of the kids giggled.

"Of course," Ms. Jones indulged, effectively cutting them off. Ms. Jones was never mean. When she smiled, which she often did, the corners of her lips and eyes curled upward toward the gray-streaked ponytail at the peak of her head. It made her look like a spinning top fallen upside down, waiting to be picked up and gently turned. "Corn does taste good, but what about the actual corn plant itself?"

"Well, it's a tall stalk," I said. She nodded, her smile

widening, the river of wrinkles defying gravity, shooting up, up.

Encouraged, I went on. "And it's planted in long rows, hundreds of acres sometimes, and they grow like they want to reach the sun, that tall, and if you listen, you'll hear it, if you listen, there's a noise rustling through the leaves like electricity. The leaves bend like water fountains and rattle against one another, and if you want to, you can run through it and make the corn rattle just like the wind and when you get out, if you get out—those rows are long— you'll be itchy all over. You'll be scratching yourself. But it's worth it."

"Have you ever been in a cornfield?" my teacher asked.

"No," I said, breathless, and realized that the other students were looking at me like I was crazy.

"But I know I'm right," I protested, my back straightening, each nerve daring me to stand.

"You are right," Ms. Jones said. She was delighted. "I don't know where you read that, but you are right. I used to run through cornfields just as you said. Itch all afternoon." Her lips scrunched up showing her white teeth when she said *itch*. "It was fun." After a pause and a deep breath of her own, she added, "Thank you."

I smiled and slouched back in my seat.

But I hadn't read it—and my father hadn't told me— but I knew. I did know.

I had run through the corn in my dreams, had woken up itching, had found the Saved World. Some dreams made me wish I could sleep and not see the desert any- more. I wouldn't leave my desk, even if the class bell rang and rang, even if I got slugged. Other dreams came to me over and over, a riddle in them I couldn't quite under- stand. Since I couldn't answer their riddles, they wouldn't go away, and it frightened me that all of my dreams could be so real.

CHAPTER 3

The Dreams

When I was young, a boy in a passenger seat carrying two lunch pails, the dreams began and kept coming back. They happened on the way to school, or in class, or in the morning hours, when school was over, when the sun started to blister everything. Breakfast had been eaten, eggs and grits, and I always slept heavy through the day. Five, maybe six dreams returned again and again—I cannot remember them all now. They mix and break apart on my way to work. But I don't know if I truly dreamed or if I only heard my father talk to himself and dance in the kitchen, his movement, those sounds playing over and over in my head.

The first dream, the one I call the first dream, was of the fields, the fields I had never held, the ones my father said he and Uncle Wayne had worked.

There was barbed wire, just as Father had said. And

plants in rows in black dirt, black like Sumner's Hill, like night. And rain—soft rains, not just storms. And white clouds. In the dream, real clouds jigsawed between each other, opening like bread pulled apart, then reversing, swallowing up larger and larger white pan-fish clouds, closing up the blue river mouth of the sky.

The scene stayed put for a long time, a still picture, then the earth started rolling like a map uncoiled from a tube, showing me green leaves, peanut bushes, and the smell of pine, peanuts, everything wet. The winds were not strong—just lulls, and there was no sand except for a white dusting mixed with the black dirt.

In the field stood a John Deere tractor like the one Father had kept, that had been Grandpa Sanford's—only this one was new, not "a piece of junk" as Daddy called ours, our tractor moving with us until it gave out completely. In the dream, in the center of the field, the tractor had stopped but still shook loud like river water, and in the driver's seat, a man sat.

I called him Grandpa Sanford and didn't know who he was except for the white-blond hair and blue eyes he had like my father—the Scandinavian blood we had in us, that was strong in everyone's appearance but mine. Grandpa Sanford didn't speak or seem to be looking anyplace. He just sat, his hands relaxed at his sides as if asleep. Or as if he had been shot. I couldn't tell. But he was comfortable, and the still picture kept rolling past him so I couldn't see if he was bleeding—rolling further and further down the rows until the tractor and the man were not there, and suddenly in front, a dust storm began to twitch and in one huge avalanche, the storm swept down, turning all the green to sand.

CHAPTER 4

Fatama, June 2044

It's been three months since my father's death, but still
I look over, expecting him in the passenger seat, eyes shut,
mouth fallen open. He slept that way to work in December
and February, his body so tired I had to slam the door or roll
the windows down to wake him. It's been three months, and
yet I expect him here just as Jennifer says, just as she has
seen, and I've told her she is wrong.

She's at the trailer, waiting for me, but I'm only one
mile along Highway 28 and already I spot the ground lights
for the new dig.

"The new site, Father." I point, whisper as if his body is
slumped over and ready to snore. A whistle huffs from the
top of the window on the passenger side. One end of the
glass has sagged from overuse and never closes fully.

When I look down at the seat a second time, instead of
my father, I see a small boy, his body wrapped in the truck

belt, his own leather belt too big for him. His hair, a dirty-brown, rough, and splintered, has been cut at home with dull scissors that pulled the hair more than cut it, and small strands jag way below his ears. He has a few freckles, a mole bolted right in his neck holding it all together. He stares at the dash, two lunch pails in his lap, acting as if he wants to say something, wants to breathe. He's got something bottled in—I can see that in his eyes. He has such dark eyes, brown like Jennifer, like his mother. They draw in every mile of the darkness that eats up the flat land.

"You learn something at school," I order him like my father ordered me.

Still, gently, he reaches up, presses a kiss, places a black pail in my lap.

"See you, Father," he says. "Mamma," he giggles, and whatever was bottled up is gone. His breath smells of eggs and milk as he digs out the clay I can never wash completely from my face. He rolls a small piece into a ball, then a worm, then flat between his fingers. He'll keep it with him all night at school, rolling the clay while learning in class. His learning is what keeps me moving through the tunnels, pushing away mud, sand, the rotting roots and soil. Already I have special permissions, a visa I've purchased and kept in a small pine box so he can travel past the Birmingham checkpoints. He'll graduate, go to college or at least find a different job in the Saved World. One day, he'll be able to leave.

"I love you." I kiss him twice and push at him slightly. He disappears through the whistle at the top of the window.

Suddenly, the whistle goes from a huff to a kettle boil, becomes sharper, flashing the road into a blur. Just as quick the highway becomes full again, sand sweeping against the windshield like a body breaking on glass.

The truck shudders, and I clutch the wheel and brake so hard that the engine stops.

"What're you doing?" I rub my eyes. "Stop it. Keep your eyes on the damn road!" My voice is gruff like my father's and my face burns as my vision brightens and dims, dims and brightens until it fixes. The seat is empty. The boy—he, too, is just another dream.

"Nothing's wrong with you. You're fine." I feel silly for talking out loud, and my face burns more. "Nothing's wrong with you." But every night I hallucinate. Every night these ghosts become more intense, fill the empty spaces in the cab. Sometimes I see the boy holding on to my father. Sometimes I see my father sleeping and know that if I tap his shoulder, touch the clay in his beard, he will wake and begin to talk, so I leave him alone, afraid of what he will tell me, afraid that he will die again.

The sign to Birmingham, the dried-out dog wheeling back and forth in the scrap heap—they come looking for me, too, flashing teeth and metal, warning that the distance, the 35 miles from Birmingham, the 200 from Fatama, any distance I reach for, try to cover with sand and rock is too great. Just like when I was sixteen and first came to work in mining, when I was twelve and learned about my mother's death, Daydreamer Mathew, when I was twenty-one, twenty-seven—

"Stop it." I shake my head, and the years jostle until they slip away, but it's only temporary.

I find the work lights of the Millers Ferry dig and start the engine up again. For a second I think of Jennifer sitting on her bed, watching the blue light. At 2:30 she'll be on the bus to Chicago. I could turn around now. I could go with her, and maybe in the Saved World, maybe these hallucinations will stop. I don't look at the passenger side.

There's no time for these ghosts, but as the truck gathers speed, I manage a smile. The child's kiss has secured me, that ghost kiss has given me warmth, something of myself, of who I remember I was.

The ground lights trap a sweep of dust. It swirls and swirls furtively higher and higher like the long throat of a snake twisting and splitting open in the sky. I reach over to the window, run my finger across the whistle—back and forth, whistle, forth—but the boy is gone.

CHAPTER 5

Sumner's Hill, 2030

WARNING: Restricted Area
Mining Operations
Camp 132
Lock and Dam Night Operations Only
No Admittance Except Authorized Personnel Only

—Sign posted at mining site, September 12, 2030

At sixteen, I drove past my school in Red Hill, everyone already hushed inside, no one to stop me from going to the mining camp at Lake Martin. Before the rivers became our only source of water, we traveled through Alabama emptying all the ponds and lakes. We had been stationed at Lake Martin for over a year and the last of the springs were finally beginning to run dry.

I checked the floorboard more than once to make sure I had on my boots and not my tennis shoes—the boots were a heavy brown pair that had been too big for my father. I had laced them to the last hole tight, rolled the cuff of my best jeans down, and tucked my whitest T-shirt in. I was ready.

About a mile from the lake, the wind almost knocked me off the road into a ditch, but I sped up, slipped away from its whirl and warning—the wind wasn't going to stop me either, and a few minutes later I cleared Sumner's Hill—a mound of black dirt that hadn't given in to the weather. My father joked that night started at Sumner's Hill, that as soon as the sun went down behind it, the black dirt rose up and swept everything in Alabama into night. He said that if you wandered in its howl long enough and breathed without a rag to your face you would choke to death on the dust. When they cut you open, they would find your lungs and throat full of the black dirt of Sumner's Hill, full of night, of Alabama, and not the coarse sand that had managed to migrate here from those bastard western states.

On the other side, the grade sharpened, sinking and sinking and drowning you into the middle of the earth. If the wind had a mind to it and enough of a strong back, you would be sent tumbling and tumbling to the lights, the devil's lights I called them, waiting at the bottom.

Since the government had restricted work during the day, all mining had to be done in the evening and early morning. The devil lights anchored the mining dig in a wide stadium circle from towers bolted to the backs of diesel trucks, guiding the workers like huge eyes toward a ring of equipment—irrigation lines and engines, slush pipes, and finally rope pulleys for the bags of rocks. The pulleys dangled over each of the five hundred mining holes—which just a few years ago had been six hundred— twenty to sixty feet deep littering the dust field, jostling up and down like miniature oil rigs while the hoses and pipes snaked inside and took root.

The caretakers drove the huge ore carts from the mining craters past the only other sign of life: the flags stabbed along the edges of the holes, black numbers on crimson cloth. I spotted 21, 18, 133. My father's number was 40, and after a while, I found it, too, opposite of where I had parked. The monotonous creak of the pulleys reassured me that he was trapped inside. But I didn't trust it, couldn't shake the image of him impatiently waiting to catch me — my father contained an unfair dose of intuition—so I double-checked his truck. It was one of only two reds in the whole outfit, and I found it bunched with the others, empty. So maybe I was safe. I decided to get on the move before I felt unsafe again.

The door of my Chevy, however, was beat-up and didn't work worth a damn. My best friend, Ray, had backed into me. I warned Ray that I owed him, and he just smiled, promising to keep an eye out.

As a general rule, whenever your transportation went dead, or the sand rusted through it, if you happened into an accident that couldn't be fixed, then you left the broken hull on the side of the road like a carcass, and picked up something else. The government faithfully sent down a corral of junk cars and trucks like blankets for the Indians to buy us off.

Since the accident with Ray, the door had worsened, grown more and more cantankerous. I knew that soon I'd have to start using the passenger side, but I didn't want to. I jiggled the handle, beat my shoulder against the metal, and immediately felt the reluctance of a chronic bruise until the door popped free.

Closing wasn't nearly as difficult, and as the door clicked neatly shut behind me, I spotted Bossey walking from behind one of the diesels. He came rushing over.

"Little Mathew," he said, reaching his huge arm around my neck and tightening a hug. Sometimes, Bossey's hugs left red streaks that burned for hours. I could never breathe until he let go.

Bossey was crew chief, had been the chief since clay mining started. Wide and towering, he was the biggest man in Alabama. No one ever gave Bossey a hard time or told him no for long. He decked himself in dark blue overalls, tottering across the dig like a walrus, and all night he shifted across the sand, checking on people and equipment, his brown curly hair shimmering with clay mica, smelling of fresh cooking oil. Some of his friends, those who had known him longest, simply called him Curly, his wrestling nickname in high school. He kept his locks fastened behind his ears away from the wind with bobby pins, and underneath, his round olive face gave way to his eyes, bullfrog eyes with dark centers, dwelling intently on some long paper list, or his walkie-talkie connected to the irrigation house, some problem or matter needing his attention.

Finally, Bossey let go of me and I straightened myself, muffling my coughs and trying not to rub the back of my sore neck.

"What're you out here for? Something for your father?"

I shook my head. "I'm quitting school."

Bossey was the first one to hear this.

"Now, wait." Bossey's breath hadn't slowed since he greeted me. Though he kept trying to calm, trying to suck the night air in slowly, he couldn't. This wasn't unusual — Bossey was always short of breath, his voice possessing a whispery quality that had never caught up with the deep reservoir of his body. "You're not planning on coming out here. Mr. Chris won't have that."

"I am working here. I'm old enough." I stepped closer. "My father can't stop me. I can sign my own papers."

Bossey didn't flinch. Carefully, he looked over my clean shirt and jeans, his overalls splattered with mud and filth.

I had to do something, so I yanked at my waist to make the white shirt more creased and rumpled. But maybe I looked too young, too puny, so I stepped up on my toes to even our height, bowed my shoulders, and slanted my eyes stern, wiser, older.

Bossey just shook his head, wheezed out a laugh, and walked to the network of hoses and moon craters, the square flags flapping above them, the pulleys inching up and down.

"Wait up," I said, but the broad silence of Bossey's back said it all—he didn't have time for some young man's macho. I followed him anyway, watching carefully the carts, the cropping of tunnels, those flags sticking up like elusive cemetery stones. Especially, I kept my eye on number 40.

Bossey picked up a dead hose curved on the ground like a snake, like rattlers that used to live here, that would kill you with one bite. He sucked in a deep breath and his overalls inflated with air.

"This what you want? You sure?" he asked, his voice growling. "Clay mining is a shitty job. It will kill you, Little Mathew."

"This is what I want," I assured him, relieved that he wasn't going to turn me away.

"But you can get out. You can go to Birmingham. Chicago. Anywhere. The government's promised."

"They've promised a lot." I smirked, thinking about seniors who had graduated from Red Hill that I had known, who had gotten scholarships to colleges, only to be stopped at the border from leaving southern Alabama. It wasn't so simple to leave. You had to have special permissions, a special visa, and it was hard to buy those now that the government paid in scrip instead of US dollars. But my father had a visa for me in a small wooden box that his father, Sanford Harrison, had made. Grandpa Sanford crafted the box from long-leaf pine, pine now extinct, and as I stood there, I could smell the rosin that had gotten on my hands the one time I secretly touched the mitered lid and edges. My fingers twitched, brushed against one another, trying to rub the smell of that sticky rosin into the air. Inside the box, my father kept his personal things, including my visa. He had saved up enough money to buy it, and Bossey knew that.

Bossey put the hose down, his jaw hanging open, showing a perfect row of tiny teeth, early corn sewn neatly into a cob, his eyes dull and stewing.

"This what you want?" he said again. " 'Cause you sure don't act like you do." Bossey started up his walk, grabbed his walkie-talkie from his pocket, and spoke into it.

"Hey," I shouted to get his attention. When that didn't work, I stepped up, put my hand on his shoulder. "This is what I want. I'm serious."

Bossey looked at me like I was crazy, like I was a fish too young, one that should be put back in the river and caught later. But our rivers didn't have fish now.

Then Bossey just barreled in on my eyes. "Okay, Mathew," he said, and immediately seemed to relax. Something inside the man had come to an agreement. Then his look changed altogether. He put away the walkie-talkie and dusted his pockets. He looked like a businessman, like I was someone he was just meeting.

For hours that night and the next and the next, Bossey trained me in the simple work, the passing of hands over a hose and digging into a mudded wall of a mining hole, stretching down to the core of the earth like the shed skin of a snake for clay rocks.

"You put your arm and your wrist here," Bossey explained quickly, snapping my hands onto the hose. "You push the nozzle down—dig with it around the sides and the bottom—circle and circle back—make sure you've got the water pressure full when you're digging."

He screwed the nozzle out. "It'll be hard on your wrists and arms for a while, but the fuller the pressure, the more rocks that come loose. More rocks means more money. The more money you make, the drunker you can get, and the sooner you can forget about this damn place, about who you are, and why the hell you were so lucky to be born here." He chuckled, catching his breath. Then he paused a second more, waiting for me to nod or say *yeah* or something to indicate I was paying attention, that I was *serious* as I had said.

"Yes, sir," I finally obliged, but Bossey looked disappointed.

He growled a few words before he went on. "Use the pipe to get rid of the mud you don't need. Works like a vacuum cleaner." He grabbed a piece of the sludge line, flipped a switch to show me, then turned it off. "The sludge water gets filtered at the barrel house and used again." It was how we survived—using and reusing water—and still, my father said, it was all wasted, our last resource wasted on mining holes in the ground. "The Saved World wants us to stay put," he declared. "They want us to tunnel in and dry up in the earth, and they want us to hurry."

"Dig, dig with the nozzle," Bossey said. "The water takes the sand out whenever it settles into the hole. And don't stop; don't give the sluck time to dry and bury you up to your waist. Then you can't move, and if the sluck gets heavy enough and bad enough, it'll take all night to get you out. Ankle-deep water is okay. Helps take out the sand. You don't want dust pneumonia—the dust pneumonia blues, like Woody Guthrie sings. But he calls it pneumony. Have you heard of Woody Guthrie?"

I shook my head and Bossey cleared his throat. "*I got that dust pneumony, pneumony in my lung; And I'm a-gonna sing this dust pneumony song. Down in Texas, my gal fainted in the rain, I throwed a bucket of dirt in her face to bring her back again.*" His voice was rough and croaking and nothing like the polished voices of Nat King Cole and

Frank Sinatra my father listened to. "Have you heard that?" He chuckled.

I just looked at Bossey. I didn't know what to say.

He exhaled a long, frustrated breath. "Leave the sludge pipe by your side for the mud, the rising water—I don't want anybody drowning either, especially someone so green," and he shoved the pipe through a shallow hole at my new boots. It was straight like the old irrigation line my father had talked about.

Bossey and I had already taken a shovel and pick, carved out a shaft deep enough to bring in the pipe and the fireman's hose. And he showed me the wet drills everyone shared to break the layers of shale and siltstone that appeared the further you dug.

"And that's it until you get down to the clay. Use the nozzle like I told you—angle it so it doesn't splatter up in your face too bad, use the guard on the helmet, and dig and dig at full pressure until you're at least twenty feet, Mathew. Then you start pulling out the rocks. Sift them through the pan." He gave me a dented pan with a tin mesh on one edge for the water to slip through. It felt like a huge unmanageable plate, so light, as if the aluminum at any moment would melt into air. "Cut down the water pressure to do this." He screwed the nozzle back in. "It's as if you're a dentist, going into a cavity, gutting the earth, cleaning it out, a regular root canal—seven hours' worth in the dark." Bossey wiggled a tooth in his mouth, then magically pulled it to reveal a smaller tooth, a sliver of bone that had been filed down. He put the false tooth back in and laughed and wheezed. But I kept thinking of miners in California twisting the water from their pans looking for gold.

"Don't lose the rocks in the vacuum," he growled. "Keep them in the pan. Sift through the mud, get out as much as possible. Put the rocks in the bag and send them up." The bag was a heavy leather pouch with a tin screen sewn into the bottom so the water could drain even more. At the top, the pouch flipped into a tank before coming back down empty. The crew of caretakers dumped the tanks into the carts, hooked the carts together, and drove them to the trucks. "The pulleys are always ready, and it's a dollar a bushel—takes two bags to make a bushel and ten bushels to fill a tank. Plus you get something of an hourly wage—you're working for the government, so there's no worry about your paycheck."

It hadn't always been this way. In the beginning, people in the Saved World protested against the desert jobs. But once it became obvious that we all couldn't live in the Saved World, that some of us had to live in this blistering place, the dissenters dried up. The president gave several speeches, and each time at the closing he declared, "The good people trapped in that part of the Southeast must stay and sacrifice for the rest of the country. Their misfortune cannot become our own." My father had taped the speeches when I was a baby, before the government censored what news we received. He brought them out from time to time and played them—not so much for me, but to remember how his own fortune had come to this; how his wife, my mother, had died; how I had been born. It was the only use my father had for televisions—"Misery boxes," he called them, and "Devil's decision," he used to say about that president dressed in his navy-tie suit and all the presidents after, my father spitting at the ground, sometimes even spitting at the screen, but he wouldn't have left Alabama no matter what they said.

On the videos, the loud cheers caused the TV speakers to crack, people clapping who I couldn't see clearly, clapping with such enthusiasm. Whenever I thought about being there, being in that crowd with the blue sky and the podium sticking above all the heads, whenever I thought about clapping with them, it was as if I were clapping in my own face, clapping loud and hard, clapping out my own eyes, my father's eyes, draining my blood into the earth against all of us, against everyone I knew in Alabama.

For hours that night, Bossey rifled through detail after detail, each with its own warning, until his shortness of breath got the better of him and he had to take a break.

He dropped the pipe, grabbed my shoulders with his strong, plump fingers. He started to speak, stopped, drew in his breath. Bossey roughed his hands over my back and stomach. He compassed my head with his hands, but not squeezing too tight. "Medium should fit," he said. "Waders and helmet. I'll see what I've got—haven't had to fit anyone in a while. Probably going to have to dig out some boxes."

We all kept half of what we owned in boxes. There was no need to unpack, we moved around so much, even things we couldn't do without, what we deemed most precious—gifts, deeds now useless, letters, souvenirs, and photographs (I had one of Mamma, half a picture of her holding a blue ribbon the color of her dress, an award for her dancing). Best to keep them hidden away, bring them out only in the mind. And when we worked, when we ate, those half moments between resting and waking, we recited the contents of our boxes, the colors and the words, to our psyche—that way they could never be really touched, never lost or aged.

"Clay mining is hard work, Mathew—that's all. But you need to tell Mr. Chris. Number 40." Bossey pointed into the morass of flags flapping like battle flags from an English war, stained in blood with all the soldiers fallen—not a battle on green grass, but a war in northern Africa. "You can't start until you talk with him. I won't have it—

sixteen years old or no sixteen—I don't care about your rights on this one."

We shook hands and I nodded reluctantly in agreement—I didn't want to do this part.

I walked around five or six holes, trying impossibly to digest all that Bossey had said, until a crimson flag posted 40. Then I sat at the lip, my pants and boots caked in cool mud, listening to the loud cranking noise of engines, the whirr of water below the surface, the wind above it echoing Bossey's words, waiting for my father to come up.

CHAPTER 6

My Father's Hands, 2024

Since the only people living in the desert were the min-
ers and their families, school was held according to the
mining schedule: ten o'clock in May and seven o'clock in
December after the setting sun. My father dropped me off
every night and I was home two hours before him. When I
heard his truck pull up, a knocking in the engine, a special
sound it always made, I quickly started the record player
and began cooking breakfast.

One morning, my father opened the door and said first
thing like he always said, "What did you learn?" still wiping the sluck from his face. We had just moved to a farmhouse in Dothan, and I handed him a glass of water as he
sat down.

"We did multiplications to thirty," I told him. He always wanted to know about the math.

"Only thirty, again?"

I nodded and waited for him to comment on the music—sometimes he would say, "You're playing Billie," his voice lifting, or just "Billie," then he would smile, relax. But not today.

"When are they going to teach algebra? Geometry? You'll never get a job with multiplication tables. Not one that's going to get you out of here." He had been dabbing his neck with the washcloths I placed in the warm bowl on the table. Usually six were enough, but the clay was stickier and thick today, so I went to the bathroom for more, the eggs almost ready.

"What do the inside angles of all triangles equal?" he asked when I returned. He dragged his breathing, wouldn't let me touch his head with the cloth when I tried. His elbow shot out to block me. Then carefully, he combed his own fingers through.

"Smooth and sparkly," he said, his voice raspy, barely chuckling, but enough to let me know he wasn't angry or annoyed with my attention to him. He rubbed his hands through his wet hair several times, the black and red and beginnings of silver clumping off in strands like the currents of a river.

"Your mamma hated my hair when it was wet with all the clay. She said my head was yucky." He laughed then, the light air catching in his throat, scratching into a cough. It took a lot of energy for him to laugh, to do anything after work, and I didn't want him losing his energy, to fall asleep too soon. I liked the way his laughing made me feel, made something in me run with no direction, no finish, and I wanted to hear him talk more, that part of him, to hear it again and again.

He slumped down in the chair, his favorite easy chair—the laugh had relaxed him, and he settled deep into the cushions. "I'll tell you this, Mathew. She wouldn't kiss me until I had bathed—that's the truth. She used to turn her nose up, used to scold me, 'When you took this job, I didn't know you were going to be so damn muddy.'" He raised his voice in a high pitch and pointed his words at the air, pretending her voice. "She was pregnant with you, and she didn't want my sticky clay hands touching her belly. That was *holy ground*. But later I saw her eat clay, eat it from my clothes or take some straight from the earth. Pregnancy gives women a taste for things." He laughed again but not quite as hard, a whirring kind of laugh, his eyes looking forward, but where?

I searched the kitchen, the greasy smoke coming up from the frying pan masking the single-bulbed light. I searched the wall, some shape in the plaster, some object to fix on, something he would notice. It was important that I knew everything my father knew.

"So what do the inside angles of triangles equal? Answer."

"Three-sixty," I said.

The smile vanished from his face, and he held me firm, squeezing the cloth in my hand.

"One-eighty," he corrected as water dripped into the bowl. "Three-sixty is the circle."

My father drew a circle on my stomach, pushed his finger in the middle for a bull's-eye. "Holy ground," he said, the humor returning like a match struck quick to metal, his streams of hair catching the light with sparkles, the hard lines erasing.

I watched for those lines in his forehead, afraid they would come back. His hair, however, was always magical. The clay trapped the wetness like gel the older boys used in school to hunch into their coats, possessed with a cool distance like their fathers. My father wouldn't let me use gel—not yet, and he always cut my hair with a bowl just above my eyes, concealing my forehead with its broken center, the same mark as him.

Through his yellow-white and silver were streaks of red iron minerals—when he moved, the mica sparkled for the kitchen lights, sequins for dancers—rubies, silver, quartz—all of it a frozen motion like the currents of rivers painted.

"I don't think I'm going out this weekend," he decided, though he never went out. "I'm going to sit in this chair and read extra. What are you supposed to be reading?"

"*Dog Day*," I told him.

"*Dog Day*? What kind of book is that—a children's book?"

"It's my week to pick out a book," I reminded him, and pointed to the stacks from the library bumping against one another, rising and rising. I kept waiting for the whole mess of them to collapse.

"Oh," he said, then "All right," satisfied a little. "I'll find something for you—when you finish."

Dog Day was actually a story about a World War I airplane battle—a battle for Queen and Country—but I didn't elaborate after the fight we had had just a week earlier over invasions and drafts, what the government might do, and he became quiet, the motion in the clay taking on a dull calm like the desert after a storm.

"Tell me stories about Mamma."

"Yes," he agreed, his head tilting, eyes already nodding off into sleep. "Your mother was a great dancer. We used to dance all the time. . . ." He paused until it lengthened into silence, and helplessly, I watched his eyes close.

"Father," I said, touching his chest. His eyes didn't open.

My father rarely told me stories about Mamma, about her dancing, but I knew because of his steps alone in the kitchen, because he told me she was a dancer. He would never reveal how she died either—my Uncle Wayne did that when I was older. So it was always through the dancing that I saw her—my mother and my father as one person. And the dancing, the records on Grandpa Sanford's player in Peggy Lee's voice, in Nat King Cole's, they carried some piece of my mother, some lyrical movement that was her body, that each time I listened passed into me.

I wanted to ask my father about the time she was pregnant, about his clay hands on her stomach, about the stepping and twirling on the floor, about holy ground. But he was too sleepy today and I would have to do the reading hour alone.

Suddenly, my father jerked his head up. His eyes flashed open as if he had just felt the push I had given him. Then his eyes rolled shut, and slowly, comfortably, his head fell back. "A great dancer. She was beautiful, Mathew," he murmured. "Go read now, sleep. But remember the angles equal 180, Mathew. It's 180."

"Yes, sir," I whispered, and pulled his boots off, flicked the record player lower, the words and music popping.

> I say I'll go through fire
> And I'll go through fire
> As he wants it, so it will be
> Crazy he calls me
> Sure, I'm crazy
> Crazy in love, you see

I cleansed his face with one of the warm rags. In the corners of his eyes, I saw clay and began to pull carefully, lightly until I pulled his left eye half-open, bloodshot and blue, the lid heavy, wanting to close. The eye gazed straight ahead like a fish sideways in a pan of oil bubbling up into no place, his breathing deep, deep inside that I wanted to bring up, a large hook reeled in on a string, a hook to tickle his throat into laughter. I let the eyelid drop, could smell sulfur and grease. The eggs were burning, and I ran to the kitchen to turn them off.

CHAPTER 7

Dothan, 2024

"The new dust bowl," Ms. Jones said, walking back and forth in front of the class, "that's what they called us at first. The scientists thought the small ozone holes would heal themselves and there would be rain, but they widened over the Southeast, connected together, scorching the fields and trees." Her pacing was one long step, two long steps, not the same grace as my father, just straight, straight lines, a single unimagined rhythm. "No more crops." She lifted both her hands and flitted her fingers as if covering the entire expanse of the South. "Nothing. On the surface we have nothing to give. The sand dunes—though the sand dunes can be quite beautiful," and she nodded steadily in an attempt to get us to nod, "the weather is unbearable for tourism. But we still have resources underneath, our special opportunity to excavate!"

"Tourism?" One kid popped a laugh so loud, I turned

to see if his cheek had burst. I think his name was Toby or
Talbot. His father worked with my father. I had seen them
together at the mining dig. "Why would anyone want to
come down here?"

"They wouldn't," Ms. Jones stressed, and narrowed her
eyes at the class. "So we excavate resources, like I said. Do
you know the meaning of *excavate*?" She looked around the
room for nodding heads. "It's what we've done since 2014."
But still no one responded, as if the desert had seeped into
our bodies, filled us and numbed us and clogged our
throats—we weren't going to admit to any knowledge, give
up anything. "Most of you were born that year."

"That's when everybody died," another kid said. His
name was Ray.

"Not everybody," Ms. Jones corrected. "We're all
here," and she floated her arms graciously outward, her
spinning-top hair pointing straight up. "Over a thousand
people live in this camp, and there are mining camps all
over the Southeastern Desert, flourishing."

Flourishing—I let the word swim through my head
with the chalk dust and the strong lemon cleaner used on
the floors. Somehow Ms. Jones could make the most dismal facts sound plausibly optimistic.

"My mother said that everybody died trying to escape.
My father and brother died trying to escape. He left us and
drove north."

"Some people left, but not everybody. Most people
adapted."

"Sun got them fast," he said. "That sun's a bitch."

And Ms. Jones froze, her swaying motions had ceased
altogether, her spinning-top head. Some of the students
whispered and Ms. Jones just stood.

"You shouldn't say the word *bitch*," I said to the boy,
this Ray, with all the moralism my father had used on me.
His hair was greased brown and black on his head, and his

face was raw behind his glasses, as if it had been washed too many times. Those glasses—the lenses kept making his eyes switch weirdly—and he had the smallest frame, like a tuber box, he was so thin, but he was all seriousness.

"Killed my father, my brother," he declared. The boy behind me slugged me in the back, and my shoulder caved in immediately—I was getting used to the punches.

"I'm sorry," Ms. Jones told him. "I'm sorry about your family."

"I didn't know them. I was a year old, hardly born, like you said." Ray shrugged. "My brother, Jeremy was his name, was the oldest." And he looked down at the loose papers on his desk.

Ms. Jones cleared her throat and started a new discussion, this one about cooking: how to cook cheese toast without burning down the house when your parents were at work or running errands. The minute she said "toast" I gazed down at my book again, the page open to a photograph of the Red Baron's plane in fresh red with black crosses on the tri-wings and tail. On Saturday, my father and I had raided the empty Dothan library, hauling as many books in his truck as we thought we could read before the camp moved on.

Eighty kills before his death, the book championed in bold, and next to the plane was a picture of the Baron, Manfred von Richthofen. How do you pronounce Richthofen? I wondered, and whispered the name with a long *o* and the *f* like a *v*. Richthofen in a black cap, and his eyes, his eyes just stared and stared into mine as if he were speaking or getting ready to speak. There were no words, yet I felt words, felt them shake through my body. I had to stop looking at the picture. My back hurt a little, and I looked at Ray. I kept looking at him.

———

After class, in the hall, I caught up with this Ray.

"I've got a father," I said.

"Good for you," he said, like I was foolish or unimportant, and I felt like both. For some reason I thought mentioning my father would make him happy, but it didn't, and he kept walking.

"I don't have a brother. And I don't have a mother either." I had to yell this time because he had gotten far away, like he was hurrying to catch up with someone, anyone.

He stopped and turned back to me. "I've got one of those. She's a prostitute. Works at Lula D's." That was the bar the miners went to. And Ray said *She's a prostitute* straight up, like nothing was wrong with it, but I knew what a prostitute was. My uncle had talked about them. He knew some of their names: Alice, Patricia. My uncle liked prostitutes, and I wondered if he knew Ray's mom. I started to ask for her name, but no words came out of my mouth.

The other kids shifted around us like we were a sandbar and they were fish and dust and moving and moving, and I said to him, "I've got a tractor."

"A tractor?" He garbled the word. I could tell he didn't believe me, so I nodded.

"A John Deere." I stretched my hand above my head, the height of the tractor's smokestack, then brought it down to the flat-nosed body—that's how I remembered it—and the seriousness, all the seriousness on his face kept brewing and brewing, trying to decide what to do with me.

CHAPTER 8

2014

Dust storm approaching from eastern Mississippi. Do not go outside. Do not travel. Wind—90 miles per hour possible. Low visibility. School, government, and mining operations canceled. All travel restricted. Repeat: Dust storm approaching from eastern Mississippi. Stay indoors. Do not travel. Listen to this station for further updates.

—WDMZ 1610 AM, 5:05 p.m.

There are many stories about what happened in 2014. My father would only say, "Everyone tried to escape but they failed to make it." The year was lost to him, any explanation of my birth, of that moment of my mother's death. Whenever I asked, his body closed down, his mind drifted, and he wouldn't speak. Ray told me what his mother had said, and Bossey explained that he had actually driven to Birmingham and was stopped, and later my uncle told me what he recalled. But the schools wouldn't. They maintained that we had become a desert and likewise a desert people, as if it were a natural phenomenon, expected, as if the world had shifted while we were too preoccupied with living to notice or care what had happened to us.

"Ms. Jones can't tell us the truth or she'll get in trouble," I said.

"She won't tell us," Ray disagreed, "won't." He didn't

trust teachers and he hated the sun. But this was before Ray turned seventeen and his mother left with a government agent, before starting his caretaking business and running the irrigation house. He has too many secrets now. The Ray who told me what he thought, emptying his mind without hesitation—I miss him.

And every year in school, the teachers repeated the directives the government sent, what could be said, what should not, how to explain our existence. But spilling around that absent history were the many stories of how we became what my father called an unsalvageable country, no longer Americans.

Ray said his mother told him before going to work in the next room. She reminded him to lock the door when she left and do not open it even if he needed something, do not open it, the lights barely on already—her bed, he could see it through the doorway, the brown sheets pulled to the side, and sometimes a man would already be there, sitting on the bed, shirtless, waiting quietly, looking back at him and his mother, waiting for her to come in and shut the door, and she said, "What could we do with all that dust? The storms kept coming and coming on, and there was one storm that lasted twenty days. We were stuck inside the house, the one Wendell's mother, your grandmother, bought, and you barely a year old." She smiled as if she was happy to remember Ray an infant, but the smile flickered, too brief to latch onto and believe in, Ray said, as if that moment of joy was a marker of her sadness. She started again. "You cried and the storm howled back, and when we lost the electricity, I held you close because even in the daytime, so much dust was blowing, I could hardly see you, black like all the doors in the world had been shut on top of us, and there was a fog of dust in every room. For twenty days we were filthy, hungry. Dirt, all that dirt. Every meal covered with dirt. And Wendell's crops, your father's crops—not that they had been growing, the sun had already killed them, parched them yellow and brown—they were covered in sand as if your father had planted nothing at all. We had truly become a desert.

"That day after the twenty-day storm, while the winds had calmed or at least disappeared into Georgia or the Gulf of Mexico, the day after, the sun was out boiling, and though the government had advised us to stay put, Wendell left to check on things with your brother, Jeremy, said he was tired of the crying, and couldn't I make you stop? He took Jeremy and they walked out, and pretty soon I heard cars, so many stuck on the road—we lived off Highway 43 at Demopolis, what remained of it—as if they were fleeing a hurricane, driving north. And you kept crying even when I fed you. And no matter how many times I washed your face with a cloth, I couldn't get all the grit from your eyes.

"Then—I think it was just before lunch—I was wondering what to cook—but then I remembered we had no electricity, and you were quiet for the first time. The quiet spread into the house as if you were breathing out the silence, breathing everything back in—the furniture, photographs, chairs, windows, the tracks on the dust floor, your father and brother's boots, their ghosts—breathing them in, just you, this small one-year-old I carried. But it was terrifying; I couldn't relax at all. I heard the cars and your silence, the two mixing, I couldn't separate them; I didn't want to blame you for not stopping your crying sooner, but in my gut I knew your father and brother had become ghosts already, and empty. Your father, I was certain, had seen that traffic and left us to go with them."

Bossey shook his head. "Crazy traffic," he told me like he always told me when we finished the night's digging, always some story to tell. "You can imagine me, all three hundred pounds of me wedged in that traffic." He chuckled. "You have to understand—before the dust storms happened, the government kept saying, be calm, everything's going to be all right, this is just a tiny, tiny drought." Bossey squished his fingers together. "For three years that's what they said, and called us the new dust bowl, the southern dust bowl, like the title was something to be proud of, like we were continuing an important tradition." Bossey huffed.

"You'd get outside in the light and cough like you do now, gulping in the white haze. We had the haze then, too, but there'd be bettering conditions. We'd get some rain, stuff would grow back a little, but it was like hair on a bald man—never lasted long." Bossey pressed the bobby pins in his curly hair tighter. He wasn't bald, would never be.

"As soon as we got a little rain, the drought started over and made us restless. We tried to stay calm. That's what we had been told to do. But once the dust storms started . . . they were hateful storms. I'm used to them now, but in the beginning I thought the earth had emptied itself into the sky, swirling and swirling red and black and dirt clouds that smelled like oil. There was no way to drive through them, to stop them—hateful storms—you had no chance but to wait them out. And then that one, for twenty days the wind and just black dust, a mess of dust. Everybody who had stayed put, who had tried to be calm—we were shaken, and once the storm passed, everybody who could get in a car, who could leave, did. It wasn't like we had discussed it. We just got up and left like birds when they head south or north. Our instinct said, get out, and so we tried to, okay?" He slowed down to catch his breath.

"You got to understand, it was crazy traffic, and it was June, sweltering June like it always is. Some people baked to death in their cars, and the rest of us were stopped before we reached Birmingham—the same thing happened in

Atlanta and Memphis, and in Florida, the roads were bot-
tlenecked so bad, most people stayed put, just died in their
homes. Without electricity, the dust had cut into everything. You've seen those bodies?"

I nodded. When we arrived in ghost towns searching
for places to live, sometimes we came across bodies, their
clothing wrapped over bones and dry skin, decayed into
chairs or in beds, still staring up at the ceilings, still waiting
for the heat to subside.

"That's when I knew," my Uncle Wayne said. He took
a toothpick from the small box and cleaned his teeth. "Our
earth had had it with us. You were about to be born, and all
we had to give you was a desert—your grandfather's land,
my father's land, what me and Chris had grown for years—
for you, all this for you—it was worthless. And everyone
left on I-65 and the state roads because that was the only
way—the airports had been shut down. A good number of
people made it, but then the army and the national guard
set up roadblocks as if we had no right to travel. Your father
said that's when we became expendable, no longer
Americans, though I don't know what else to call us.

"People pulled up exhausted and upset, and the army
wouldn't let them through. Along the highways the police
tried to turn people back, but the lanes were crammed
with one-way traffic—no one budged. The army wouldn't
budge. Some people just parked and began walking to the
city, and from what I understand, the national guard and
the army spread out and stopped them. They did a good
job of stopping them, Mat."

"All I'm going to tell you, Mathew, is that the army was
ready." Bossey looked at his feet and shifted until he found

his balance. "They made barriers. I was maybe ten miles out in Saginaw, but the traffic wasn't moving, and you couldn't pick up anything on the radio, so you didn't know what was happening. That's when the government started jamming radio signals, cell-phone signals, everything. They had made this barrier, and they planned to keep us in. I know it's tight now, but at least we have some communication with Birmingham."

Just you, I wanted to remind him. Like Ray, Bossey had connections with the Saved World and kept more secrets than he revealed.

"Your father and Jeremy, they were up there. Now, you have to believe me, you have to believe me when I tell you this," Ray's mother shut her eyes and she would not look at him, she would not touch him; the blue eye makeup she wore seemed like quarters pressed into the circled bones, "and don't ask me how I know, and don't ask me who told me, but they were part of those people who walked up, who left their cars and tried to leave by foot and get across the desert, get to Birmingham, and someone told them to stop and they wouldn't stop, and shot them with the others. The army killed your father. They killed Jeremy."

"But I thought the sun got your father and brother?" I asked Ray.

"Sometimes she tells me the sun got them. Sometimes she tells me they were shot."

"What's the truth?" I asked.

"I don't know," he said. "The sun or the army or both of them—I don't know."

"I was in Saginaw and some people in the cars around me opened the doors and just started walking. Hours later

I heard rifles. Warning shots, I thought it was, but it was too late for that. Through the afternoon and night some returned and told us about the killing—how they had walked and walked and would not turn even when the army said to and so the army fired overhead until it did no good. When we heard about the killing," Bossey hesitated, "we knew the government meant business. At first you get angry, but then you just want to survive.

"Everybody headed home. And I did as well. But even when I did, what I remember were those empty cars jumbled around my truck, boiling in the sun. Empty and going to stay that way. For a moment, I wanted to find those lost people and bring them back, no matter what. But I don't know why I wanted to bring them back. They were nobody I knew." And Bossey stopped.

"All the cars, they returned on 43 by our house. I went outside in the evening because it had cooled some and I held you and watched the cars, the faces on those people—I won't forget it, they looked as if someone had unmade them, robbed them—and I waited for your father to come home with your brother, but then I heard what happened. Now, don't ask me again, but I know that they are dead."

Ray explained that when she got to this point, she was gripping his arms or his collar or the sheets, gripping so tight that she sometimes bruised him, but he couldn't say anything when she was like this; he didn't understand how to calm her, and how his own words so easily could fail and dry up.

"When everyone who didn't escape, who didn't get shot came home, we asked each other, what're we going to do?" My uncle shook his head and spat the toothpick at the ground. "We couldn't be farmers anymore. Most businesses were bankrupt or going bankrupt, some places just stayed empty, and there were no rescue efforts. They even took the capital from Montgomery to Birmingham, and we were left to figure out the desert on our own. But just for a while. The government was afraid we'd get agitated, organized, so they focused on the mining. A lot of people, especially the older people—the heat was just too much, and the rest of us, well, here we are." Uncle Wayne smiled broadly when he said that, as if there could be a smile to any of his story.

"And all of this happened, and I didn't even know it?" I asked my uncle.

"You were too young," he said. "Trust me, it's better to be ignorant about some things. Just don't be a fool about it now, Mat. Get out of this place when you're older, like Chris wants."

CHAPTER 9

Dothan, 2024

Ray didn't believe me about the tractor, an old green John Deere my father couldn't abandon from Grandpa Sanford's farm, and though it wasn't a red tri-plane, it would do. So the next morning after school, those few hours before my father got home with night still disguising everything, Ray came to the farmhouse.

"How long have you had it?" he asked. The tractor was parked against the east wall, covered by a blue canvas dusted in sand, but better the canvas than the engine, my father said. Ray and I removed the stones anchoring the bottom and pulled, letting the blue and dust slide with an eerie easiness from the smoke pipe to the large back wheels.

"My grandfather used to drive this," I said proudly. And even though we kept most things in boxes, *this* was too big to go in a box—it was even more real, an even deeper testament that I belonged here. The whole of the tractor, the largeness of it was barely visible in our flashlights, just streaks of metal we pieced together into a shadowy frame.

"Do you drive it?" he asked. "You drive it a lot?"

"Yeah," I said quick, and shrugged and gulped before the lie got too far away from me.

"Show me how it runs."

I paused—for one second I paused—I knew if I waited, he'd figure me out.

"All right," I answered, and we both pulled ourselves into the bird's-eye seat. Then we stood on the running boards and the center chassis because the cushion had busted out a long time ago and the rivets made the seat uncomfortable. Above the steering wheel were gauges, and to the right, a black lever, and below, some buttons, one that said *choke*, and finally on the other side of the open dash I found the keys my father left plugged into the ignition.

"We can be the Red Barons," I told him.

"Who?" he asked.

"The Red Baron. He was a World War I pilot, the best—eighty kills," but Ray looked at me as if the sun had *gotten me fast*—what he had said to Ms. Jones in school about what had happened to his father and brother, like I had turned insane in the length of a few sentences.

"It's not important," I mumbled.

"Let's see the tractor run."

So I turned the keys and kept turning them, but they wouldn't budge.

"The other way," Ray said, and put his hand on mine and I shoved him back because he wasn't as big and I kept switching, pressing other buttons, and tapping my fingers at the gauges—I had seen my uncle tap at the gauges and there was magic, some power in doing so, something that signaled to the tractor it was time to start.

"You sure you know what you're doing?" he asked after a while.

I sighed as if of course I did and he had no right to not believe me. I turned the ignition as hard as I could, then shifted my body so Ray couldn't look at what I was doing and quickly switched the key in the other direction like he had suggested. Suddenly, the tractor sputtered and wheeled and flashed into the dark.

"Turn on the lights," Ray said.

"I know, I know," I told him, but I didn't know if the tractor even had lights. I had seen my father and uncle drive it from time to time but always in the earliest morning before the sun got too strong.

"Turn on the lights," he said again, but all there was was solid black, no house or tree, no markers except for our flashlights that zigzagged before we could fix on a gauge or a button that made sense, fix on any one direction.

"Hold the steering wheel." Ray kept saying that, too, because the steering wheel kept jerking out of my hands.

"Don't worry. Just calm down," I told him, and lost my flashlight and the tractor hiccuped as it rushed ahead, hiccuped like a bronco, what I had read about Texas, what people did there, only Ray and I weren't broncobusters, not by a long shot.

I pulled the black lever on the right and the engine revved angrily and shot even faster ahead. But as I grabbed the steering wheel and tried to rein it in from swerving wildly, the tractor bucked at the ground, and off I went into the black cool air for ten yards or fifteen yards, flying, flying but not like a fighter pilot, methodical and exact, instead like a hurled rock or a turtle, a pumpkin, potato, something awkward that shouldn't be doing what I was doing, until I crashed into the sand, and I lay on the ground and my side ached as I listened to the engine shudder and wheel.

"Ray?" I called.

"Where the hell are you?" he said desperately, but I

couldn't see him or the John Deere, could not see them, and I knew it would go and go until it butted into something or the engine shut off, or maybe Ray knew what he was doing, but all I heard—that engine clawing an echo into the darkness, my side aching too much to get up.

The sun rose a thick, thick dust-red out of Georgia, and a white mist, the morning haze was already settling on the ground. The darkness had given in, and with it, I didn't hear the tractor. I looked to where I thought the tracks had gone, west, away from the sun, where it had carried Ray off into the black, but where the black was, the white haze now covered everything equally as full.

And I couldn't move well—the ache in my side had found its way into my right arm. Then I did hear a sound— the familiar knock, knock of my father's truck engine coming at a tear. The truck stopped beside me, and I smelled propane as water drizzled from the exhaust pipe into a small twist of dust.

The door swung open.

"What've you done?" my father asked when he reached me.

I grabbed my stomach and cringed, but I was more afraid than hurt.

"What have you done?" His voice was firm and steady, not loud.

"I haven't done anything," I said, but I was lying and he knew it, and his eyes were too hard to disagree with or look at. I looked at his waders covered in mud, a mermaid's fin—already the mud was cracking and drying. His boots were stepping one-two, one-two in an impatient rhythm.

"I don't know what I've done," I told him plainly, and since my father didn't answer, I thought my response had satisfied him.

"Don't know?" he finally said. "The tractor— What did you do to the tractor?"

"Nothing. I was just trying to ride it."

"You don't know how to ride it." His words flashed over me and pinned me down.

"But I thought I could. I've seen you and Uncle Wayne—"

"You saw us?" My father's voice raised quick and stopped. He was staring, brewing, that heavy forehead of his like a plow broken, just waiting to open up and cut through me if I turned the wrong way, if I said the wrong thing. I winced, and he looked at my hand, then glanced at my arm.

"Get in the truck," he demanded, and slowly lifted my other arm and opened the door to help me inside—he didn't shove me—and walked around and opened his door.

"We're not supposed to be out in the sun," I reminded him of the government law, the red circle stirring and spilling against the white haze as if the sun's explosions, its solar flares were happening just a few miles east.

"You need to see Carson. The sun will have to wait." Which I knew was impossible.

"That sun hasn't waited on anyone. It never has," I told him.

He cranked the engine. "No one said you could get on the tractor."

"You call it a piece of junk, so what's the big deal?"

"No one said you could get on *my* tractor!" he said more loudly. "I didn't give you permission."

"Sorry." It was definitely time to apologize. Then I asked, "Did anyone get run over?" I was worried about Ray, but I was afraid to mention him to my father. Ray's family history was already full of unlucky dead people, and I didn't know him that well. I wasn't sure how to explain the mix-up, how he got on the bird's-eye seat, how I fell off, the fact that his mother was a prostitute at Lula D's.

"Not that I'm aware of," my father said, and he smiled just a little, just enough to let me know he wasn't totally mad. "Fortunately, you haven't killed anybody yet."

CHAPTER 10

Laws, 2021

The government sent down laws and warnings that started with *No* and *Do Not* and *Avoid* and never *Please*.

They sent them as pamphlets, as advertisements on the radio station and TV station out of Tina's store. At school, they were posted on the sandy block walls and every computer screen—you couldn't move from one permissible website to another without a warning popping up in red or bright yellow.

The first and most important was *Do Not Go Out in the Sun. High Levels of UV Are Dangerous*. You could be fined or jailed, but our marshal, Jack Thompson, said he didn't plan to enforce such a law until well after lunch, and he had no intention of being outside himself at that time.

"If someone wants to be fool enough to take that kind of risk, then let them go ahead," he told the miners whenever they crowded around, and they always crowded around when he drove up. Jack liked to comment on bureaucratic nonsense and the miners liked his sharpness. "It might as well be a natural law—*Do Not Go Out in the Sun.* The consequences will take care of themselves. And here's another." Jack read slowly from the pamphlet, "*No Mining Permitted in Daylight. Hazardous.* You're damn right it's hazardous." His eyes grew wild, his jaw lolling off its hinge. "We want to live just like they do. We don't want to kill ourselves." And everyone laughed. Then he brought the pamphlet close to his face and puckered his wrinkled mouth, "*No Government Offices Open Past Noon.* Absolutely. I close my office at 10:30, 11:00 if there's trouble. But that's it," and he folded the pamphlet firm along the creases and put it in his shirt pocket.

The government sent down new laws and revamped the old laws as much as they sent down food and supplies, and we joked that there was a special bureau for cautioning us about our way of living:

Do Not Go Out in the Sun Unless an Emergency.

In the Event of an Emergency, All Skin Must Be Covered.

Nothing Can Be Exposed.

Exposure to the Sun Can Cause Severe Blistering, Dehydration,

Overheating, Stroke, and Cancer.

Sometimes *cancer* appeared first on the list, sometimes *dehydration,* and the pictures in the background held a black X through the orange core of the sun. When I was six and seven, I was never sure which affliction would happen to me first, though I was certain each would attack sooner or later and maybe all causes would attack at once, leading to my certain death.

But this is how we communicated with the Saved World: they constructed and controlled what was sent down, what we sent up. Telephones and shortwave radios and cell phones had been banned, their signals blocked at the border. Two-way communication was restricted to the camp, so every house, every vehicle had a CB, and only when another camp was in range could we talk with them. The Internet was available but only at the schools and we were allowed access to a small number of sites. We could, however, receive mail that had passed what the government called a check-inspection, in Birmingham. Each week, the supply truck delivered envelopes slit open, with black lines drawn through sentences and pictures cut out—certain information was not for us to handle. And any mail we sent north had to pass the same check-in before going on.

The television and radio aired news from the Saved World. "What they want us to have," is how my father put it. Occasionally, the news anchors would mention us, but as one collective, like Death Valley and other deserts, as if this dry, unusable land didn't possess people at all. "They've erased us so no one has to worry. Do you think the people in the north know who we are any longer? That we still exist?" my father asked, and shook his head.

But the government workers knew what was happening throughout the desert as well as in the Saved World—they carried special long-range walkie-talkies and traveled back and forth and told us nothing except for the weather, except for Jack Thompson's wisecracks. Each day the radio posted the highs, the lows, the amount of dangerous white ozone we had to inhale and ingest, and sometimes we were notified to stay home or quickly prepare to leave for a new town. But since they told us nothing else, we had to invent our own knowledge, our own sense of what was happening around us and beyond us in the Saved World, our own rumors.

Was the Saved World mending as reported and promised? Did the people smile as much as the people on TV? Their motions and gestures made from room to room, from one locale to another, whether on foot or in a car, alone or together, each actor and actress containing so much trust and ease as if the world around them was safe and would hold them and keep them safe—was that possible? Was that true?

My father rarely let me turn on the "misery box," the "want machine." Instead he excavated books out of abandoned libraries because the pages held real truth, he insisted, as much of it as anyone was willing to admit. The books remained trapped in 2014 and years earlier, and many of the spines had busted with dry rot and were polished down with sand. "But real," he said, cracking the spines open, rubbing his fingers over words as if he were blind, as if he could draw language through his body using his fingers as straws. And one afternoon my father found something worming down the page, some small bug. "The only insect left in the desert," he laughed, "eating a book to survive. Fitting." He looked happy with himself, as if he had uncovered something profound and silly in that small bug. And for me, I liked reading to my father's music: Billie Holiday and Nat King Cole, their voices looping through the words. But every time, every time I watched television, the conviction of those moving bodies, their clothes, the rooms wasted in breathable light and color made me thirsty, even if the Saved World was destroying itself like my father claimed, the programming and news a fabrication, propaganda, even if we were truly erased in their minds.

I couldn't, however, totally erase my father's allegations. Like the time in class when we learned that New

York City, this gigantic city, was recovering from a year-long flood. "The Big Apple is the Big Apple again," the TV announcer explained in a mudless coat—an anomaly in Alabama. The dikes were holding, dirt and sewage had been cleaned away from monuments and buildings, and the people had moved back. They showed clips of boxed streets full of determined New Yorkers marching into one another and together, as if preparing for war. But until that moment, we had never been told of a flood in New York City, and I wondered, what other disasters hadn't been mentioned? that couldn't be fixed? that we would never learn about? I opened my book to the Red Baron, his red plane against a blue sky—*eighty kills*, the book said, and all that sky was his, the whole expanse of it. I was envious. I wanted to fly there, brushed up in the wind, looking over fields, the gravity unable to reach me.

But there was so much hope in Ms. Jones' voice, the announcers,' the footage of a perfect world, or at least a mending world, always mending. They couldn't all be lying. And the older I got, the more I believed in my own dreams. They were the most authentic, even the parts I didn't want.

Whatever the truth, the information the Saved World provided was where we began. Each night at school, we absorbed the directives, the canned news, the prepared documentaries, the laws, each *No* and *Do Not*, and determined them lies or half lies or possible truths, and then filled in what was missing, what was needed to make the information fuller, to create the second half of the lie, the second half of the conversation they didn't want to hear. But it was how we made ourselves kinetic, how we moved upriver.

For the warnings, we created gossip about children in other mining camps who drowned in deep water and shoals, or picked up crippling diseases from swimming, or who wandered into the greedy sun and parched to death, the rays blistering off their skin. And following extremely gruesome stories, a rash of death-stories that built upon each other would be told throughout the camps for two or three months, each death more horrific than the one before it, until the fever for such stories, the fear of them had passed into boredom and something new replaced our appetite. The weather especially cycled rumors in and out—dust storms that led to choking deaths and dust pneumonia, and houses filled to the roof with fine-grained sand, and in the hottest months when no one could bear the heat, children in Mississippi and Florida died miserably and instantly, lost in a flash to the devil sun.

"Is it true?" I asked my father. By the time I was seven, I had taken every precaution, done everything thinkable to stay away from sunlight, to the point of covering myself in the thickest blankets, layer upon layer no matter how hot it was. As I shuffled from room to room—like a loaded-down mule, my father said—he agreed, "The sun's dangerous," trying not to laugh at my mulish appearance, "very dangerous. But it's not going to sear off your skin like a bolt of lightning, kill you outright. I'm not saying children don't get lost in the desert or trapped in cars. If you stay out too long, you'll dehydrate, the ozone will stick in your lungs and throat. You can overheat, but the sun doesn't work like lightning." He reached for the blankets, and I stumbled safely back.

"Nothing grows," I said as possible evidence that my father was wrong. "Even next to the water, plants won't grow."

"The sun's too much for them," he nodded and pulled dry pieces of clay from his beard, throwing the pieces at the floor like tiny nails, "but if you run through it right now and run inside, it's not going to kill you. Not for those few seconds." One day he opened the door, pulled the blankets off my body. "Come on, Mathew, let's go in it."

"I don't want to," I answered, and grabbed at the blankets, but he yanked them away.

"We're going. Have faith in me." And so I walked ahead, touching the hot doorjamb and holding there until he pushed.

The rays flashed on my skin. I shivered and waited for both of us to boil over and melt. Inside, blood pumped and pumped—I could feel heat, but it was hotter in my own brain than from the sun. Still I wanted my blankets, the coarseness and thickness of the sheared fabric as my father strolled lazily and held me enough to make me keep in step. We walked a circle around his truck, and as we did he started whistling—*Just found joy, I'm as happy as a baby boy*—I recognized the tune, "Sweet Lorraine" by Nat King Cole—and eventually we walked inside.

"If you go back out and stay, you'll get sick," he promised. "But you can survive for a while. If you were lost in the desert, stranded, the sun would eventually wear you down. The sun is more about endurance and water than anything else. Even here. Do you understand?"

I nodded yes. My skin was still my skin, had not melted like the cheese sandwich I had imagined, and yet my brain was clogged with the words *Do Not Go in the Sun. High Levels of UV Are Dangerous.*

The pamphlets prescribed: *If you are dizzy, go inside and sit down. If dizziness persists, contact a doctor. If you have recurrent vertigo, contact a doctor immediately and lie down*—The words withered and swelled, changed from red to yellow, and I waited to tumble or faint, but I didn't feel dizzy at all. The warnings, however, kept churning and would not vanish:

Do Not Cook with River Water.

Do Not Drink River Water.

Do Not Drink from Ponds, Puddles, or Surface Water Until the Sewage Is Treated.

Contamination May Lead to Diarrhea, Dysentery, Cholera, and Death.

Rivers Are Dangerous.

Avoid Drinking Too Much Water.

Avoid Sand Storms.

Dust May Cause Pneumonia.

Do Not Go into Rivers.

Keep Water Close By.

Drink Three Quarts of Water Daily.

Do Not Look Directly into the Sunlight.

On and on the instructions came down, until we began to think in terms of *Do Not, No,* and *Avoid,* as if the language had changed, as if there was a proclivity toward sentences starting with these words, with what should not happen, what should not be done, what we should never, never do.

CHAPTER 11

Millers Ferry, June 2044

It's 11:15 p.m. when I reach the new site. The truck has coasted in perfect, sandwiched between two other trucks, but a body brushes against the side.

"Hurry up." Bossey slaps the hood. The noise startles me and I fumble on a good answer, but he's not looking for one. He just keeps walking.

Bossey's been waiting on me, I can tell, even as he strolls back to the stadium lights and diesel engines, his walkie-talkie to his ear. He won't turn around, won't act like he notices, but since my father's death, Bossey has kept close to me, asking every night how I'm doing, asking more than a few times. It's hard to believe that he's been crew chief for thirty years now—since the beginning of the Southeastern Desert and clay mining, since the government subsidized the lost farmland, said they needed clay rocks to build highways and dam rivers.

"A straight-out lie." Father had wanted to laugh. He kept the official notice from the government about his employ and the need for clay mining in the pine box and took it out occasionally to read, the paper stiff with age, tearing at the edges, turning yellow, and smelling of rosin. As his eyes wandered down the page, his wrinkles toughened his lips in a strict line. "They throw this shit in a dump," he insisted. "Clay rocks are good for nothing but the money and for us to die quick, be out of their way." I watched his eyes, watched them harden, could feel them burn into me—I knew he was thinking of his brother, Wayne. Wayne drowned in one of the holes where the Coosa and Tallapoosa Rivers come together near Santuck. Whenever Father thought of my uncle, there was no use in talking to him, his words venomous for days.

"Come on, Mat." Bossey slaps the truck hard again like some god, like Zeus, making it shake like the wind shakes. "I can't pay you if you don't work," and he walks off once more.

I didn't see him coming.

His fingers hug the walkie-talkie, plump as grilled franks and swollen raw from the ropes he has pulled—the biggest man in Alabama, using those raw hands to pull people out of the dark airholes, telling whoever is around of the lives he has saved.

"Grabbed Tom out," he told me the first week, my training week. He pointed to a scar on his index. "Got him out of the suction just in time. The walls caved in around him and the pulley had tangled.

"There was JP. We were pulling him up, but the rope broke and he was balled up inside the shaft. I reached down far enough to get him, with five people holding my ankles. I don't know if I should have been going in," he gave his stomach a wallop, "but I had to." Bossey curled three of his fingers, revealing a scar cutting across, shaped with the thickness of twine and snakeskin.

"Wayne, your uncle—" Bossey shook his head. "He was a fool. I don't mean anything by that. No reflection on you or Mr. Chris. He just—don't take it personal, Mathew—he just . . . just didn't want to come up." Bossey held up his pinkie, the end tip missing.

His walk is slow, walruslike, and hard, too, shoulders leaning as if a rope is always in his hands and he is about to pull someone to the surface and back to life. His shortness of breath is chronic, and since my father's death, he watches me and circles me, won't give me any room.

There's two hundred of us, two hundred that used to be five hundred—the ground lights rolling between pipes and hoses and the wobbly aluminum pulleys—overhead the towering stadium lights. I see one miner clinch his rope, jump down a tunnel.

"Like swimmers diving for the coral reef," Father had said of the ritual and chuckled with satisfaction. Before we became a desert, my father said coral reefs died every year and he wondered how many were left, if any were left. "Living rock," he called it, "becoming as dead as us."

I turn to the passenger seat and he is there again—the shade of my father—staring through the windshield. I don't want to disturb him, afraid he'll turn, will notice that I'm here, but his eyes broaden quick.

"Grab the steering wheel!" he demands, his hands reaching over, and I wrap my hands through his, steady the steering wheel, realize I'm in park, look across—the image gone.

"Stop it," I say angrily, but not too loud. I'm afraid Bossey will hear. I'm breathless. Like my dreams when I was young, ghosts have crept into my waking life. Daydreamer Mathew, the kids used to taunt, and the daydreams have caught up.

The sand sweeps across and slips away, covering everything, infiltrating every speck. You can't tell when you look in the distance, how far to the end of the desert, the end of Alabama, the whole earth. In the dust storms, you can't find any light, can't recognize the steps behind you, the ones you just took. There is no path, no echo of your own, nothing familiar to connect you back.

And I need to go to work, need to keep moving, not think about the desert, Jennifer, her bus leaving at 2:30, my father, my uncle. I need to not think of this place—that's the key to an unsalvageable world. My father had told me that enough times, and I know it to be true, so I jump my hands to my work belt—if I can get out of the truck, if I can just get to the dig and dive like swimmers for the coral reef, slip into one of the tunnels, a mirage through sand and dust.

But why do I keep seeing my father's ghost?

His hands on the steering wheel—I felt warmth from his skin—our hands twining together to swerve this truck that had already stopped. On the dashboard, the smell of clay, fading sparkles, an emptiness. The wind is wild, beating sand against the grill. It stops, then picks along the wheels, gathers itself, and washes over the hood.

Two more men give Bossey an okay signal, fade to the earth. Another checks his water pressure, the toughness of his rope. I'm trying to get my hard-hat light to work and I hear mud gurgling, the sludge-pipe engines being filled with gas, sucking the muck into old cement trucks, spinning, scraping, and the heavy sound makes me feel safe. If I can just get outside to the dig.

"On seventeen, this is Ray. Pick up, Mat, if you're still driving. Over."

I reach down for my CB, flip the switch.

"Hey, it's Mat. You've got me. Over."

"Late to work again, huh?" Ray jokes, and the static cuts his voice in and out. "At least it's been easier to reach you."

I watch two more men dive. "So how's the water look-ing? Am I going to be able to work all night or not?" For thirteen years Ray has managed the irrigation house where the water is pumped from the river to us and the barrel houses where water is treated in huge vats, stored, and reused. He's the first to know about the shutoffs.

"I think she'll make morning, but the river's getting low and muddy. We're having to clean the filters a lot. Going to have to start rationing water, again. In a few nights we'll need to move up to Cahaba. But, hey, I've got some good news." Ray's voice is suddenly upbeat. "I got another bonus."

"You mean a dead body." My helmet lights up. I flip it off, back on.

"Coming in on Tuesday from Alaska. Alaska, Mat. That's some distance for Mr. George Peagrass, going to McRae, Georgia. Ever heard of McRae?"

"No," I answer.

"It's a good distance—almost to the Atlantic, according to my map. I could use your help."

"Sure," I tell him. The static cuts in and out, but as I watch another miner dive, I'm unsure of what I'm say-ing yes to. Something about the ocean—but vaguely— something about the Atlantic Ocean, and Ray's other job—burying people in the Southeastern Desert.

"One other thing. When I was in Birmingham last week I bought a dresser—"

"I thought you were supposed to sell dressers—"

"Couldn't pass this one up—made of maple. I really like maple."

"But is it in good shape? It's not another piece that needs stripping?" I'm suspicious.

"No, this is a Queen Anne. And it's going to be beauti-ful. But it does need a little help. What do you say, partner?"

"Partner?" The goodwill in his voice is the clincher.

"After work, what do you think?"

"Yeah, I'll help you with that, too," I tell him. It doesn't matter—Jennifer will be gone. I hear her whisper, *Come with me*, reaching over, nibbling on my bottom lip. *Four a.m. Breakfast on a Greyhound. Sex in the bathroom.* But that's when she was younger, was twenty-one and we married, when she wanted me to touch her.

Dust sweeps across the windshield. My light hits the mirror and blinds me for a moment.

There's something old in your eyes, she said, and I see it now, see it in my reflection, the blue diamond light, Jennifer's face turning toward the window at the trailer, the light outside flashing, flickering through. And my eyes close, my father's eyes close.

"See you then. Over and out." Ray clicks off.

CHAPTER 12

Desert Ceremony, 2035

"I do."

"By the powers invested in me—"

Jennifer grabbed my shoulders, biting my lip in a kiss, her veil hooking the wind, tangling for a moment, then billowing open like a bird in mid-flight. The veil dived suddenly hard to the sand, and Ray shoved the ring box he had been turning in his palm into his pocket and went after it. He snatched at the lace and small flowers, but the whirlwind caught the veil a second time, lifting, darting, just out of his reach, preparing for a long voyage.

How high would it go? we wondered. How high would the wind carry?

Then a downdraft crumpled the small flowers and dragged the veil down a mining hole.

The strips of decoration paper—blue, green, yellow—tore from the ground lights, as did the yellow roses my father had ordered from Birmingham and attached to the folding chairs. Everyone shut their eyes, waited for the wind to give out of breath.

"Man and wife," Bossey finally got to say, and he laughed—choppy, deep laughs, as if he had been saving every ounce of his strength just for this moment. He shut his book with a loud clap and put his arms around us.

"Now, this is a good thing, Mathew." He shifted inside his large black robe.

The workers, including my father, stood up, clapped, and whistled.

"You're going to be good for him," Bossey said to Jennifer. "He's luckier than the first day he came to work for the government, I can tell you that. Blessings, blessings," he squeezed us tight, "I give you all my blessings." Then he patted us both hard. "Now give me a second to clean some champagne glasses," and Bossey walked off in his shuffle, the smell of cooking oil leaving with him.

Jennifer pushed her body to mine, pulled my arms around her, then up and down, warming her back against the cool wind, unexpected, even this late in August.

"I wish these winds would quit," she said. "Just for a moment. But they won't, will they? Not even for my wedding dress and your nice tux." She trailed a finger down my coat sleeve, pointing to my black pants and shoes. The shoes had been purchased for my high school graduation, though I had never worn them—the leather too hard, cramping my toes.

"You do look nice." She smiled, her knee and calf easing between my legs.

Her embroidered dress was pulled at the zipper, the fabric puckered and creased; I wanted it to feel like her skin, so my hands could sink down and be warm, rubbing away the flecks of sand and lights, but the more I smoothed over the material, the rawer my hands became. I could taste blood where she had bitten my lip, and the soap Jennifer always used, its fragrance of lilacs washed with the blood.

"I love you," I kissed her, "here in our Alabama," and I smiled. It was a joke between us—with so few people, it felt like all of Alabama belonged to us.

"Only Alabama?" she asked, her voice trailing off, distant and dreamy. Chicago, the promise of blue skies and Lake Michigan to swim in—or maybe it was her mother she was thinking of, or her stepfather.

Jennifer's family had moved from one of the Mississippi camps only a year ago after the Pearl River dried up. After six months, her stepfather came up from a tunnel in Blacksher, flag number 270, coughing. "I can't breathe," Terry Philips said, and gasped and then his voice failed. Bossey pulled the alarm and we gathered around to calm him. We tried water. We put rags to his cheeks burning purple and red. But Terry was suffocating in front of us in the thinnest of air, and we felt guilty for each breath we rationed. In his swelling face, we could see ourselves, could feel the dust burning in our throats. When blood and clay began to spill from Terry's mouth, Bossey put him in his truck and drove toward Birmingham. Carson, the doctor the government sent down to help us, went along, too, but Terry died before they made it. "We were two hours from the hospital," Bossey told Mrs. Philips. "It was too much to ask of him. I'm sorry."

Mrs. Philips didn't nod or anything, just looked blankly at Bossey as if he had said something about the weather. She had carried a stricken expression from Mississippi, her deep wrinkles folding up her dimpled cheeks and her small dull eyes that seemed to dig at her skin, making us feel awkward in her presence. After her husband's death, she kept us even further away. She didn't know us, didn't want to know us.

But Mrs. Philips had a sister in Chicago who had written the asylum requests and could pay the cost, and so the government granted two visas—one for Mrs. Philips and one for Jennifer.

"Let's have the wedding in Chicago," Jennifer had pleaded. "Just think about it, Mathew. We could be someplace that's alive. We'll never have that here." My father had given the same reasons. As I grew older, his reasoning fermented with his anger. But Jennifer rarely stayed angry for long.

When I didn't respond, she simply pulled her black hair to her eyes and lips, let her arms dangle loose from her shoulders. I could grab her shoulders and hold them, but they wouldn't move, like the monarchs my father had told about—orange, yellow, and black wings like paper beating faster than your heart can catch. "When you watch them flutter," he promised, "you smile."

Jennifer wouldn't touch my body, and her eyes became her mother's, growing distant behind her curtain of hair, as if she had lost trust, had lost who I was completely.

When her stepfather died, the mood didn't pass for weeks.

She had already lost her biological father in a mining accident at age four. "I didn't know him that long," Jennifer used to say, and shrug as if it didn't matter. Terry's death wasn't as easy.

"I'm sorry about your father," I would bring up, but whenever I mentioned Terry's name she just nodded, never talked, and her skin became so cool, as if her body's spirit had left to roam the desert until my words were forgotten.

When the government promised visas, her mood had shifted back, the color in her skin, the way that she reached for my shoulders and touched me as if I were a part of her, all of it came back from her absence and wandering.

"Come on, Mathew. Let's marry in Chicago. We can be alive." Jennifer asked and asked, until finally she gave up that hope, too. After her mother left, Jennifer slipped deeper into depression. There were days with the sun popping the wood and wires of another temporary house, days stifled with heat that I held Jennifer's body naked and stiff, rubbing my hands slowly down slender arms, legs that wouldn't cross over mine, and the small bell of her stomach and back, shoulders set in covers, hard river stones I tried to warm to me until I fell hard asleep, dreaming that I was in the desert, too, looking for Jennifer. If I could find her here, find her wandering, then maybe I could bring her alive, force her awake. But I couldn't. I only found my own dreams, my own apparitions.

Then the wedding dress arrived from her mother with a letter. Our wedding day drew closer.

Tonight, her warmth had returned, was underneath her white dress, trapped in her skin. If I could slip my hand underneath the dress, each kiss, pancake makeup and lipstick lifting, this skin I could hold and curl into.

Jennifer locked her legs, her elbows and hands.

"Let's send everyone home and have sex." She gave me a sly smile, happy with her suggestion. Jennifer liked to catch people off guard and shock them, especially me.

"Now?"

"Yes. Send them all home," she said, her voice rising.

"But the sand . . ." I started. Jennifer hated the sand, said it never came out of her clothes or her hair no matter what she did.

"I can deal with the sand," she promised, and tugged at a button on my shirt, causing the entire shirt to move.

My father had starched the shirt into cardboard, sprayed and ironed and sprayed it. The buttons were almost impossible to loosen. But I knew Jennifer. I knew she wouldn't stop until my shirt was pulled out and open, flapping in the wind. I tried to turn my back to the workers, but her arms tightened around me.

All the workers had broken into small huddles, some around Bossey, who was serving champagne and cake, others returning from their trucks with cans of beer.

They came up, one by one, the few who had spouses came together, and patted Jennifer and me on the back or shook our hands, hugged us, said congratulations, and made toasts to our future more vigorously than either of us believed, all of them glancing at my shirt looped open in the middle where Jennifer had pulled a button completely off. Afterward, they slipped back into their circles, for the evening shift started soon.

But my father didn't step up. He stayed at a small table, fiddling with his record player, trying to get it to work. A musty square box lacquered in brown plastic, the player's coating had grown wavy in places where it had come unglued, scales peeling off fine as snakeskin, leaving splotches of oily plastic and metal until the brand name RCA could no longer be seen. The lid opened on hinges to a simple turntable, arm, and needle. Underneath, two heavy brown knobs (one labeled for 78, 33, 45 speed, and one for volume) commanded a built-in speaker that accented the cracks and pops in his records. The player had belonged to my grandfather, and my father grew up listening to Ella Fitzgerald, Billie Holiday, Nat King Cole, Peggy Lee, each night as he went to sleep. Grandpa Sanford played them in the kitchen and they filled Father's dreams. With my grandfather's death—he died a few years before I was born—my father inherited the player.

Once I started mining, I bought my father a new stereo, had Ray bring one from Birmingham as a peace offering for no longer going to school. My father uttered a perfunctory thanks and never once took it out of its box. I wanted to be upset with him, but I, too, preferred listening to the voices popping high and low, the crack of horns and strings on Grandpa Sanford's musty record player each night as I fell asleep. It was as if the popping added layers of history to the music; the more popping—the more static and crackle—the more you had to decode, years back, words, those people, their lives now lost.

I watched my father in his tux, his heavyset body, his attention on heavy knobs and the spinning black record— Benny Goodman's "Little Brown Jug." The sound streamed forth for a moment, the needle peeling off a layer of horns and clarinet, peeling the sound away, then the arm skipped and lost itself just like it did the first time I played something for Jennifer. "Does it still work?" She had lifted the arm and inspected the diamond needle. "I thought these things were only found in museums."

"It works," I insisted, wiping the album with a cloth. I dusted the needle and started the album over. My father did the same thing now. This time the needle dug into the groove.

"Come on," Jennifer ordered, and began to spin me around. I had watched my father dance but rarely danced myself. When I did, I held an invisible back just as he had done in the kitchen. I understood the circling, the turning, the rhythm in the feet. It felt good to finally hold someone real, and we started to spin faster and faster, beating out the tiny dust storms—our only competition. Even when the trumpets and drums abruptly halted, we kept spinning and spinning, until Jennifer spilled champagne on my sleeve.

"Sorry, sorry, sorry," she said, then gathered up her gown and wiped the spot.

"I love you, Mathew," she said suddenly. "That's why I stayed in Alabama." Her words caught me off guard as if something between us had skipped, as if all this elapsed time between what I had said minutes ago about *our* Alabama and now was some other motion, some other conversation, two other people suddenly returning to their beginning place.

"I'm glad you stayed," I told her. "Besides, you make me feel dizzy." For even as our bodies came to a rest, the circling went on and on in my head. I felt like a horse on a carousel, lighted reins twisting, music out of tune. I was six again, twelve again, and the small traveling fair had drifted along the other mining camps finally to ours. I wanted the world to slide around me as I walked through the Midway, beaten up by gravity, carousel horses, too much cotton candy, trying not to fall—all of that in her dress now—the champagne, folds of white.

"And being dizzy is important?" she asked.

"Especially here, don't you think?"

Jennifer shook her head as if I were crazy.

"I'm sorry your mother didn't make it."

"It's okay. Mom told me she couldn't come back. I knew she wouldn't." Jennifer dabbed at the spot on my sleeve. "She wishes us well, though. Told me that in her letter. Said we should come see her."

I was about to say, *and live with her*—that's what Jennifer's mother really wanted—but Ray grabbed my arm with a handkerchief.

"Don't mess up the white dress," he scolded Jennifer, wedging his body between us. "It's the only one in the whole camp. Someone else might need it when they get married."

"There's no one to marry but Jennifer," I pointed out.

"Yeah, yeah," Ray sighed, and pushed his glasses on straight, "there are a few girls—they're just too young, still in school. And besides, you never know. Women might be moving down here from Birmingham any day now."

"In droves," I added.

"And for what sane reason?" Jennifer smiled.

"The weather," Ray explained to us matter-of-factly, as

if there were some weight, some truth to his words, something that we had neglected to notice. He looked up at the lights—it was hard to see the black sky beyond the glare and pink glow, but Jennifer and I looked up, too, as if maybe the sky would actually heal, as if, for a second, we believed him.

"Stop," I finally said. "No one's moving back here. You're too damn hopeful."

"And silly," Jennifer added. "And you're in my way." She pushed him so hard that he fell back to the edge of a crater.

"What you got against hope?" Ray asked, his voice rising at the end.

"It's a good night to be hopeful," Jennifer said, and pinched me, but I didn't feel it. I had already started toward Ray, because in all the joking he was about to fall in the crater. More than a few people had died, most of them drunk, falling forty, fifty feet, their bodies heavy with gravity, breaking, plopping down against the hardening mud.

But Ray grabbed the horse pulley and steadied himself.

"Don't be so damn rough," he scolded, the pulley's flimsy aluminum frame wobbling more and more as Ray straightened up. But Ray was just as wiry, just as wobbly, had always been that way in school, a year older than Jennifer and me. The round gold-rimmed glasses he wore swallowed his bottle-shaped head, especially now that he was losing his hair at twenty-two. "Twenty-two!" he said in constant disbelief since his birthday a few weeks earlier. "I'm too young and too handsome not to have hair."

I told him it was because he was so greedy.

"I'm just an opportunist"—that's how Ray put it.

"You used to be a pessimist, or at least indifferent," I told him. "What happened to you?" It was when his mother left five years ago. That's when Ray changed. He oversaw the barrel houses, which were old warehouses that pocked the desert, and the irrigation house where they pumped water out to the clay mines. The irrigation house was a huge square building that we disassembled and re-assembled at each stop along the river. No one could start digging until Ray said we could. He had connections with Birmingham, a visa that allowed him to travel back and forth between the Saved World and our world, but unlike when we were younger and the two of us guessed about the Saved World, what it was like, Ray knew the truth and wouldn't tell—he said only that the Saved World was fine, doing just fine, just not as beautiful as the desert.

As for the greed, for his opportunities—he sold an-tiques to a dealer in Birmingham. The minute we arrived in a ghost town, he searched through every home and store for anything valuable. He purchased antiques off of the workers as well, whatever they found in the temporary houses they moved into. Ray had tried to get my father's record player.

But he made his real money with a funeral service for people in the Saved World who lived here once, who wanted to be buried at their birthplace, in cemeteries with their grandparents, spouses, and great-grandparents. He would make the journey for them to the underworld, bury anyone for the right price, anywhere in the Southeastern Desert. You could find his undertaker service online and in phone books listed in the Saved World. In Birmingham, Nashville, and Atlanta he had huge billboards staked out. Ray picked up the prepared bodies at the Greyhound sta-tion and Birmingham International Airport if they were Out-of-Towners, as he called them, and funeral parlors and residences throughout the city, in his big black Suburban, carrying a map, surveying equipment, shovels, posthole diggers, a chiseled headstone, taking them wherever they wanted to go.

I had been along with him on trips that took us into the

desert in the heat of day, a time that hardly anyone traveled, that the government had restricted—if you got stranded and couldn't reach anyone by walkie-talkie or CB, couldn't get back, then you'd die. But I didn't care about the risk—when I was seven my father had taken me out in the sun and nothing happened. I was too young for death, and Ray was too young.

"It's crazy that people want to be buried here, don't you think?" I often asked. After driving for hours our conversations circled around to the same questions. "They've already left once."

"I couldn't tell you if it's crazy," he said, "but dead people have lots of money and last wishes they can't take with them. That's where I come in."

"Greed always gets you into trouble," I reminded, and tapped his shoulder to make my point. I was a true disciple of my father at times and couldn't help it.

"Opportunity. Opportunity," Ray answered, tapping my shoulder back. "You've got to make the best of this place. One day, you'll realize I'm telling the truth."

But I couldn't see things his way—all his optimism built on other people's loss, the draining of rivers, on furniture and jewelry people left in their rush to escape. And I couldn't understand their wishes either—people escaping this death only to want to come back to it.

Winter was his busiest time. Most people seemed to pass away after one more autumn, he observed. And most weeks in January he looked haggard, thinner than usual from driving in the sun, working all night at the irrigation house. Ray had a small crop of skin cancers on his neck, arms, and face that had to be burned off every few months. "They're a bother, but they'll never kill me," he promised, and I never asked him how much he made, just took my hundred in US dollars on those trips in which he needed my help. Without a doubt Ray was fairly rich, especially compared to the rest of us in camp. He had found some use for this dying place and uncovered new uses all the time, though his being an undertaker with a black Suburban made the other workers a little uneasy. The Death Machine, they called his truck, refusing to park near it. And some called Ray the devil himself, though the nickname got mostly laughs. He wasn't strong enough to be the devil—maybe a feeble death with a scythe. He was harmless, a little weird, most said, and why did I hang out with him anyway? I'd shrug my shoulders—a few times I started to protest, but always I managed not to answer. I didn't have an excuse. What do you say when your best friend is the devil and you like him?

The pulley kept wobbling even though Ray had let it go. He quickly moved from the mining hole to Jen and me.

"You almost knocked me in," he accused her. At the limestone areas around Santuck, some holes went ninety feet.

"I had faith you wouldn't fall in," she said, no concern in her voice. "Those kind of holes are for all your dead people, not for you. Where would the dead be without you?"

"I guess you and Mat would take over the business. There's no one else I'd want to have it."

"Not those routes in winter," I said. "No thanks. You'll have to find someone else."

"Things change, Mat. Trust me about change." Teachers had given the same speech proudly in school, especially Ms. Jones, noting that we river people were a great example of the consequences of change, but they never went much further with their mantra. It would be too depressing. "You've just got to have an open mind about this place."

In the background, Grandpa Sanford's record player finally appeared to be warmed up, going through an entire

Peggy Lee song without skipping. "It's a Good Day" started, and Jennifer hooked my arm.

"Let's dance some more, Mat."

"I'd like to," Ray cut in. "I mean, the best man does get one dance, right?" He cleared his throat and straightened the glasses against the bridge of his nose.

"Yes—one," Jennifer said politely, then turned to me and whispered, "Let's go to the Gulf right now. I don't want to stay here any longer." We had planned to go to Mexico Beach for our honeymoon. "I want to see the ocean. They say you can see the sun setting, maybe even blue sky in late summer, sometimes dolphins will come into the water." She spun on her heel, squeezed my fingers. The flash of sequins and white lace kept my head dizzy, kept me thinking of the carousel, of white birds, her black hair in sparkles of dust.

"All right, let's go," I said. When she was in such a good mood, I always felt better. "I just need to tell my father."

She nodded and grabbed hold of Ray. "Come on, Best Man. This is it for you," and they started.

I called after them to watch out for the holes and looked over the dig, its boundary of sludge trucks, pipes, and generators, until I found my father. He was picking up a glass of champagne from Bossey. Bossey uttered his toast faithfully like a priest giving sacrament, then the two men drank. He refilled my father's glass, and it seemed that my father was looking everywhere except where I was standing. Slowly, however, his body turned, and he trudged over.

"Congratulations," he said, his voice rough like a car engine starting cold, a smile trying its damnedest to wash the tension from his face. He hadn't wanted us to marry— not here. He had wanted us to leave, go with Jennifer's mother to Chicago, and I watched to see if his grin would rise or wither, for the way my father and I smiled had grown very much alike. Now that I was twenty-one, people told us that we could be brothers—my father's grin still young-looking despite the hard work and clay, despite the crow's-feet gathered at his eyes, the roughness in his voice—all that dancing, I told him, all that dancing before I was born had kept him young at heart. The trick with my father was to get him to reveal it.

"You got one thing right in this damn place. Now take her out of here and have children—do that for your old man."

"But you won't leave," I said. But I rushed the words, said them too harsh, and regretted it immediately. The truth was, all of our conversations turned bitter sooner or later.

"No, I'm staying in Alabama. Ray said he would bury me at the farm with your mother—"

"That's where I'll be buried."

"You don't know the farm."

"I was born there."

"You don't have to die there, do you?" he said, but he wouldn't look at me. "You're young, Mat. You can still escape the desert, can have a life, at least until the whole earth burns itself up."

"What good is it without you? What if it's all domed cities like you tell me? the air ruined? How long do we have anyway before the earth burns up?"

He shook his head. "I don't know." His voice had lost its edge and become quiet. "Probably won't happen until you're fifty or sixty," his words shaky, unable to convince himself. "It's no good trying to predict this world. You should go to the Saved World while some of it is still saved."

Then he raised his champagne flute and cleared his throat in an attempt to smooth his voice. "Good luck, son." He drank, but the happiness of the occasion had passed, and I didn't answer him.

"It's strange," he said.

"What is?"

"I'm telling you good luck when all there is for you and Jennifer in this desert is death. What kind of luck is that to be wishing someone, especially your own son?" His voice was metallic and bitter, drying out, sinking even rougher— I was afraid that soon he wouldn't be able to talk at all. In the past, his voice had vanished for weeks at a time, vanished more and more on a regular basis, his only option to scribble messages onto strips of paper. He seemed to know it, too, and his face locked up.

My father gazed past the equipment into the flat land, the wind blowing huge whirls of dust into a single hill, what we called whalebacks, that could go on for miles and miles. I looked, too, as far as the ground lights would let me, looked for some way to answer him, to turn the conversation and start again.

"Mr. Chris." Ray raised his glass in salute. He and Jennifer spun in front of us, and Father lifted his glass.

"Now, there's someone who can make money off a dying situation."

I watched my father's smile, his yellow hair and beard silver-slicked. No, this smile was too hard to be my brother's.

His wedding tux was cut close to his waist, making his stomach more in line with his chest; on his pants' legs, marching-band stripes, his knees twitching, a movement always in my father, ready to dance.

Earlier, at the house as I worked the buttons on my shirt, he had come into the kitchen.

"This," he said, pointing to the suit he was buttoning. "Your mother said if I wore this, she'd dance with me every night." My father slammed the heel of his foot down and spun, his hands grasping a chair back before he fell.

"You look great doing that," I said.

He laughed. "I look ridiculous," and he recovered his balance fully. "But I looked great at one time."

It was true. I had seen pictures of him and Mamma with ribbons and trophies, pictures of them in step, with horn players blaring.

He snapped his fingers, the coat sleeves cuffing down into place, and he laughed so fully that I almost believed he had been happy once.

Suddenly the wind hurried down, scratching the needle across the record. Peggy Lee's voice tore, and my father stopped.

"I've got it," Ray shouted, and started Peggy Lee again.

Jennifer was already walking over. "Dance with me, Mr. Chris. Can I have a dance with the groom's older brother?" She tugged on his elbow. "I know how much you love to dance. Let's see those feet moving." I could make out a row of sweat along her hairline. I wanted to lift the thick strands in back, allow the heat to escape, the grassy smell mixed with perfume.

"Sure," he answered, a little embarrassed, "I'll give it a try." And this smile *was* contagious enough to be my brother's. Jennifer had the self-confidence to do this to anybody.

My father lowered his champagne to the ground and rubbed his hands together, those short chubby fingers not as big and fat as Bossey's. For some reason, my father's hands had never fully grown. Carefully, he placed one hand to her back. My hands felt raw thinking of the puckered material of Jennifer's dress. Raw and empty. He waited, was waiting for something in the music, I knew, some beat to begin. Then all at once they shifted.

I watched, his hands perfect, guiding their feet between dust swirls and craters. It was like watching Ginger Rogers and Fred Astaire dance on the moon, studio lights all around them.

I watched my father move and thought of all those nights when he didn't notice me watching—the spin, spin, sudden stop, unfurling of Jennifer's body like the empty woman in the kitchen between refrigerator and table, between his fingers, above them a single bulb, a makeshift chandelier. Then tightly he pulled Jennifer in, their feet making cuts into the earth, forcing the dust to fall away.

Bossey unzipped his robe. "Work in fifteen minutes," he yelled from behind the table, "fifteen minutes," his trousers and galoshes showing.

"Guess I better get over to the irrigation house," Ray grumbled, and shot back his glass of champagne. He looked out across the mining field.

"Your father," he started, "and Jennifer," but didn't say any more. He, too, was mesmerized.

I told Ray, "I've always wanted to see him dance with somebody. I was hoping."

And it wasn't just us. As the workers fitted on hats, gloves, and tightened their boots, they formed a crescent around Jennifer and my father, the spotlights overhead, the song going into its conclusion:

'Cause it's a good day for payin' your bills,

And it's a good day for curin' your ills,

So take a deep breath (Ahhh!) and throw away your pills,

'Cause it's a good day from mornin' till night! (Say that again!)

Oh, it's a good day from mornin' till night (That's what he said!)

Yes, it's a good day from mornin' till night!

My father dipped Jennifer, taking her arch gradually up the string of his arm until straight, their shoulders locked. Then the spin unraveled, and their hands let go. He clapped and she bowed, dust swirling around them, dust dying, rising and dying, over and over.

CHAPTER 13

Dothan, 2024

> High today 102°. Tonight's low 65°. Air stagnant with
> the ozone index reaching 210. CODE RED. Currently
> 85°. Ozone index at 160. Do not go outside after 10 a.m.
> Repeat: CODE RED. Travel restricted after 10 a.m. This
> report is updated every hour.
> —*WDMZ 1610 AM, 9:05 a.m.*

The white haze wasn't so thick yet that my father
couldn't see where he was going, and we soon made it to a
small huddle of shops—a strip mall, my father called
them—used for the mining securities office, the doctor's
office, the marshal, and Tina's grocery store. All the
smaller government agencies were here as well, except for
the school, which had been kept at Dothan Elementary.
The one place you could get liquor, Lula D's (named after
an Alabama River steamboat), sat a few doors from the
Church of the Brethren. My father said you could get
saved, get drunk, and go to jail all in one block. "That's
easy living," my uncle added. "Have your spirit lifted twice,
then sleep your spirit off in jail."

In some towns, the downtown districts were used, and
in others, the buildings were in such bad condition that
work had to be done out of the back of trailers or from the

homes of the government agents. But in Dothan, the
Gatewood strip mall had held up against the sun, and at
the center stood a C & T bank, where our physician,
Carson, and Jack Thompson, the marshal, had their offices. The bank peeked out like the head of a goose, ready
to carry the whole flock of buildings south with its A-frame
and plastic emblem, the red and blue C & T colors faded
to a gray pink. On this morning, a sprawl of trucks jutted
out into the plaza in front of Tina's grocery. Each cab was
empty.

"Let's go," my father said as soon as we parked, and I
reached for the handle with my good hand. My right arm
was purple now and achy and kept swelling and shrinking
back a little. I tried not to bang it, touch it, but the morning
air made me cough, which made my arm hurt more. If the
ozone didn't burn, it would seem like a harmless fog, but
both of us were coughing, and everyone was standing in
front of Tina's with rags on their faces, gazing to where my
grandfather's tractor had reared up and shot through the
glass front doors and windows, no longer sputtering, but
stuck, unable to wiggle inside. Tina had built a pyramid of
cans in the left window—green beans were on sale—and
the display had completely fallen.

"What are you going to do about this mess, Harrison?"
she shouted from inside the store, and at first I thought
Tina was shouting at me, calling me by my last name like
some of my teachers did. Usually she called my father Mr.
Chris, but Tina was talking to him, putting the blame on
him. She said "Harrison" like it was something nasty she
had to spit quickly from her mouth.

"Harrison?" she demanded. I couldn't see her behind
the tractor, but her voice, high and jangly, was scary
enough, and the bruise on my arm went cold.

Everyone turned and looked at us. No one else in camp
had a John Deere. When we said nothing, they turned back

around and mumbled and shook their heads. And I looked hard into them, slowly searching through the mudded clothes and hands, but I didn't find Ray.

"Came clear across the desert," one of the voices raised up above the others.

"Lucky someone's not killed. Flying in here without a driver. I saw it without a driver." It was Bill Tilson who answered. His daughter Katherine was in my class. He gave me a look, and my father a look, like we had done something, bewitched the tractor or messed with its gears. We were guilty. And I wondered if what happened to me had also happened to Ray, if he got bucked off somewhere between the farmhouse and Gatewood. I started thinking of those government warnings and the children dying in the sun.

"How far you think it went?" another miner said, and coughed into her rag, paisley and blue, glancing at my father, but my father refused to speak.

"Come on now, Chris," Jack Thompson said, "tell us what happened," and he thumbed his hands into his belt, his shoulders stretching, and he sighed. Jack didn't wear a badge, but the slope of his shoulders gave his entire body a strength and caution people backed away from. I was always amazed at how that same body could just as easily pull in a crowd when Jack wanted to tell his jokes.

"About five miles, six miles," I blurted, "that's how far," and my father glared at me. He bit his jaw in tight, scolding, and I looked down. My father didn't like spectacles to begin with, and I had put him at the center, then spoken up and drawn even more attention. I knew better than to say anything else.

"And without a driver." Bill Tilson shook his head. "Six miles without a driver. That's something."

"Divineness of God," a man said. He had on waders like my father, his hair all tangled in clay, and everyone looked at the Church of the Brethren with its cross leaning against the chipped wall. No one had been brave enough to climb and nail the cross to the roof since the preacher's legs got snared in rotten boards a few months earlier in Andalusia.

"There's nothing godlike about my tractor," my father told him.

And I should've spoken up, too, should've said something about Ray, that he was missing, but I could tell that the tractor and me, my father, that we were becoming a mini-legend, and possibly, eventually a full legend like the Red Baron in his long flights over enemy lines. I wondered if he ever let go of the gears, let his plane fly itself.

"Can't you see the hand of God in all this?" the man said. "Six miles without a driver and no one's killed?"

"Luck," my father shot back. "God doesn't have time to drive tractors."

"He's too busy making deserts and fools," Jack Thompson said, and some in the crowd chuckled.

"It could've killed me," Tina shouted. She was pacing from one side of the front wheels to the other, slipping in and out of view like a shooting gallery duck, being careful around the broken glass. Despite the haze, I could make out her scraggliness, the red-brown curls that draped over her thin neck, and underneath, all bones and wrinkles wrapped in loose overalls that she wore like many of the miners did, like Bossey did. Behind her stood aisles of produce and tools and clothes she had organized into perfect displays—more cans stacked into pyramids, handkerchiefs and gloves grouped by size and color, and boxes of candy straightened into rows with even the candy aligned. She kept her arms crossed. "The sun's going to ruin everything if you don't get this tractor out soon. It's your responsibility, Harrison."

"Wayne's coming, and Bossey," my father said. "They're

bringing the winch from the dig. But I've got to see about Mathew right now. He's hurt."

I was glad to be of some use, even if it was to simply get us out before Tina's attacks became sharper.

"Aren't you going to arrest him?" she snapped at Jack Thompson. "His tractor could of killed me, flying like it did. I'll have to find another place. You know how long it'll take to get my stuff set right?"

"But it didn't kill you," Jack Thompson said. "You're fine, and the boy's hurt. Let's just take it easy until we can get the tractor. Then we'll look for another shop or fix this one. It's an accident anyway." Jack's voice was soothing and low, and his voice grew lower and lower as my father walked me to the bank, but Tina's voice jangled louder, until all her words became an impossible constant ringing. I was afraid she might try to hurt my father if she could only get out, but Tina was pegged in, and I knew I wouldn't be able to buy groceries or anything else from her for a long time. And Ray, why didn't I say something about Ray?

The bank was split into two partitions by a quickly made wall of plywood and tacked-up covers and old quilts—the left half was the marshal's office, empty now, but seeing that empty side, I wondered what laws I had broken, as Tina had suggested. Would I have to go to jail? Our jail was literally a cage that Jack lugged on his pickup from town to town and had unloaded into the front portion of the bank, closing off several teller windows. Jack said the longest anyone had sat in his cage was a week. "You'd go stir-crazy if it was any longer," he assured us. It had a small cot and a bucket, and even with the open view through the bars, it was obvious that all the emptiness in the room was held inside that cage. The bars went up and down, most of them straight, and they didn't move, and neither did the small bars on the teller windows. Brad Sincs had the same kind of window on his Airstream trailer we called the Silver Can.

The Silver Can stayed at the mining dig and each Friday Brad Sincs parceled out the weekly earnings in scrip, what my father called Monopoly money. Later he told me Monopoly was like cards or checkers, except you used fake money to play. The scrip was only good at Tina's, Lula D's, Teal's Gas, and the government agencies in the camp, and because it was useless in the Saved World, some miners traded the scrip for US dollars on the black market. My father had done this for my immigration, though it was illegal and the exchange was never even—six scrip dollars (an hour of digging) got you one US dollar. But the truth was, we had been paid in scrip so long, we no longer knew how much our Monopoly money was worth outside the desert, if it was worth anything at all.

In front of the teller windows stood Jack's cage and his table and black swivel chair, and to the right of the partition was Carson. We went to the right, and Carson got up from his sofa where he had been half lying down, watching TV. Each time an actor or actress said a line, the invisible audience roared with laughter, but I couldn't tell what show it was since we didn't have a TV at home. "The want machine. The more you watch, the more you want stuff," my father declared, "and in a place lacking stuff, that's not good." But that didn't seem to bother Carson. He stood up, lightly twirled a duster at the sofa without letting the feathers actually touch the surface, as if the motion itself could remove dust from the leather seat, and the smell of wood and steel became the smell of antiseptic and plastic.

"I hear your tractor got into a little trouble this morning," he said. "What else is wrong?"

"Mat injured himself," my father explained.

"How?"

When I didn't respond, my father pushed me.

"I fell off of it," I told Carson, and cleared my throat, and brushed my good hand through my hair.

Carson nodded and walked up to us. "Lucky you didn't get run over. Where did you fall?"

"At home."

He shook his head. "Your body—where on your body."

"My arm and side," and I turned, but before I finished, he had my arm in his palms, rolling it with the duster back and forth. The feathers tickled a little, and their looseness reminded me of Carson's white hair and cotton candy. But his palms—they weren't smooth as I expected them to be. They were rough like my father's, as if Carson was a miner and only pretending to be a doctor.

"Yeah, your arm's swelling bad. Scoot over to the table." As I sat down, my butt crinkled up the paper, and my father sat on the sofa, doing everything he could not to look at the television, the loud obnoxious giggling that echoed through the bank.

Carson told me to take off my shirt, then he wrapped my arm in a sheet of cool plastic, an imaging sheet, and took a larger one and wrapped it around my stomach and chest—it gave me chills as he tightened them.

Each sheet had wires attached to separate monitors, and I watched, waiting for my arm to appear, first the skin, and next, slowly, layer by layer, all the way to the bones. The same thing happened to my ribs—images of blood pushed through, constricting with globs of white, black, and red flesh as the monitor zoomed to the center of my body and back out. I felt like I was watching a science experiment, and I made myself breathe and breathe until I recognized the swimming flux and constriction of blood, the pattern as my own. Carson changed the angles on the monitors as my skin grew sweaty and hot with a murmur happening inside, radiating out.

Then the door opened, and in came Jack, followed by two patrol deputies, a woman and man in flat brown suits that had been made, it seemed, out of Alabama soil, and between them another man in handcuffs. Jack worked on the gate of the cage, switching the keys until it opened while they removed the man's cuffs chained at the stomach and below, ankle cuffs. When the woman kneeled, the knot of blond hair under her cap began to fall and she pushed it back in. The other deputy held a club to the cuffed man's neck. He was in a black jumpsuit and carefully he twisted his arms and stretched as they led him and shut him inside. I knew he was a deserter. That's how they looked when they showed deserters on television at school.

"Sit down," Carson demanded, and pushed on the top of my head to hold me in place. "You have to be still so I can do this." I hadn't realized I had moved up at all.

"So where are you taking him?" I heard Jack say.

"To Quitman, Georgia, the gravel mine," the woman said, and handed him the documents. Initially deserters were sent to the new prisons along the border. Supposedly, even some criminals from the Saved World had been sent to the prisons—a whole network had been built and continued to be built. "Imagine looking out of your cell every day and all you see is sand and blowing wind and just that sea, that hard dry sea," my father said. But the government had also started to use prisoners in mines. There was the Quitman Mine, and one in Mississippi near Jackson, and two limestone mines in Florida. My father called them chain gangs, called it slavery, "Only they don't care about the color of your skin now, only where you're from." I had a visa, I had permission to leave, but without it, you were a fugitive. And if they found you, they brought you back.

"Your body's all right," Carson acknowledged in a whisper. He had brought his voice down so he wouldn't disturb the deputies, or maybe just to listen in as much as he could over the television.

"But your arm," he unwrapped the sheet from my chest, "has a fracture in the radius." He placed his finger on the monitor and ran it down the white part where he had zoomed in, and I could see a thin split like a twist of smoke. "I'm going to have to put it in a cast." He nodded to my father when he said this, but my father wasn't paying us any attention.

"Hopefully we'll get started back to the station tonight," the woman said. "The haze is too much right now."

"It'll be fine by then." Jack nodded and signed the last sheet of the documents. "Lula D's, the little bar, has some rooms for sleeping."

"You're not talking about the building with the tractor in it? How did that happen?" the other deputy asked.

"I haven't gotten the full story yet." Jack glanced at my father, then me. "It's been a weird morning, but we get those. Lula D's is on the other side. Just tell them I sent you. Probably Stacy is running the bar now, Stacy Cochran. And don't mind the drunks when you go in. They just finished digging all night. Lula D's has a few rooms, and if you're interested, some of them with prostitutes." He handed the documents to the woman.

"I'm too tired for prostitutes," she said, and looked at the other deputy, but he said nothing.

"How far did he get?" My father pushed himself up from the sofa and began to walk.

"We drove from Memphis. All night, pretty much," she explained, turning to face my father.

"No. How far did the deserter get?"

"Kansas," the woman said. Her voice drifted, had an ease to it—laid back, what everyone tried to imitate as laid back at school, a West Coast voice, and not at all sharp like Tina's. I wondered where she was from. "He went from Mississippi to Kansas."

"How did you catch him?"

"Just walking, I believe. A deputy picked him up."

"All that time in the sun." My father's expression went blank, and he put his hands on Jack's cage. He looked right at the deserter. "So you took a chance to enjoy the North?" And I got up, 'cause all I could see now was my father's back.

"Stop it, boy. Be still." Carson hushed me as if I was the one speaking and not him. He was busy wrapping gauze around my arm, but I kept moving, and he trailed behind, and didn't force me back to the table.

The deserter shook his head. I could see half his face, then more and more, like pieces of the moon or an apple, until I saw the tiny moles, so many on his splotchy black skin. And there was something hollow and drooping about his eyes. I stood and watched.

"Nothing to enjoy in Kansas," the man in Jack's cage told my father, and his accent was so thick, so different from ours—*Mississippi*, I thought, and wondered how Alabamans sounded to him, as if the dust had twisted his tongue and made his words come out strange. "It's like it is here. That's why they caught me. There's nothing there to hide behind."

But what about the fields? I wanted to ask. The corn and wheat Ms. Jones had talked of, that I had dreamed of.

"Come on, now. There's stuff in Kansas," the other deputy said, and chuckled. It made his full red cheeks jiggle, what my Uncle Wayne called jowls. "Watch out. This man's a liar, been lying all the way from Memphis."

"Are you from Kansas?" my father asked.

"My wife," the man explained. "She's free. They didn't catch her." He gave a strong nod.

"Oh, we'll get her," the deputy assured him, and pulled at his cap until he had it at the angle he wanted. "But you'll never see her. She'll be at the women's prison."

"She won't get caught," the man insisted. "She has people in Kansas protecting her. She'll get smuggled out."

"They didn't protect you," the deputy reminded. "We got you."

The deserter looked at him. "She has people in Kansas," he said again, but the deputy just smiled confidently and nodded.

The man shut his hollow eyes and brought himself slowly down to the bottom of Jack's cage.

"Did you see anything?" my father asked, his voice desperate. "Anything that was good? That was worth leaving here for?"

"Leave him alone," the woman said firmly, then looked inside the cage. "Don't speak. You're not supposed to. I don't want to have to use this." In her hand she had a flat piece of metal, a rectangle muzzle hinged with a metal bolt and lock in back. I had seen them on television, how they fit over the deserters' faces, making them into muzzled dogs.

But the man wasn't speaking, and slowly in that silence, slowly he put his hands to his face, and he started to cry. In the background, the television audience kept laughing, making me dizzy.

"You better go see about your tractor," Jack said.

"So you'll send him to Quitman for trying to leave, for just doing that?" My father kept his hands on the cage.

"He broke the law," she said.

My father just looked at her, then the other deputy, then Jack, and no one would respond, and I felt dizzy, a sign that the sun was getting to me, and Carson had stopped wrapping my arm, but I felt his hand holding my arm, just holding there lazy.

"Did he kill someone?" my father asked. "Did he hurt someone?"

Under my breath, I whispered, "Pick up the cage." I wanted my father to pick up Jack's cage and take it from the bank, as if my father could do that, as if there was that much strength in him.

"He broke the law," the woman repeated forcefully. "Is there something you wish to declare?"

"Don't."

And the word, that single word was something that should've come out of my mouth, at least that's what I decided when I thought about it later, but at the time I wanted my father to pick up the cage and carry the man. But it was Carson, Carson who said *Don't*, who yelled it, who understood what might happen if my father said something treasonous. You could go to prison for speaking against the government. You could go to one of the prison mines. Inside the camp, we said what we wanted, but this deputy had just come from Memphis, from the Saved World, and she was waiting.

My father looked at Carson, and then me, and then back to her. "He didn't do anything," my father said. "Anything." And my father's voice was low and deep and he let go of the cage, which he wasn't supposed to do. *Pick it up*, I almost whispered again, shouted. My father sighed and seemed to shrink down. He looked back across the room. "Just send him out when you get done."

Carson said he would and my father left and there was a huge emptiness in that building, just the man sobbing and the laughter from the television as if the TV were laughing at him, as if that crying had become part of the show.

CHAPTER 14

Honeymoon, 2035

July 17

My dearest Jen,
    Your wedding day. First, I must apologize for not being there. I never thought I would miss my daughter's wedding, but I can't return to Alabama only to leave you a second time. I'm not even sure——————————
————————————————————————
————————————————————————
————————————————————————
—————————————————but somehow I feel that I
abandoned you there, even if it was your wish to stay.

I've only been here a few months and already I'm having difficulty——————————————————

——————————————————————

——————————————————. It's not the same as the constant dust storms——————————

——————————————and, of course, I only know——————————————————

——————————————————————

want you and Mathew to come. Chicago is a good place. There's another room your Aunt Bobbie uses for storage right now. I just don't want you to come and expect——

——————————————————

——————————————. It takes some time to adjust, but you'll do that.

I'm enclosing a wedding dress from a bridal shop— they have many shops here. It has the lace and the design like we talked about before I left. The size I hope is still right. If not, ask Julie Oliver to look at it. She did some work for me. I'm enclosing money, too, so your trip to Chicago will be easier.

I hope to see you and Mat soon. The wedding, I'm certain, will be wonderful.

Affectionately,

Mom

After the wedding, while everyone clinched their ropes and plunged into the earth, Jennifer and I snuck into the cab of my truck and drove all night into the pitch, following a highway that was barely there. It was one moment of real possibility.

I still had the gray Chevy. A week earlier, Ray and I had taken rubber hammers and crowbars and things you shouldn't use on a truck—and pulled and snarled the metal door, made it bend, made it work. The truck itself had become as familiar to me as my father, as the pine box he kept under the bed filled with old pictures and government documents he would never use, as the ghost dance steps slipping from the records, and I wanted to keep the truck as long as I could.

My father insisted the truck smelled of sweet corn feed, what he and Uncle Wayne had fed to horses that disappeared when I was born. They were long gone now, but my father told me, "It's sweet corn feed, that's for sure," and whenever he crawled inside the cab, he drew in an exaggerated breath, telling me he could see the horses walking, the slow clopping of hooves approaching, the heads of horses roan and appaloosa—he gave them names sometimes with his eyes closed, "Blaze" and "Zodiac" and "Hummingbird" bending long-down into the trough that the wind worked on, sifting and sifting, the horses rolling their tongues, carrying the lightest dust of the feed away.

The weather had been promised good for the next week or two—no dust storms, no disturbances. There was even a lull in the wind, and the desert had become dead quiet. We wanted to honeymoon as long as we could on Mexico Beach and brought the shortwave radio Bossey had loaned me to keep the weather in check. We had coolers in the back full of food and candles, small Ti-generators, propane and gas tanks, sleeping bags, and a tent in case the abandoned hotels had all crumbled as we had heard.

"I've got to get out of this wedding dress," Jennifer said abruptly, and put her hands under her hair, allowing its full curtain to fan out and down, her hair so thick, always beading sweat at the roots. Wherever we went, Jennifer was drawn to air conditioners and would throw her head against them, gasping, the fine black strands spreading over the vents like iron filings around a magnet, or when we had a freezer, we would make buckets of ice for her to dip in or if the heat was too much, she'd snatch a pair of scissors and threaten to cut it off, every length of it, and eventually beg me to do the cutting.

"This hair is a curse," she used to say, wagging the scissors, lobbing pieces of ice at me. "You don't understand what it's like to have this kind of hair." And I didn't, but I loved her black hair and would hold handfuls of crushed ice above her ear until she went numb with too much cold, behind her neck, her forehead, and hide the scissors, and she knew that and threatened and threatened and kept her hair for me.

I checked the vents, kept thumbing the louvers open, but the air conditioner was weak, and the night hadn't cooled down enough yet—we needed the same north wind from the wedding.

The compass bobbed due south, and the road, Highway 1, began to clear up in patches. You could make out strips and triangles and squares of blue tar and reflectors nailed into the center and signs that were no longer needed and markers gobbling up the distance traveled—27 miles, 36, 53, and on, from ghost town to ghost town.

"You don't mind if I take the dress off, do you?"

"No," I answered, trying to sound uninterested. "Go ahead." I had already taken off my coat and well-starched frilly shirt and crumpled them in the extended cab. I felt much better in my T-shirt, the holes around the neck ripped wide and thin from being washed so much.

Jennifer grabbed at the zipper in back of the dress, but after a couple of attempts, she scooted around and I loosened it, my finger opening a tiny stream of skin.

"Keep your eyes on the road," she warned before she did anything else, then pulled away and pulled the sleeves down. They made a sliding noise like sheets being pulled from a bed for cleaning.

I glanced at her skin, the longer and longer stretch of arms, the trunk of her stomach, freckles and two brown moles and rounded knees. I touched the mole on my neck and suddenly felt warm. I turned back to the road, put my hand to the vent, could smell sweat, the back of her neck mixing with sand and ice and perfume and music I had yet to turn on, so I flipped on the radio. It was all static—we were too far for Tina's station, which she ran in the back of her grocery—so I popped in the cassette hanging halfway out. Johnny Cash started in singing,

> *I fell into a burning ring of fire*
> *I went down, down, down*
> *And the flames went higher*

his voice gravelly and certain. It was music that Ray liked and I had gotten used to on our trips into the desert, but the fire was just the sun's unbreakable heat on those trips. Here the fire was something different. I turned off the stereo.

Jennifer reached over and turned it back on and up more loudly. Then she pushed the dress all the way to the floorboard, its wide skirt plopping over my shoes and everything, sending up a poof of dust that tickled my throat.

Next she hiked up her knees and stretched over the seat for her bag. I glanced over the long bend of skin, the panties round-pink, a band of pink, satin pink, and only the bra now, and I could taste the blood under my lip that she had bitten earlier at the wedding.

> *And it burns, burns, burns*
> *The ring of fire*

and I looked out at the highway, the full of her back to the markers. I could feel her body cloud over mine, shift down into me, stretch through the dry heat, the music, her blood and skin shifting inside my fingers and toes, filling my body out completely, layer on top of layer, two bodies times two, and even though no one was coming the other way, there was no one, for a moment I thought that someone might notice her, and the cloud lifted, the spirit of her body up and up, leaving me to shiver. I looked over at her skin, the two moles, her skin, wanting to draw her back, and

> *down, down—*

"Put your eyes on the road," she caught me. "I don't want to die in the desert. Patience, Mathew."

"Patience?" I laughed and shook my head. "You're taking your clothes off right in front of me and you want me to have patience?" I flicked the stereo out in one quick turn. At the same moment, Jennifer twisted around in the seat and spun a long red cotton shirt over her arms and down her body. As she did, she spoke through the fabric, "Hey, I like that song."

"It's too much," I declared. "If you want patience, the song has to go."

Jennifer sighed. "All right. Just calm down. I do expect *some* patience from you. A little bit." She pinched up her fingers like an inchworm getting ready. Jennifer touched several drops of sweat on her face, rubbed them into a strap, and started to work on her bra. Immediately, her black hair fell over like two dish towels hung on a rack.

"I hate bras." She pursed her lips and leaned her head into the dash, working her hands behind her as if cuffed. "It's like putting something of your body in a box. No, it's worse than that—a steel pipe. You can break out of a box." She pulled a strap down one arm, reached and pulled the other strap down the other arm and then the whole contraption through, its shiny loops and strips of pink, all in one fluid movement. She gathered up her dress and the bra and reached over and laid them in the back with my tux.

"Be glad you're not a woman," she said.

"Just don't wear bras," I told her simply.

"Ever?" She seemed surprised at my suggestion, something in her voice rising up, confirming that I knew nothing about being a woman.

"Not as far as I'm concerned," I clarified my position. "Ever. Looks better without them, if you ask me."

"Calm down, calm down," she laughed, and pinched her nipples so they poked against the red shirt, its thin fabric. "This what you like?" she laughed.

I nodded, then changed course and shook my head. "Are you trying to torture me?"

"Just keep your eyes on the road, Mathew," she admonished, but lightly. "I don't want to die on our wedding night."

"I'm trying," but I could hear the anxiety in my voice surging, and I started over. "I just want to hold you," I explained. "I need to. You've been so quiet these past months. When I see you like this now—"

"Shh," she said, and sighed again, but softer as she inched across the seat, fitting her arm around my neck. She watched the highway with me, the oncoming black and black and pitch that seemed endless, that would hit the ocean's salt, and hit us with it, the markers flashing like mica, and the smell of sweat and perfume, and her skin I could feel working through me, and when Ray had looked into the sky as if it could be healed, and Jennifer had danced with my father—I had always wanted to see him dance like that, as if there was something in this place, some reason for hope.

CHAPTER 15

Sumner's Hill, 2030

I sat at the edge of my father's dig and waited for him to come up. Next to me, the sludge coursed through the pipe, stopping, gurgling more, and I touched the hose, felt the shaking of the water, the roughness of the cable stretch and give. Meanwhile, Bossey was busy walking around each dig, pulling the cables to see if there were any satchels of rock ready for lifting, any snags, the workers okay. He was making his way back to his office for some waders and a miner's hat, but he was too slow. I sighed. Bossey wouldn't get back with my equipment until I had talked with my father. And I sighed even longer. My father stayed inside number 40 and I thought about everything he had told me which, like the government warnings, was always *No.*

"A college degree out of Birmingham, Atlanta, before they have to shut them down, too. That's what you want," he emphasized whenever we drove in his truck or sat at home for too many hours, any space where we were boxed in and he could turn anxious. "You don't want to be doing what your old man's doing. I'm dying," he would say, his eyes hard, pressuring my ribs. Finally, his glare flickered down like a lamp, the generators in his brain sputtering, and he let me breathe.

Instead of going out with the other miners after work, my father stayed home. If he had the energy, we read together, and later from my bedroom, I would watch him dance alone in the kitchen. But those days when he couldn't sleep wore him down and were always followed by days when he collapsed in his favorite chair. While he slept, I reached for pieces of clay from his ear, sometimes still wet, squished the minerals into a ball and rolled them into shapes, gems and worms, his face and hair a frozen river encrusted with garnets and rose quartz of kitchen lights.

"Tell me about dancing," I whispered to him, twisting the clay, watching him as the voices from the record player popped and climbed and drew me down an entrance circling to his inner ear—the inner ear wet and muddy, the ropes out of it, the pipe and hose. A small light sparkled from the bottom with hands pulling rocks in.

"I want to know about dancing," I said, but this was only half true. When he started to snore, I asked him, "How did Mamma die? Was she skinny? Fat as a pig? Tell me about when she was pregnant? When you were happy?"

Most of the time his breathing grew deep, and he slept, didn't hear me over Peggy Lee and Billie. But sometimes he abruptly woke, as if I had interrupted him by taking the clay, and I was guilty, guilty for my words and my asking. He knew what I wanted.

On those mornings, he kicked the chair back hard, and "No," he would begin to pace, the blood in him building.

His walk reminded me of the dancer in my dreams—

step one, step two, a kick of dirt—the kick of another chair, just as deliberate, just as strong. But there was war in him, too—what I had seen on the faces of the men and women in the history books, my father in a crisp marine uniform, charging. But no matter how much of him I saw in that light, his steps were never in unison, conformed. They circled and swayed almost to the point of falling, yet he never quite fell, and the uniform never stayed put, became instead a tuxedo to match his sparkling hands, his steps that needed a partner.

"Tell me about Mamma. The dancing—" I didn't say it, but he knew. He seemed trapped by my questions. They burned through his motion. He couldn't escape them.

"No. I want you to have an education. I don't want you working in this clay. I don't want you to keep foolish dreams of this desert and me."

He stopped pacing, looked over my body where I had smudged the red pieces on my shirt and arms so I could glitter in the lights like him. Then he shut his lips tight, pulled me into the kitchen, and pulled my hands to the sink, turning the spigot all the way on. I felt my fingers pried open, the clay washing out. The water went from cold to hot quick.

"It's important to have an education. To have something in this world—at least that." He yanked my arms to the towel rack and began scrubbing. "Stop crying!

"These hands aren't yours—they don't belong to you."

He opened his own short fingers so I could take a good look.

"Do you understand this, Mathew? Do you understand that they belong to me? Just me? That I want something different for you?"

He scrubbed my fingers harder, rubbing so hard that the remaining water burned my skin and blood. Then he put the towel away.

"And I don't want them either. Not without your mother." His palms were sweating, upside down to the kitchen lights, leading as his voice raised.

"Don't stare at me so hard," he demanded. He sat down in his kicked chair, breath exhausted, and hid his hands in his pockets. "It's not that I don't love you."

For a moment there was a recognition on his face that he might have hurt my feelings. Then he said, "Your mother. I should tell you more about your mother," as if now he had heard me; my buzzing and asking had taken that long to reach him. His face had changed, however: I wasn't in the room anymore, not any place in his mind, not even on the surface of his clay beard, no longer something to be washed off.

"Whenever I was around your mother, close to her — always I wanted to dance because when she moved, when she spun into my hands, I could hold her. She never wobbled on her feet. I never stepped on her small shoes, somehow. And I forgot about other people in the room when we danced. I let them all go. I didn't think." He laughed, uneasy, but then with more confidence that this was the right thing to do, that we could make amends. "I couldn't. I was mesmerized by her. I just wanted to spin your mother perfectly with my hand-holding." He looked at his boots for a long while, the two of us watching them shift heel, toe, one-two, one-two and in tiny step. My father was moving, always unconsciously moving.

"I met her at a dance — it was a VFW, some church — I remember they were trying to raise money that first night we met. She was so beautiful — Shelia, it's a beautiful name, don't you think? And the way she spun around on the floor and her dress would lift just enough like the roll of a hill, then fall down and rise with her hair, and just — I remember this, Mathew — when I first danced with her, our hands fit like we were two pieces, two pieces that had found the right connection, the right body. I was lucky. I was lucky for so long.

"I wish she could see you, be here. She would love you," he said, the expression on his face more and more resolved about something. "You can call me Mother, if you want. And Father. If you need both, it's all right with me. But promise you'll never do what I do."

"Okay." I nodded, dancing my hands to the kitchen lights, pretending that my fingers were my parents spinning each other, crossing in step, the red streaks dissolving back under my skin.

"Stop," he said.

"Yes, sir," I told him, and wanted to ask him how Mamma died, but he was calm and I didn't want to lose his calmness a second time.

"Mamma." I smiled and laughed—it seemed silly to call him that, yet for some reason it made me feel better, two pieces that had found the right connection.

My father stayed where he was and didn't approach me, still afraid of his anger, I guessed. My hands still burned, but the most important thing was that my mother had existed, had been alive, and I knew that for a moment without any doubt. Her name, the way she danced, her dress—was it yellow or red? He hadn't told me, but it didn't matter. I made it yellow, full with a bow and lace. Then I re-created her steps, one-two, one-two, a mirror of my father's that first night, cutting and spinning, building in my mind.

Sitting at the edge of my father's dig, I knew what he would say, or knew he wouldn't say anything, but that expression, the disappointment—I saw a light shining from the hole. I looked down. My father was coming up.

CHAPTER 16

The Dreams

Rising from the sand and dirt is one dancer, kicking his feet in circles—he dances as if there are two, as if his partner is visible. Lean in with the right, step one, back—two, forward with the left—three, spin, elegant, spin, let go. I know all of these movements, though I don't know how to dance, and the crops are dead, choked in the dust. Occasionally, the dancer kicks up leaves and roots. I'm watching his hands jerk slightly at the invisible back, groping for the spine. Slowly, I'm closer and closer. The dancer pays me no attention. His arches and breaths are strong, purposeful, but his face—there is no complexion of eyes and nose, no lips or even faint bones to raise or lower. I want him to show me how to dance, so I can be as good as my father.

"Your face?" I ask, tapping his shoulder, and I try to wake up. If I can wake up, he will help me. But the dancer quickly spins away, takes off across the desert—step one, step two—kicking up dirt. So I follow him. I stay close behind, and when I finally catch up, he has a partner.

He leads her left, then to one corner of the desert, then another—swirling, swirling, her dress in sequins, his cotton gloves sparkling with jewels. The dream moves closer, the desert shrinks until they are in a hole of clay with ground lights flashing down. I see his shoes, sharp black, polished stripes up his pants legs, gold cuffs. He keeps his chin at an angle for her to hold, but she doesn't hold it, and the tops of their heads flash with mica. There is music—"Sweet Lorraine:"

> *Just found joy*
> *I'm as happy as a baby boy, baby boy*
> *With another brand-new choo-choo toy*
> *When I met my sweet Lorraine, Lorraine, Lorraine.*

Closer and closer to his back, she moves round and round as they arch in deeper and deeper—twenty-five, thirty-five feet—spiraling into the dig. It's difficult to make them out; I lower my head and pebbles and dust and mud fall from the tunnel's edge where I'm watching. At that moment she looks up. And I wait for her to speak to me as the song echoes and curls:

> *Now when it's rainin'*
> *I don't miss the sun*
> *Because it's in my baby's smile, whoa ho*

But he pulls her face back down and they spin and spin until I can no longer see.

CHAPTER 17

Millers Ferry, June 2044

"Are you going to work, or are you quitting?" Bossey is at the window and pulls on the door handle. I push the un-lock back and step out. Even though it's June, the air's cool enough to shiver me a little and wake me up. "The night's getting short. I already clocked you in."

"Thanks," I answer, and try to think of something else to say, but I can't get the words to form and Bossey doesn't force it, so there's nothing else, no small talk as we walk past the mixers and engines to the web of moon craters, to number 19, my number, the crimson flag flapping over. Last night I dug thirty feet—the clay has been soft, the rocks more mushy than good. The best clusters should be five feet more.

"How're you doing?" he asks, catching his breath.

I stare down the crater and my head grows dizzy—the

shaft spirals like an ear, the falling sound of ocean water rising with salt, hollow, black.

"It's rude not to answer when you're being talked to, especially if that someone is your boss." Bossey's half-kidding, but there's an edge to his voice.

So I look at him, and his eyes, those bullfrog eyes are intensely set on me, studying me, trying to understand.

"I'm sorry, Bossey," I tell him, and I mean it, but the words flatten out into nothing, so I turn away.

"That's all?" he says after a while, his voice rough and agitated. The biggest man in Alabama, and I've gotten him mad. "Damn you, Mathew. You can shut this place out of your mind, but you can't shut me out." Bossey grabs my shoulders, lifting me off the ground slightly, making sure he has my attention before he plants me back. "I'm not going to let you burrow in so deep that you don't ever talk. It's just stupid. Hear me? I've seen it too often, and I'm not going to let you." Bossey stamps his foot. "And Mr. Chris, if he were here, he wouldn't let you either."

I smile like my father, the smile that kept him young for years and looking like me—the wide grin that settled people down. "I'm all right," I assure him. It's the answer he needs in order to let go of my shoulders, to get back to his own work.

"We've got to evacuate this area in a few days, Mat," Bossey says. And he's fidgeting, scratching at a mole on his face. "The river's drying up faster than last year. The desert's on the move again."

This is something I haven't heard, something Ray hasn't mentioned. And Bossey doesn't have to say it: he's got a lot of pressure on him, more than just worrying with me.

"Bad news, but it's true," Bossey says. "After sitting on top of us for thirty years—thirty years!" He raises his arms at the domed lights. "Making me an old man in the process—after all this sitting, the sky's opening up above the ocean more, and from what they tell me, getting closer to Birmingham. I heard the government's setting up road-blocks north of the city to keep the people there, to keep them from panicking and flooding the Saved World just like thirty years ago." Bossey shakes his head. "The government's not going to save anybody. That's just like them."

"What will the people do?"

"Hell, they might head toward us. When you're running scared, who knows."

"But what about people with visas?" And I almost blurt out Jennifer's name, tell him the whole thing: she will be gone soon on the bus. *Should I stop her, Bossey?* I want to ask him. *Should I take the bus with her?*

"I don't know," Bossey says. "They've always worked, but I don't know. You thinking about leaving? Is that it?" His voice gains momentum. "You still got that visa of your father's?"

"In a box," I tell him. *But that's not all of it, Bossey*—I want to give in, tell him everything.

"Well, if you want to go, you better. The desert is about ten miles from the city. They don't know it, they're not even aware—but it's going to sweep into Birmingham sometime this month, anytime. All it'll take is one good storm. It's going to be a mess when that happens."

The wind slips across us, bringing the memory of the yellow dog swinging in the dragon scrap heap with Birmingham, 35 miles away, fangs poised, all of us ready to slip over.

"If I left tonight, I'd be okay?"

"Should be." He nods, yet there's still doubt in his face. He's weighing things, I can tell, trying to figure out what to tell me next. "This week should be okay. The roadblocks haven't been set up yet. But you've got work to do tonight, unless you don't want it. And if you don't want it . . ." Bossey doesn't finish his sentence, just moves back a little, enough to let me walk past him. The biggest man in Alabama, and he's willing to let me go.

I nod, stare down the tunnel, don't shift an inch, the sludge pipe already in place.

"Did Jennifer get the job with the store? I talked with Tina. She said they're moving the groceries out tomorrow." Bossey takes a bobby pin out and repins a loose curl of hair flat to his broad head.

"Tina told her she could work fifteen hours a week," I tell him, and it's a lie, but it's what I wanted to happen. Jennifer took the application from my hand without a thank you and later I found the paper in the trash.

Suddenly, I hear a bus—I can make out the loud diesel engine shaking through the tunnel at my boots. The hole spirals like an ear sinking, driving further, then bubbling from the bottom sluck. I adjust my light to see, and pick up flashes of mica, hardened clay clumps, a pair of hands slowly digging at the wall—the hands are pale, almost purple. The wrists dissolve into pitch, then fade into flashes of mica just as the bus engine dies without any light, without barreling up like a rocket. It never comes close.

The sludge pipe is all the way in, and I grab it to steady myself. I shake the pipe where the hands had clawed and clawed until the dirt is erased so the hands can't come back, are truly gone.

"I guess I'll see you in seven," Bossey says, but he mutters the words slow and uneven as if he's witnessed what I've witnessed, or seen the cold sweat, the reflection of those pale hands in my face.

"I'll be out in seven," I tell him. *But that's not all of it, Bossey. Jennifer's leaving. She's taking the bus—* The words hum and twist—I should tell him, but I don't say anything.

He sighs, moves his trousers around, checks the rope tight on the pulley.

"You can shut out this place, but not me," he says one more time, no doubt in his voice. "And if you're going to Birmingham, you better go tonight. Tomorrow. Don't think on it too much. Just go." His plump fingers pop open as I take the rope. We nod to each other, and I wait for him to disappear into the equipment and ore carts and engines before I go down.

CHAPTER 18

35 Miles from Birmingham, February 2044

High temperature today of 68°. Low tonight 19°. Ozone index at 150, CODE ORANGE. Outside work restricted from 10 a.m. until 6 p.m. Winds easterly at 45 miles per hour. Avoid sandstorms. Dust may cause pneumonia. Visibility 100 feet. Outside work restricted until 6 p.m.

—*WDMZ 1610 AM, 8:05 a.m.*

My father grew old so quick. That smile became snagged in deep wrinkles, deeper ravines, that youthfulness from his dancing gone after my marriage. We no longer looked like brothers, but father and son again, and eventually grandfather and grandson, like a river blooming full into an ocean, spilling and widening, my father and me on opposite beaches, less and less recognizable to each other.

For eight years I left him after work and went home to Jennifer, watching him deteriorate in snapshots. Then Carson called me, said my father was having problems with his heart—there was dizziness, fluctuations in the timing, the beating, and he needed medicine every day. Carson emphasized *every day* and told me that I must take care of him.

So after eight years of living with Jennifer and listening

to television—she hated television but liked the sand and wind even less—after eight years, my father moved in with us. In the mornings, I lay in the bedroom next to him, listening to the old songs on Grandpa Sanford's record player creep through the walls as if the dried insulation and plaster had formed a special conduit for the static and popping, as if the music had waited patiently inside every house I had lived in, waited for me to be next to my father so the sand and cadences could resume. He kept the music quiet—I think he didn't want to offend Jennifer—and we kept the small TV in our room low and placed another TV on the Formica table in the kitchen.

When Carson told me about Father's heart in December, the rivers dried swiftly. Before long we reached the scrap heap and rusted sign near Birmingham. It was February and my father had said little about the new arrangement. He talked less and less, the rough scratching in his throat so packed with clay, the vocal cords my father had told me about and made me learn about, their vibration of wind and filament unable any longer to shed the thick clay and vibrate into words. When I cornered him with Carson's warning, he said nothing. My father only had a few things—mostly boxes and his easy chair and the record player, so it didn't take long to move him, and now his music trickled through the walls.

"Do you want children? Or do you want to fuck?" Jennifer asked, shutting the door to the bathroom, the lights already off and the curtains drawn so the sun couldn't breathe through. In her hand, she shook a small plastic bottle, the arch of her arm flickering in and out like a lightbulb, its tungsten dying, creating different shades of darkness: a gray-black into purer black that became a bruised indigo.

"Separate—I want them separate. I don't want children, but you do?" I said it halfway as a question. She hadn't mentioned children, not since we married.

She frowned, "Your enthusiasm is contagious," and opened the small bottle, sliding a birth control pill into her palm and swallowing.

Jennifer said nothing else, and I slid warmly under the covers, waiting for her to finish undressing. As I watched the robe fall from shoulder and elbow, my own breathing picked up. I wanted her next to me, that turn of skin so familiar. And I wondered, as I had always wondered, how could desire exist in this place? Not without Jennifer—I was certain of that. It seemed to begin in her body, in her words and her motion.

Then the music, like some faint net, began to spread over my mind. I made out a saxophone winding through the smooth rise of Ella Fitzgerald's voice. Then a second net and another covered over me with drums and guitar, layer on top of layer, the weight of the instruments, their sound, the rise and fall of Ella's voice.

"I just want you," Jennifer whispered. She kissed my arm, my neck, her kisses small pecks like stitches in the sleeve of a shirt as she rolled one leg across my stomach. I shifted my hands to her back, but the music numbed my touch, and I dropped them to my side.

"Look at me," she said, forcing my attention away from the wall. "He's asleep."

"I know. I just don't want to wake him."

"I'll be quiet," Jennifer promised, letting her hair fall across my face. The strands smelled of spicy mandarin that Jennifer and I had cooked together before work and had eaten chilled for breakfast while watching a TV show on southern catfish. Occasionally, catfish floated belly-up in our rivers, washed from the Appalachian dams, useless. But on the show, they were battered and fried and I still heard the pan popping them, full of grease. Her hair swirled and dampened the clay in my skin, and the healing was working, erasing the seven hours in the tunnel, the tiredness I had brought home and thought I still carried. She lowered down to kiss me again, but through the thick curtain and warmth, the music untangled itself and slipped inside.

"Mathew," her arms straightened, "you're not paying attention. Is it something I'm doing? something wrong?"

"No," I said, but her expression didn't change.

"My father doesn't want me to take care of him," I offered reluctantly, and gazed at the wall for cracks to shut off, a way to eclipse his music.

"He's never wanted you to take care of him. He's very independent."

"But he hardly talks to me. Have you noticed at dinner? or breakfast?"

"Your father's sick. And he's tired from the work. Besides, you don't say much either, Mat. I'm sorry if that hurts you, but that's the truth."

"I talk to him—he's the one who doesn't. And I know why. My father wants me to go back to school. Can you imagine going to school now? I'm almost thirty."

"You should." Jennifer's body grew more tense, a battle in her getting ready.

I turned my head to the window for an ally—maybe the sun, maybe the wind weaving dust into a fence taller and taller, but Jennifer caught my chin. "You need a degree. The GED or something. Something more than this desert," her tone darkened just like my father's.

"I like working with my hands. I've always liked—"

"There's plenty of jobs for your hands, boy." She flushed my palms to her hips to demonstrate the point. "What if the rivers permanently dry up? This mining job isn't going to be around forever."

"I'll work the Gulf."

"I don't believe it," she said. "You had your chance." We had spent our honeymoon on the Gulf. Jennifer had wanted to stay, but I refused. "Besides, it's killing you to stay here. That's all this mining is good for. And you know it." She sat up. For a moment she was perfectly still, then she shook her head. "I take it back. You're too stubborn to see how living here is killing you, killing us. I need you to see it, but you won't. And you know what else, Mathew? You've shut me out. It's not just your father. Since he's come, you've separated yourself and won't talk to me at all."

Her voice had risen so high, I was afraid he might wake up. I whispered, "Don't you like my hands when they touch?" caressing down her back. "Their strength?" pressing into her sides, massaging. "Their holding?" and I forced her back down. "I'm not separate," I insisted.

Something in her wanted to give, wilt like a flower, let me caress longer. But her body stiffened, and I felt that coolness in her skin where I had tried to press a warmth. She pushed my fingers away. "This job isn't good for you, Mat. It never has been."

"It's money." I twisted back to the window, traced the line of sun along the curtain's edge. "Besides, what good has your college degree been? You don't have a thousand calls for jobs." Jennifer had taken six years of correspondence with a college in New York, a diploma in business. She had finished in November and was already talking about getting a second—this one in history or science, for teaching.

Jennifer crossed her arms—her motion, golden-black into gray into purer black and bruised indigo again, too distant for me to reach.

"That's not fair. It's because we live in a wasteland. There're no jobs here. None. Chicago or Detroit—if we lived at the lakes—they have water. So much water." Her voice became rough and dry and she had to swallow.

"I can't leave him."

"Your father doesn't want you to stay. Mr. Chris never has."

The heat from the blinds drifted closer. The sun was scorching the glass, even though it was February, impossible to escape.

"Mom wrote me from Chicago."

"Did she send money?"

"Yes," Jennifer said, leaning over. She snatched her shirt from the chair and rolled off my stomach, then plopped down on the opposite half of the bed.

"I'm not spending it."

She sighed, "I know you won't," and she began pulling at the shirt, wrapping herself, jabbing the buttons through. "I'm going to buy some dance music—Doris Day, Rosemary Clooney—that Mr. Chris likes. Now that we live with him, I thought I'd add some records to his collection—there's a place in Birmingham that sells old records. I'm sure Ray will pick some up for me. Besides, I'm tired of watching TV, watching what the rest of the world looks like, everyone so damn happy, so damn absolutely positive that it's a wonderful, beautiful world. Some joke, isn't it?"

I started to answer but could feel my muscles weaken, my bones pooling under my weight into the soft curve of the mattress. *Just shift the fillets around with a fork*, the man said on the catfish show. He had splotches on his hands like pepper, and he kept poking at the fish. He wouldn't let them rest. *Just shift them around until the cornmeal's crisp and—Walah! It's ready.* But I was too tired, the hours spent digging had crept back into my body. I was too tired to speak now.

"For me it's a joke," Jennifer answered herself, and said nothing else.

She lay back, and we stared at the ceiling, my father's music covering us, filling all the space in the room that had been silent for years, except for the shuffling of making love or the backdrop of television promises and commercials. Then the music ended and it was just the static and popping noises intruding on us, changing us, the stiff arm of the record player at the album's center, refusing to lift, or unable to lift, and return to its home.

A rhythm started: endless, monotonous. I knew it would go on all morning like the clicking of a watch, scaling away time, wearing us down into sleep, and we would wake up still angry.

Jennifer rolled over to touch my face. She snaked a line from my eyebrow, the heavy ridge, down my high cheekbone, opening the skin back so it could breathe. Then she draped her arm across my chest.

I wanted her body on top again, straddling. I would be quiet, would let her black hair come down, let her kiss like water splashing like stitches in a sleeve like warmth but not like the desert's hot-dry, her warmth full like water splashing, warm and total.

Jennifer found my fingers and rubbed them, pulled at my wrist, pulled herself in tightly. "I hate being in this house, the one we lived in a month ago, all of them, Mat. While you're working, I'm awake all night with the wind whipping everything around. I need you, Mat. I need you to talk to. I hate this house. I can't even plant a garden except for those few indoor pots." She pointed to three small terra-cotta pots with parched leaves and stems. The darkness in the room made them heavier, like eyelashes set into the dirt, the lashes closing, blurring into a small hedge. "They never make it long because of the wind. Then the sand gets inside. It's so dry here."

"If you watered them more—"

"Don't." Her arm stiffened. "Nothing grows here and

half the time water has to be rationed. It's illegal to have plants anyway." The government prohibited animals and plants—it was too hard to keep ourselves alive, much less any other living thing. "So don't insult me," she continued, "not while I'm holding you. And don't remind me about the water. Mom says the weather is good in Chicago, and she swims in the lake once a week for her legs. Said it would be good for my legs, especially if I want to have children."

She had slung her new dress over an open drawer on her vanity, a design of red and green camellias. Jennifer loved floral print dresses, had loved them since her mother sent photographs of petals in vases, real flowers, and when she had tried it on for me earlier, the dress was twice her size. Even with a belt it swallowed her up.

"That's why you bought the new dress."

"It's from Tina's. It's not like there's a lot of choice. She only had that size with that pattern. I like it, and I'll wear it, Mat, like I told you I would. Don't worry. But if I did get pregnant . . ." Jennifer tugged at my elbow, pulling me away from the ceiling, the blinds. "I know Mom wants a baby. Mr. Chris would like a grandchild, too."

I shook my head. "He doesn't want another child." I thought of his clay hands on my mother's stomach, on holy ground, what Uncle Wayne had told me, how Mamma screamed in labor, the complications, how she collapsed and no one could wake her.

"But what if I want a child? I'm getting older. I'm not going to be able to have a baby in a few years. Besides, we wouldn't have to raise a baby in the desert."

"I know we can leave, Jen. Do you think I don't understand that we can leave?" I shut my eyes and tried to block everything—the clay; my family; the tick, ticking of the record player needle; the sun and its dust; everything—out.

"Sometimes," Jennifer said, her voice barely audible now.

"I know we can leave," I said, but my body stayed pinned to the mattress, my bones dissolving into dead fish. I was too tired, and Jennifer didn't respond, was silent again like when her stepfather couldn't breathe and had broken apart, when she had roamed the desert in my dreams before the wedding. If I just went to sleep, maybe I could find her, find the two of us in that empty landscape, able to touch each other. But my father—it was the one thing that had been on my mind—what my father had told me a few days before.

"He won't make the winter."

"Don't say that."

"He told me, Jen. He said, 'Go back to school. The winter won't be so cold this year. I won't feel it.' When we drive to work, when we eat, he doesn't talk, but his face and arms and hands, they're telling me it's over. They can't keep up. Especially with his heart like it is."

Jennifer shifted her pillow behind her. "Then let's drive to Chicago or take the bus. Mom will send us tickets. We already have visas. We're so close to Birmingham right now."

"I can't leave him."

"And me? Can you leave me?"

The record player scratched and popped, longer and longer seconds.

I needed to hold her, and I reached around her back, but Jennifer pushed my fingers to my stomach and sat up.

"I've already lost two fathers, and I know Mr. Chris is dying. Your father said to me in the kitchen for us to get out of here, to get the hell out. But you won't do it." She hit me in the shoulder where she had planted a kiss earlier.

"Why won't you listen? You stay to be near him, but you won't listen."

The scratching static stopped, and there was a fumbling noise in the other room, some heavy piece of furniture scraping over the floor. It was my father all right, stirring around—we had woken him—and I held my breath, slipping back to when I was younger and shouldn't be awake, slipping into that skin that was too tight to stay inside for long.

Then the scraping ended just as sudden, the tick-tick of the record player. I waited, but the walls, my father— nothing—and I exhaled a little more comfortable back into my skin.

Jennifer whispered, "I'm not going to die in this place, Mathew. I can't listen to you say *no* forever."

I touched her neck. Her skin gave a little, enough that I could fit my palm inside the cotton blouse, pull the heat from her body into the quilts.

"I'm sorry," I said, and moved over to kiss her, but she pulled away.

"I love you, and I've stayed for you, Mat." Jennifer tried to slow her breathing. "But I need more than this. You've got to be willing to give me something more."

She stood up from the bed, the long blouse unfurling to her knees, and she walked out of the room, yanking the door shut. I heard the TV in the kitchen click on—*Love Connection, The Dating Game.* I put my hand against the blinds—people were clapping, laughing, clapping like the people on my father's video who had come to hear the president declare this place a wasteland before I was born.

On the windowsill lay two of her turquoise bracelets and my watch. I put the round base of the watch next to my ear. A voice so sure the date would go well kept asking—

What kind of food do you like?
What is your perfect evening?
What will you wear?

Silver rings, topaz, jade, neck chains, gems, so many gems—but why can't I leave this place? I waited for some-one to ask that question, but no one did, the tick, ticking of voices working their sand through me until I fell asleep.

CHAPTER 19

Dothan, 2024

By the time I got out of Carson's office, my arm stiff as rock in the new cast and aching still, the tractor had been hauled out of Tina's store. Some of the miners were nailing up huge patches of canvas and the sun was no longer red, but invisible except as a white ball, a large white drop in the consuming haze. Some men had on masks, but most had rags or handkerchiefs, bandanas, tied across their noses and mouth, the cloth hanging down as if they had green and blue and red beards.

"Come on," my father called out. He was in his truck and Uncle Wayne waved from the wrecker, the tractor hooked in back. He was sitting shotgun with Bossey, who also waved and then grimaced when he saw the cast on my arm. Then a hand grabbed my shoulder. It was Ray.

I was surprised and immediately felt guilty. "What happened?" I asked, looking at his body for dents and bruises.

My father pressed the horn down. "Come on," he yelled.

"It's all right. I jumped clear," Ray said, and stretched his thin frame to show that he was fine. "Didn't see the building at first, but I jumped clear. What did you tell everyone?"

"Nothing. About you." I hadn't said anything to anyone about him, that he had been driving the ghost tractor. "Everyone thinks the tractor made it across the desert without a driver."

"Crazy," he snickered, "but that's good. I don't want to get in trouble." He tapped the cast, its wet sheen. "Are you all right?"

"Like new in six weeks." That's what Carson had told me, but for some reason I wanted to hide my arm, wanted some of Ray's luck. I wished I had jumped clear, too.

"There's a deserter in Jack's cage," I told him. The deserter had stopped crying before I left, his head still bent to his pulled-up knees. He sat next to the cot, but he wouldn't lie in it.

"I thought something was going on. I saw the patrollers." Ray frowned. "Doesn't do any good to try and leave this place." And I thought of Ray's mom, wondered if she had seen the deputies.

"Sorry," I said, but he looked puzzled, like what was I apologizing for?

"I just hope your tractor's not messed up," he said.

"Tina's shop." I nodded at Tina's, and Ray's mood shifted.

"Yeah, it's something. We did all of that." His small frame stretched out again to meet his smile. And I giggled. All my fear and shame, he had none of it—look at what we had pulled off, what we had accomplished—Ray started to laugh again, and he breathed in the ozone as if it could never hurt him, as if nothing could.

"The tractor will be fine," I said confidently. "Not even a tire got busted." It didn't look smashed up, and my father hadn't mentioned anything about it.

"I thought you said you could drive it."

"Mathew." My father opened his door, and if I didn't start walking, he would come out to get me, embarrass me.

I shrugged my shoulders and moved toward my father, trying to stop my giggling. "I'll see you tomorrow in school." Then I turned and hurried to the truck, with my face lowered so my father couldn't see my expression.

On the way home I closed my eyes and thought of the Red Baron flying over fields, but not in Kansas—there was nothing in Kansas, the deserter had said. Tomorrow he would be working the mines in Quitman. What was left? The Red Baron flying overhead, looking and looking for green fields, and never coming down.

CHAPTER 20

Porch Stories, 2026

March 8

My dearest Jen,

    The weather has been good for a whole week and Pearl has wanted to go outside. She always gets that way in spring—playful, like you were. Yesterday, when we started out, the city siren———————————
————————————home. Everyone has————
————————————————when the siren goes off. According to Bobbie, the military—————————
————————————————————————————
————————————————————————————

———— *but that is the only bad news, if it's true. And since it happened over a mile from the apartment, I feel safer. Bobbie found this place before the army compound was set up.* ————————————————

————————————————————————

————————————————————————

————————————————————————

————————————————————————

though it is still difficult ————————————

————————————————————————

————————————————————————

————————————————————————

————————. *Then the town closes off, each apartment its own fortress or*————, *Bobbie calls it. And Pearl stays quiet under the bureau all day. Today I'll try to get her out again. Hopefully the siren won't go off*————

————————————————————————

————————————————————————

————————————————————————

————————————————.

I'm glad the money I sent got through Birmingham in the last letter. I wish I had something more good to tell.

Affectionately,

Mom

My father was the thick one. "Low to the ground like a pig," my Uncle Wayne used to say, though my father wasn't that short. Uncle Wayne, it was true, was a tall, lanky light pole, his shoulders always hunched over, his body needing to prop up on things: the side of buildings, truck beds and truck cabs, cars, sometimes even me. My build was somewhere between the two, and when I was young, I thought they both were my father. No wonder. We spent so much time with Uncle Wayne.

He had never married and was one hell of a great cook. My father warmed stuff in the oven, boiled dried bricks of things into edible shreds, but several times a week, we went to Wayne's, or he came to our place to make real food.

What I remember most was him in the kitchen, every kitchen, and me creeping to the tiled edge or wood or carpet, depending on the house, just to glimpse the chop-chopping I heard, the roiling noise from silver pots, my father calling me back from the scent of onion and salt and basil, sometimes even fresh basil that grew sweet and sharp with each step I dared to take.

"Mathew, get in here and read," my father would yell. "Let your Uncle Wayne alone." Sometimes I'd catch him glaring and snarling—books were important and not to be discarded, not even for good smells from the kitchen.

Uncle Wayne fired back, "He ain't bothering nothing, brother." And I would catch a glimpse of his eyes breaking from all the boiling to look me over with his long chin jutting out like a sandbar in the river, those months when the river flooded, that short-straight hair of his blond and bushed up and full of the same clay as my father's but without the same strides and lines—Uncle Wayne's hair did have a few sparkles, but they were more random and carefree, a patch of tangled points.

After a while, Uncle Wayne would wink. "Now go do what your father says before he gets us both." With that, there was no one to turn to, and I'd trudge to my chair, banished. But I liked the idea that my father would have to get us both—that meant Uncle Wayne and I were partners.

Like other supplies, we mostly got the food the Saved World didn't want. Many of the items were delivered out-of-date, but somehow Uncle Wayne could make it taste better than it should, even when it was dried-up rations and beans and canned meat from Tina's store. When we moved past Montgomery and in range of Birmingham, the government workers would go through the checkpoints, bring back coolers of fresh fish we could never get, and my uncle knew some of the black marketers pretty well and put in special requests for basil plants and strawberries. All year my uncle traded his scrip for US dollars so that when we got close enough to the border, he could get fresh food. Tina carried some fresh items, but it was rare when they came down with the supplies, and often they were spoiled by the time we got them.

But as soon as we set up camp above Montgomery, Uncle Wayne cooked great huge steaming pots of food, frying pans of steak, real squash in real butter, not margarine—which my father preferred—catfish filleted and blackened, lima beans and crowder peas that settled warm in my stomach with cathead biscuits and rolls and always cold sugar tea that for some reason made you sweat more, made you thirstier. But the best part about eating with Uncle Wayne was after the meal. He and my father would talk for an hour or half an hour until my father fell asleep—any conversation was taxing on him after a night of work. Uncle Wayne, on the other hand, was always wound up—he didn't like to rest and told me so. As soon as my father started napping, we slipped into the kitchen to do dishes and talk.

On weekends, on nights off, we ate midnight lunches on the porch—Uncle Wayne loved porches, especially wraparounds, and always managed to find a home with one. We'd sit on the porch, watch the black sky. Sometimes there'd even be stars, the markings of a map, pinpoints of distance to take if we could just step far enough into the night. Instead of that journey, however, we settled on talking.

"How's school?" Uncle Wayne would begin, his voice always ticking a pace faster than everyone else's. And I'd oblige, tell him all about school, but it was easier than with my father. Uncle Wayne never demanded anything, and I felt like he mainly asked because my father would want him to. Uncle Wayne nodded and said, "That's great, that's great, Mathew" at most everything I said, or "Sorry to hear that" if I told him something somber, but I mainly told him the good stuff—I wanted him to think well of me.

After my schooling was out of the way, the conversation shifted, and he'd talk about my father, which always led to talking about my mother.

"Your father was great," Uncle Wayne said, and passed the toothpick box one night while Father slept in his favorite chair. "When he and your mother showed up, everyone started clapping. 'Come on, Chris.' 'Get out there, Shelia.' We loved to watch them dance.

"Of course," Uncle Wayne stretched out on the step, reached his hand around, grabbing hold of one of the banisters on the porch, a rotting wood piece with white paint chipping off, yet sturdy enough to hold him, "your father had the big head. He knew he was good. That's all right, because he could dance like Fred Astaire. Ever heard of Fred Astaire?"

I shook my head. "But I can imagine him."

"All right, all right," Uncle Wayne nodded, "I got you, nephew. Focus. Close your eyes," and I closed my eyes. It was a game of my uncle's—with everything gone in the desert, this was how he communicated the past.

"Astaire was maybe the greatest dancer. You got that? Thin like me, but nimble—which I ain't. In the movies, he'd come flying down beautiful, spiraling stairs, dance with brooms and make them sway like a partner, away from him and back into his hands. He loved tuxes. And he smiled, a long smile that stretched into his long, long chin. He had a casual grace, seemed always up for dancing. That's all he wanted to do. You could tell that made him happy. Yeah, he was thin like me. A great dancer like your father. I remember everyone expected me to be able to dance because I was Chris' younger brother, and maybe a little bit because I was thin like Fred Astaire."

"And you got a long chin," I pointed out, opening my eyes just a little.

"That's true, that's true, my mother's side of the family, you know?" Uncle Wayne nodded his chin into his palm and rubbed at his jaw in agreement. "But I guess you wouldn't know about her—Mrs. Estelle, we called her, everyone did because she made us. Tough woman. Gave your grandfather fits and that wasn't easy. When Mrs. Estelle died, Daddy stiffened up and was meaner. He missed Mrs. Estelle. She died when I was young, just like your mamma did."

My eyes opened fully, waiting for him to go on and talk about my mother, about her death.

"I couldn't dance anything like Chris," he said, was all he said, and I was out of luck. "The first time I stepped on the dance floor," Uncle Wayne raised his hands as if circling an imaginary back, "I broke my date's arm." His hands collapsed to his stomach, and he laughed so hard, his toothpick fell out of his mouth. "Just landed right on top of her. She screamed, too. Screamed and screamed— bawled like a cow, I tell you, Mathew. The band playing came to a halt, she screamed so loud. And Daddy wouldn't let me leave the house until her arm had healed—this girl. I can't even remember her name now." He chuckled a little more, picked up the toothpick, and let it click and roll from his lips and teeth.

And I laughed, too, since it seemed all right to laugh.

"Mary, Amanda . . . something like that. It took two months for her bones to set right. So while I was home, snapping beans and shucking corn as punishment, I had to watch your father prep up for his dates with Shelia. I wanted to go so bad, but 'No, no,' Daddy said." Uncle Wayne's voice bottomed out gruff and deep like I imagined Grandpa's.

" 'No. You're not getting out of this house until the girl's healed.' " Then Uncle Wayne's voice lifted. "Your father isn't the only one who's strict. He gets it honest, I tell you.

"So for two months I watched Chris leave and come back. Leave and come back. Me, snapping beans, boiling peanuts—" Uncle Wayne turned, made sure Father was still sleeping through the door, then he spoke steadily. "And in all that coming and going, your father's hands sparkled. Have you ever seen it, Mathew? They still have it. Like precious stones. I would go to the mirror, put my hands to the glass, and pretend I was holding Shelia. I had a big crush on your mother—she was so gorgeous. I'd touch the mirror, then pretend to dance, but I wanted to hold her with his hands." He smiled, winked his blue eye—that's how I knew when Uncle Wayne had finished, he gave his patented wink. "*His* hands, you see?"

"I see," I told him, and gave him back the toothpicks. But as soon as Uncle Wayne headed for the door, I examined the insides and outsides of my hands with great seriousness and anxiety. In fact, I stared so hard that my vision blurred. I was unable, however, to find any sparkles, any remnants of Fred Astaire, my father, or my mother, even when I closed my eyes.

Another midnight lunch, the mining crew still empty- ing the last ponds in southwest Alabama—another week- end evening off, not long after telling me how my mother died, Uncle Wayne pointed to the brightest star he could find.

"You see that?" he said.

I nodded.

"Well, guess what?" he asked.

When I didn't respond, he went on. "What do you think it looks like?"

"A small sun," I told him, because I had learned that in school and wanted to sound smart.

"Well, hey, you're right, nephew." He tipped his hand to me, brought it back to his mouth, and wielded a tooth- pick between his white side teeth.

"But you know what else?" he said. "It's like a dia- mond, too. Don't you think? Sparkling. Just look at it. And man, that would be a big damn diamond if you could bring it to earth."

Uncle Wayne lifted his hand to the sky and squinted, trying to hold the small sun between his thumb and index finger. "Do you like diamonds?" he asked.

"Yeah," I told him, "I do." I wanted to sound enthusias- tic, though I had never really seen one. I had read about them, about how people killed over them in the past, how people mined them in horrible conditions just like gold and jade, hands hunched into the ground, trying to bring up the precious stones.

"Sure you do. Everybody does," he said, bringing his hand down. "They can cut glass—they're that hard. Harder than your noggin." He tapped me on my head. "*And* can get you out of this place. Easy. This damn desert. If you could find a diamond here, you'd be a rich man. You could ride through the checkpoints in style. Have a farm some-where where it's worth having a farm.

"Now, I've got a secret to tell you," he said, his tone shifting serious. "No one knows this, Mat. You can't tell anybody. You promise?"

"I won't," I said, and felt a sudden importance that was powerful and scary like the deep reservoir of a river where you can get too far in and sink and not come up if you're not careful. No one had called me just Mat before, and I felt grown-up, felt like I had grown five or six inches inside my Mathew body and the space inside me was real tight.

Uncle Wayne leaned in, and when he did, he pulled the stars along as if kite strings were attached from his tan-gled blond hair to them. He whispered, "I've been looking for diamonds when I'm mining—blue diamonds like that star, that bright one—see how it turns blue?"

I stared and stared hard, but it seemed to turn more pink than blue. So I stared harder and hoped.

"You get diamonds when you mine, Mat. In all that Alabama mica, all that clay, there's got to be some—I know they're here. The blue ones. The rare ones. And when I find the blue diamonds, well, hell, we won't be working for nothing like my brother says. I'm going to take him and you—even if he's screaming—I'm going to take him and you out of this place. We'll buy a farm. And the skies will be perfect blue, long days with clear skies, and we'll see stars every night—thousands, that whole other world. And your father—I'm going to make him leave, Mat. I want you to know, I'm going to make him."

I thought about my Uncle Wayne all tall and lanky, my father low like a pig, and I wondered how he would get my father to budge. I wasn't so sure. So I imagined him push-ing and pushing at my father, but my father was too much of a pig, a dancing, graceful pig. And he told Uncle Wayne no, just like he told me no.

Then suddenly I understood. "You only stay here because of him, don't you?"

It wasn't the response my uncle expected, I could tell, and the smile on his face turned.

"I'm not leaving without my brother and without you," he said, determined, then reached his hand out to grab hold of mine. The toothpicks fell on the ground and scattered.

"Don't worry about that," he said, holding me down. "And don't worry about the other. I'm going to find those blue diamonds. I'm going to find them."

I nodded my head uneasy and squeezed his palm. All night my hand smelled of sweet basil; all night I dreamed about cooking great food.

Is a diamond all it would take? Could we really get out of here? I dreamed and dreamed.

When I woke up, my hand smelled even stronger of basil, and I believed my uncle even more.

CHAPTER 21

Sumner's Hill, 2030

The rope was tight, my father's hands showing first. This was the moment Bossey had made me wait for—having turned sixteen, barreling over Sumner's Hill to the devil lights, so I grabbed one hand, helped pull him up.

The first look on his face was surprise, and for a moment I thought he would accept my decision—my father knew I was here to work, it was okay. But he was only startled, nothing else, and that didn't last.

"What're you doing?" Even though his face was covered in clay, underneath, a sternness quickly took over.

"I don't know. I just wanted to come out and see you," I lied.

"Well, don't you think you should be in school?" He cleared mud from his watch, checked the time. "You can't be missing a lot of school."

"I know, it's early, I just . . . Look, Mamma—Father. I

don't know what to tell you. I can't just say that I'm—" I stopped, and his eyes locked on me, his face even more grave. I counted the flags slipping at the wind and dust— 43, 27 in black numbers. I looked again at him. "I need to tell you . . ."

"What? This break is short, Mathew. I only have ten minutes. Just get to it."

He began rubbing mud from his chest and stomach deliberately, slowly. He put his hands in a bucket of water, the liquid oozing with mud. He pushed at the liquid, tried to make a trough of clean water, then cupped his hands together, swept it up full and splashed it over his face. Somewhere in the wader's chest pocket, he kept a rag and began to dry off with it, pulling long streaks of clay from his skin.

"You need to talk," he said. "Don't be afraid of me."

"I'm not."

"Then what is it?" My father was yelling now. "Tell me—"

"I'm quitting school." I had said it, and a burning, a fuse lit through my calves, my hips to my neck. We looked at each other, and I could see the separation in his stare, the way his mouth hung open, the clay on him like a warrior now. I had lost my father's hope.

And I didn't wait for a response, for any other expression. I just started walking. There were no more shouts, no demands to turn around, to come back and listen. I knew my father was watching, but he didn't move, didn't grab my arm, stop me as I half expected, yell that I was an idiot, yell about my future, force me in his truck and back to school. Only the loud noise, the sludge lines and pulleys pounding and pounding, clearing a space between earth and sky, such little space.

I crisscrossed the field of tunnels until I found Bossey's trailer. I yanked the door hard to the wall, stepped in.

"Hey, be careful," Bossey admonished, but then there

was a grin showing those tiny corn teeth. "You're just in time." Bossey handed me some waders from one of the three boxes popped open on his desk. "Try these on. They should fit—"

But before he could finish his sentence, I was wiggling them over my jeans, trying not to fall.

"Ready for work?"

I didn't look up, just kept at my new rubbery legs and waist.

"Answer me, Mat—don't be rude. I know you know better."

"Yes, sir," I said. "I'm ready to go to work."

"Did you tell Mr. Chris?"

I nodded.

"What did he say?"

"We didn't talk."

"But you told him?"

"Yes, sir."

Bossey sighed, was all that he did in a voice like rubbing alcohol drying on skin. It reminded me of a wound clean and empty. There was nothing for either of us to respond to. Then he gave me a hat, the light already flicked on, and we walked into the mining field. I looked at number 40 but my father was not there, only a flag flapping with the others, the ground wet where the water had brushed against his worn face and spilled down with clay.

Bossey took me to the hole the two of us had dug earlier, and a caretaker steered an ore cart around us.

"Watch out," he said. "They move out of the way for tunnels, not people." Then Bossey kneeled, grunting a little. "I just need to set up this pulley." He took a can of gas and poured it in the reservoir, screwed the cap on tight, then turned his attention to the base. He had brought several sandbags and stacked them on top of the pulley's aluminum feet to stabilize it. All the while, his breathing grew heavy and more difficult, his large body covering the pulley completely.

"Can I do anything?"

"Almost done," he said. "Don't worry about all this."

I stared into the hole. It was pure black, endless it seemed. Seemed that I could fall and never find the bottom, my father, Bossey, never find myself again.

CHAPTER 22

Santuck, 2026

This area under a tornado warning until 6 p.m. Strong thunderstorms. Flash floods continue to be possible. Hail possible. Take precautions. Do not travel. Do not go outside. Stay indoors. Repeat: This area under a tornado warning until 6 p.m.

—*WDMZ 1610 AM, 7:05 a.m.*

When I was twelve, I daydreamed hard about what my uncle had revealed: my mother (the pain she went through for me), and the diamonds (through their sparkle, our escape). Two secrets, and there was one more secret to uncover, one more to know.

My father had a pine box, square, the size of a large book, six or seven inches deep. It had been made with long-leaf pine—trees, I learned in school, that had died in the drought.

Grandpa Sanford had sawed and stained and nailed the box, fit the lid tight, and inside was my visa, my ticket to leave once I graduated, no questions asked at any security checkpoint. I knew this because my father had said it was true.

From time to time my father took out the box, set it securely on his lap, his hands and arms working like the toughest locks. He patted the lid—"Your visa. It's ready. It's secure." I waited for his hands to pull a magic trick, bring the document forth like a white rabbit, but my father never did. It was a matter of trust, faith, believing in the future.

There was the deed to his father's land—useless now. He took it out occasionally and read the contents of the acres, the surveyor's entries as if talking to a judge or giving a proclamation: "The line borders Indigo Creek for a quarter mile, then turns west," my father would say, clear his voice, and continue, "250 acres total—" enough land to run through and keep on running and it never ends.

One time my father took out his contract with the government, read the words in the same flat tone, talking more to the empty room than to me—my father wanted me to hear, but I didn't exist anywhere in that sermon, in his expression.

And what I remember most was not the government's assertion that clay mining was a "good, redeemable job." What I remember occurred after my father was done, with his voice fizzled out: as he shuffled the contract back in, I glimpsed the contents. The pine box seemed full, much fuller than the few items I had been allowed to witness. What was my father not telling? An entire world existed in that box. I had merely a few pieces.

When my uncle revealed the story about my mother and the blue diamonds, I decided I also had to find out about the box.

It was late May, my last few days of school in Santuck. We were heading to Red Hill soon, the lakes there. The bus dropped me off, and once inside, I locked the door, including the dead bolt. My father wouldn't be home for two hours and that was enough time, but I checked the lock on the door again for reassurance.

We lived in what my father called a shotgun house because the rooms lined up one behind the other. If you fired a gun through the front door, the bullet would zip straight through. His was the last room, and I opened and closed each door, living room to kitchen to my room to his, a long procession of knobs clicking and hinges creaking and otherwise silence. All of it was unnerving.

I kept wondering, worrying, what if my father came home early? What if my father was already in his room, waiting? My mind spun and spun. The house began to breathe. I noticed boards swell and shrink with each step I took, boards angry and furious, infused with the conscience of my father. The house was alive, knew what I was up to, and was certainly going to stop my steps with furniture and kitchen knives and window glass. *Daydreamer Mathew, Daydreamer Mathew*—the mantra of my classmates began to build.

Finally, I shut the door to my father's empty room, and the house shrunk back down, shrunk all the way to his bed, neatly made with a quilt sewn by my grandmother. My father always kept his bed neat, which was easy for him to do because, as usual, my father had fallen asleep in his favorite easy chair and started up that way, his body cramped and shaped like an L for the first hour of the evening. Whatever house we moved into, there was always a new bed to cover with Mrs. Estelle's quilt, its square design of old shirts and strips of red and blue materials, the quilt untouched until we moved again. The beds we left behind, but his sleeping chair, like the quilt, we took with us.

Under the coiled springs, the bed was stuffed with boxes of clothes, all of them mildewed inside stale cardboard. I wondered why he kept them; he never wore them. My father had jeans and freshly washed T-shirts for the mining. He had his one nice suit—he kept these folded on top of his dresser.

The cartons slid out easily on the hardwood floors, and in the center was the pine box. It was as if my father had placed the pine jewel in first and put everything else around to protect it.

Carefully, I curled my hands around its edges and carried it out.

I sat on the bed, my father's pine box in front of me, the shutters letting in only a razor outline of the sun. I touched the lid six or seven times. I patted it like my father did, thought of his hands and arms locked, hitched like musty leather straps across it. Then I turned the box front to back, trying to figure out the best side to open.

Finally, I simply took my thumbs and lifted. The lid came up and fell back dully on the quilt. I exhaled a deep breath. For some reason, I had shut my eyes, and I opened them. Before me a thick mass of papers crowded in, yellowed and crumbling.

On top was the contract. The paper split a little, and I set it aside.

Then the deed to the land—I read a few lines out loud, strident like my father had done, but hearing my own voice was too scary and great: What if the house came alive again? Carefully, I put it down, too.

I picked up a birth certificate—my own—the inked prints of my feet small enough to tuck inside my hand. But the certificate had been dated August 9, 2014, two months after I was born. And there was a note attached at the bottom addressed to my father.

Chris,

    Your news about my sister has devastated me a second time. My daughter, Margery, died in her sleep. She was with us for only ten days. Ten days. We've locked the door to her room because we can't pack up

her clothes. Neither of us can go near her bed now. Jacy
hasn't gone back to work, and I can't tell her about
Shelia. I just wish I could drive to your home, but it's
been difficult in Birmingham since they put the border
up. Only these couriers are able to slip back and forth. I
found one to take this letter. And yes, Chris, I can help
your son—that is the one bit of good news. I'm enclos-
ing Margery's birth certificate. Use it for Mat. Then come
to Birmingham. We'll be waiting.

  Take care,
  Reynolds Oren

So the feet were not mine at all, but the stamp of
another child. Where my name had been typed, I picked
up faded marks, half-lines forming an *M*, the top curve of
an *r*—Margery and Oren, and her middle name, it looked
as if it were Leigh.

And there was my father's name—Christopher Thomas
Harrison typed over rubbed-out letters, and my mother's,
Shelia Oren Harrison, replacing Jacquelyn.

I knew I had been born in my grandfather's house, and
my father told me he had to send off for my birth certificate. "It was the only way," he said, "to make you legal in
this world." But he never mentioned the second half of
the equation—how he forged the certificate, Margery, her
parents.

So she was my cousin, I guessed.

It struck me then that I had an entirely different tree of
relatives I didn't know about, my mother's people, that my
father never talked about.

Were they dead? Were they alive?

Just the name of this dead girl, her feet inked in my absence, making the paper official, making me official. Who were they to me?

I studied the certificate for a long time, trying to imagine my cousins, the ones whose feet had outgrown the page—surely there were some survivors. I wondered if they still lived in Birmingham or somewhere else in the Saved World, if they even knew what a desert was, what it was like, if they knew I existed. How would they ever know me?

"They won't," I whispered.

There was the RCA Victrola warranty for Grandpa Sanford's record player, dated 1958, almost seventy years old. Next to it, his death certificate, and paper-clipped to the side was a picture of him and my father.

My fingers stopped twitching. I could do nothing but look, holding that face, my grandfather whom I had never met, the white hair, the rows of wrinkles across his red forehead like cornrows. His red face seemed smushed up, flattened and fat, broad more like a bull than a human. In the background stood a huge tree, a black gum, the beginnings of a field, my father much younger, hugging my grandfather, the two men smiling, teeth poking through and hanging over their bottom lips like popcorn about to burst. I had never caught my father with a smile so full. And my grandfather, Grandpa Sanford, a name I had heard so much, my grandfather was the same man from my dream, the man in the field on the tractor, not moving, not waving. It was him. He had existed, too. Here was the proof of it.

So I kept the picture to the side and scrambled the papers, looking for more pictures. Dust and turpentine rose as documents, the odds and ends, lifted and fell. At the bottom, I uncovered a gold mine.

Some pictures were of my grandfather, my father, and Uncle Wayne dressed in jeans and T-shirts and denim jackets, even flannel coats. Uncle Wayne looked even leaner and younger than my father at eight and nine years old—my father gave the camera such stern expressions. But the times he stood next to Grandpa Sanford, the sternness gave way.

In every photograph they were at work or about to work, surrounded by fields, a barn, a tractor, the 250 acres I had been told about—the place I was born.

I placed them in a square, each picture over a pattern Mrs. Estelle had sewn into the quilt, then a longer rectangle, carefully plotting my family's history.

Then I discovered a photo of my father and a woman carrying a satin blue ribbon the same color as her dress, my father dressed in his black tux and striped black pants. That woman, I knew, was my mother.

My mother—she had dark hair, and in her eyes I could see my own brown eyes, the wide oval shape, not gray-blue like my father, but he was beside her, shoulder to shoulder. I rubbed a finger down her arm and back up. I traced the elbow's curve, the neck. She was actually taller than him, her skin tawny, a shimmering brown like my skin, not red like his, blistered by the sun forever. It was true that he turned pale in winter, and I faded also, though never as fully or completely. I wondered if she did the same. She was beautiful like my father always said but had never exactly revealed, never revealed that we shared so many of the same features.

I touched her stomach, the holy ground I had come from. Her stomach was so flat in the picture, like the beds my father never slept in—how did I ever fit inside? Unlike Grandpa Sanford, I had never dreamed about Mamma. I grabbed half of the picture tight, ripped the other half out, but my hands got stuck in the middle—the photo didn't rip all the way. Something heavy was stuck to the back. I turned the picture over, and taped to the paper was the pair of earrings she was wearing, blue and sparkling, dangling from silver hoops—blue diamonds. Below, just the words *Shelia and me, April 5, 2006* in my father's handwriting.

They were blue diamonds, just as my uncle had said, and I pulled the tape and the earrings, flipped the picture back to the glossy front.

"Why won't he let me see you?" I studied my father, his smile so full, but the truth was, there was nothing open about him, the way he kept all of us hidden and separate. I gripped the picture, split it in half, and tossed my father's face, his shoulder torn a little, back into the box. I held on to Mamma, the first-place ribbon. I didn't realize I was crying until some drops plashed on the dress. I cleaned them off quickly, afraid that I would ruin her face, her ribbon, smudge it, cause the glossy paper to blur. The light edged through the windows and disappeared. It was morning. He would be home.

And though I hadn't seen all of the contents, I had seen enough, had found the other secret, and I started to put the deed and the certificates back when I spotted a document that read *Permission to Transfer*.

It was my visa. I picked it up, unfolded it, the paper heavy and green like money, smelling like money and damp, sticking to my fingers, and as I did, two more sheets, duplicates I thought, fell out as well. I began to read: *This certificate gives permission to Wayne Harrison to transfer from the Southern Alabama Zone*—

There was not only a visa for me, but one for my Uncle Wayne, and a visa for my father. We could go anytime we wanted. We could all go. But why hadn't he told me?

I remembered what Uncle Wayne said about the blue diamonds, how he was going to find them and get us out of here. He didn't have to do that now. But why hadn't my father told us?

A pulse shot to my hand and the headboard came straight into view. I wanted to smash it, but just as quick the pulse burned itself out. For so long, my father had been mad at me for not reading enough, not wanting to leave the desert enough — it felt strange for the reverse to be true, for me to be mad at him.

I felt the half picture of my mother. It was crumpled now.

"Damn you for that," I said, and the walls recoiled. Carefully, I flattened the wrinkles of my mother's blue dress, the creases in her face, the ribbon against the quilt as best I could. Then I filled the pine box and put it back under the bed, carelessly pitching the other mildewed boxes around. I didn't care if he knew what I had seen. I marched out of his room and sat in his chair, his sleeping chair, pointed it toward the door like a cannon and waited.

The bright outlines at the window curtains darkened and rain began to thump on the tin roof. I heard rumbles of thunder, but they were far off. The house barely shook. Here, the rain fell light, drizzly, rare in the desert. Any other time, I would've gone outside, run and run, allowed the rain to soak me. Not today. I waited to confront my father.

But he didn't come home.

After an hour, I got up, finished my chores and the cooking.

The eggs grew cold and stiff. I turned off the record player, turned it off before I had removed the needle, causing it to burrow and scratch into the grooves. Slowly, I lifted the player's arm, lifted Billie Holiday's *Me, Myself and I* album and placed the disc with a hush into its sleeve. The static from the record shocked me a little when I sat back in the chair, but this was good. I needed to stay awake.

What if he knew, knew I was angry, and he was avoiding me? What if he couldn't face his betrayal? I had convinced myself that I had not betrayed my father by rummaging through the pine box. I had merely found the truth; my father, on the other hand, had betrayed me and betrayed Uncle Wayne. My anger started to boil again, but it quickly cooled and turned to worry—why wasn't he here?

The rain persisted with its deliberate thump. I opened the blinds to the gray sky. I touched the glass—it was sweating, no escape from the heat steaming outside. Inside, the air was muggy even with the air conditioners grinding on.

I waited and waited.

Finally, the door turned, and I tried to find the energy I had possessed hours ago. I cleared my voice, grabbed Mamma's picture and the earrings, the evidence, ready for battle. But my father's face was swollen and solemn. He was soaked in mud.

"Mathew," he said, was all that he said. The word crumbled, vanished immediately into a deep sadness, and I knew then that something was wrong.

CHAPTER 23

Millers Ferry, June 2044

I am thirty feet in the tunnel now—a diver for the coral reef, like my father said. Each step and twitch I make echoes a circle at my boots and head, and up until vanishing. The hose is waist high. Everything's black. I need to dig five feet more and somehow manage to forget about the pine box, its contents and visas.

"Focus on your work," I whisper, shift my hands over, and as I do, I remember the advice Bossey has given on and off since I was sixteen:

"The light on your head doesn't help the mud in your eyes." He slapped the hard-hat switch off, handing me a towel that first week. "Keep your eyes clean. Goggles or a rag, either will work. There's a bucket of water at the top of the tunnel. Some people take canteens down. But the goggles will keep you from getting infections.

"And you dig deep—twenty, thirty, forty—afraid when

you hear something fall above the push of water and sucking of the pipe. You wait—second one, two, another second, still nothing lands. Five full seconds, Mat, until there's a splash on your hard hat. Usually it's only mud, a clump breaking from the wall, easy to wipe off. If there's a cave-in, if an underground stream bursts through, as happened to Tom in Suwannee, then it's over, we can't get you out." He showed the nub where his pinkie went missing.

"There's a winch used. But when we pulled Tom out, by the time his body made it through the heavy muck, he was torn apart. You wouldn't think mud could be so damn heavy, be that strong, but it is—it's like drowning under bricks."

"Yes, sir," I answered as Bossey expected, always, "Yes, sir."

"Then there are the storms. The sudden sweeps of dust that rise without warning. You have to get out before the sand comes on top—huge waves of sand, and you can't find an end to it, a place to get around the swirling and flooding and filling in of every tunnel like dirt over an open grave, and you will cough and cough until the storm is over and your tunnel is gone, except for your rope and pipes. The rope is cut, the hose is cut, and you're left in a burial, the pulley your gravestone. There isn't time to dig you out." Bossey breathed in, the air rustling in his throat.

"The same with cloudbursts, thunderstorms in February and March. When it does rain, the mud slides fast and buries you, drowns you. Jacob got hit by lightning, Jacob Shell—fried right in his hole.

"There are so many ways to die here. And every time you dig down, every foot deeper you dig, you start to think of those ways. You can't help it."

"Yes, sir," always *Yes, sir.*

For me it is war, the traps that turn into shallow graves, the traps where the earth fails and you fall into a grove of

sharpened trees. I am again in the history books, men dying for wrong causes, created mantras, for mankind. In
World War I, all those trenches, all those trenches built
into the earth, the men attempting to cover themselves, to
hide their fear from mustard gas, mortars, and death, the
nerves and shrapnel buttoned and pressed into their uni-
forms, buttoned inside their skin, shaken and ripped out
with every explosion.

This is how I think of death: people losing their
strength, having it taken from them, waiting for the sun
like a comet of metal, for God to kill us.

"You think of every possible way," Bossey explained
that first week I came to work. He still brings it up when we
walk across new mining fields, surveying acres to dig, when
it's just us two alone.

But I don't want to think of wars, count the Allies and
the Central Powers, the Coalition of the Willing—and
death tolls in my head, dying men, "Dying for nothing,"
my father said.

I need to concentrate on my work. Deep clay boots,
hard sweat, pressure on the eyes, working through the
night, seven hours. Movement is hardest on the calves.
The bones in my feet want to break. Above, the land is flat,
sandy topsoil that sustains boots like snow. Here the wet
clay sucks and drags at your feet. My father said, "You sink
into a field's black dirt like you sink in the clay, but you can
keep walking in a field." There's nowhere to move in this
crater.

My grandfather's fields held corn. "High stalks." Father
would raise his hands over his head as high as he could
stretch, then fit them around my chest and lift. "Wayne
and I shucked corn on the porch while Father slept." He
said my gray Chevy smelled like sweet corn feed, and I'd
take in long, slow breaths of dust until I could smell it, too.
I kept the Chevy until the engine wouldn't turn.

And I have run through fields with tassels clicking at the sun, dreaming, have woken up itching. And one August, Tina arranged high stalks tied in bushels, set them on either side of the checkout at her store. "From Ohio," she said, spitting tobacco in a cup. "For decoration." I ran my fingers down the narrow leaves and husks, broke them for their wet green color.

Now I place my hand on the wall of clay, rub the cool mud. The sparkles of mica break open the smell of minerals and dirt. The light fades. The switch isn't working. Everything's too black. Deep clay boots, hard sweat. I check the strength of the pipe, wait for my eyes to adjust to the dark, swish the nozzle full. Five feet more I need to tunnel down.

CHAPTER 24

Blue Diamonds, 2030

May 11

Mom,

Just knowing that you're alive is good enough. The letters themselves, they are enough, in whatever pieces they come in. I'm finishing up my course work in business—just two more weeks. Schoolwork can be so boring, but it's better than the monotonous wind. Well, I have to make this letter short. Great picture of you, by the way. The money helps, too. Everyone wants US dollars. I can buy so much with it.

With love,

Jen

"Your uncle," Bossey lowered his eyes, began rubbing his hands, "Mr. Chris and me tried to get him out. But we couldn't, couldn't do it."

Bossey checked his boots, waited for the sand and wind to fall back just enough, an opening in the weather, to retell the story he always tells.

"Pull up," Bossey shouted.

"Give me a minute." Wayne's helmet light flashed to the top of the crater, then back in.

"Water's out. Electricity's out, lightning's hitting. Now, pull up. You're holding in too long, Wayne. I said pull up!" Bossey wrapped his fingers around the rope and jerked, but it came flying by his head with nothing, like a fish, the kind Bossey talked about catching when he was younger, the kind on television that leaped from the water, too big breaking free.

"Hang on, Bossey," Wayne's voice boomed and echoed. "I've got a diamond in here. A blue diamond."

The hoses died, the siren wailed across the site, a quick wind dusted everything.

"We've got to get out of here," Bossey said. "Listen to me," and he reached into the tunnel for a better fix. *Find his light,* Bossey said to himself, his huge face beaded in sweat, trousers dirty, fingers going down, down—

"Diamond, Bossey," the echoes swirled up in Bossey's face quick with sulfur and dust, "Get the water back on, I've almost got it."

Bossey dug in his boots to keep from falling, his fingers reaching out from the walls, chipping at mud and black air. "Listen to me," he tried to reason.

"Diamond, Bossey."

"The storm's almost over us. There aren't any diamonds, you hear?"

There was no answer.

Drops of water began to plunk onto Bossey's legs, his back, and he had to pull himself out of the crater. As he did, the other men ran over. My father pushed through and glanced at the flag number—53. He glanced at Bossey, then found the slack rope and trailed it back into the hole.

"Chris," Bossey stared at the sky, black, pure black, even the stadium lights creaking and breaking from their towers like chinaberry trees about to break apart, "you can't go down there. We've got to leave."

Father hammered the stake and faded into the tunnel. The south Alabama wind was trapping dust in the ground lights. The hot rain started pouring, steaming.

"Find his light," Bossey said, watching my father's shadow swirl and swirl. "Up!" he yelled.

"A diamond. I see it."

"Bring him up!"

Echoes mixing, dissolving in the humid air.

"Do you understand?" Bossey took a rope. I clutched my hands around. "We give you one rope—over shoulder, under thigh like I showed you, all the way to the bottom. Then hook it to the bag. The pulley takes it, empties the bushels. If the water kills, you hook the cable back to you. We've got time to pull you out, but it's your choice to die. And the hole's not big enough for two men. And the holes fill up fast with rain, with dust. Don't panic."

I nodded, felt as if I were someone else, a soldier parachuting into a fog. "Divers for the coral reef," my father had said, someone else suffocating inside my new rubbery clothes, as if dead bodies were already inside the crater, waiting for me.

"Grab my boots," Father called. He kicked and spun on the cable, a spider dangling, trying to find fingers, a flash of skin, a metal helmet under the rain swirling down, buckets of rain getting heavier and fuller.

"Leave me alone, Chris." The shout boomed louder than the one just seconds ago.

My father edged a few inches deeper, my father's hands burning and numb.

"Grab on, brother," he said. "Hear my boots kicking? Can you spot them?"

"Leave me, Chris. I'm getting out of here."

"Then grab my boots—can you see them?" Father kicked into the side.

"No, I'm not going with you. I've got another way." His voice crested and fell, the echo pushed down by the water.

Father heard hands scraping at the wall, saw them in his light, in the lightning, then nothing. He could feel the mud slide around him and knew his brother's feet were trapped.

CHAPTER 25

The Dreams

I take the old green tractor spotted with rust sores that sat in every yard, in front of every house we moved into for years and years, the tractor that belonged to my grandfather and my great-grandfather, and I take it across the desert, a flat section with no burnt trees, only a few dunes, but in front is the sun rising—it's morning—and today the sun is bloodred, a sandstorm is brewing from the east, is coming at me, but I'm in a marine uniform, deep navy blue, and I have my tractor and a brandished sword, and I'm driving toward the red-blood sun to find the end of this world like explorers who thought the land was flat.

"For Queen and Country!" I say—one hand on the steering wheel, plumes of diesel smoke puffing up and up, the other hand brandishing the sword at the sky. But the sand is growing and the bloodred is becoming thick and black like Sumner's Hill, like death, like the true end of the world—and I look back, look back, but no one is behind me. When I look forward, the sand has become an army battalion, parachuters with rifles aimed. They take up a formation on the ground, point at me.

"For Queen and Country," and their yell is much louder than my own, scopes set, fingers ready on the triggers. The bullets begin to fire—first only one like a small crackle of light, then all of them like lightning, and before I feel anything, I know that the sun has shut me out.

CHAPTER 26

Blue Diamonds, 2030

"I waited on your uncle as much as I could. I'm sorry. It's no reflection on you, Mat. He was crazy. This work can do it. But I'll never understand why he thought he saw diamonds." Bossey shook his head, repinned a wild curl to his scalp.

"Your father stayed as much as he could stay. Everyone had scrambled to their trucks and left. It was just him and me and your Uncle Wayne. But now time was up—we had to leave, too. The rain was coming so hard, so thick, the winds and lightning striking close, flashing the world up. It could strike us any second.

"I yelled down to Mr. Chris. He was yelling at your uncle, but Wayne had stopped talking. I think he was dead. Which made me feel a little better. We had done our best—I'm not saying I was happy about him dying in that crater, Mat. I'm just saying we had tried to save him. And all of this took less than a few minutes, mind you. Within a few minutes, your uncle had drowned. There was never enough time for your father, especially when the tunnel walls began sliding apart.

"I said, 'I'm pulling you up, Chris. We can't stay here.' And your father kept saying, 'No, no, a little more time, okay? I almost can get him. It's my brother.'

"I didn't say anything else. Your father would've stayed as long as I would've let him. Just started pulling, that's what I had to do. I didn't have time to get the winch in, and I was afraid—I tell you this now, Mat, I was afraid your father would let go of that rope just like your uncle, would sink down with Wayne. But he didn't. It was you—I'm certain he couldn't leave you, Mat. I think he didn't want to live either, not at that moment. Your father's lost a lot of people."

"He's always taken care of me."

"And he always will." Bossey slapped dead-center between my shoulder blades, his fingers plump like grilled franks. "Bull's-eye," he said, satisfied, the muscles in my back stinging. "That's one thing you shouldn't worry about. He's a hard man, I know that, but he'll never abandon you."

I nodded. "Yes, sir." And I was glad that when we had breaks, when work ended, Bossey wanted to talk.

CHAPTER 27

Santuck, 2026

That morning, Father came home, sat in his chair, quiet until he fell asleep. For a long time I watched his breathing lapse deeper and deeper. Then I hid the photograph of Mamma and her earrings inside a pot in the kitchen, one we never used because the handle was broken.

"What happened?" I asked my father, but not loud enough, touching a washrag to his face. I had never seen so much mud on him. And he stayed put, cocooned in his wet clothes. He wouldn't answer.

Hours later, I tugged and pulled on his shoulder. "You've got to get ready for work," I said more roughly.

His eyes flashed open and the wrinkles on his forehead pinched tight, angry that he had fallen asleep or angry with me for waking him, I wasn't sure. He was so disconcerted that for a moment, I thought he would tumble to the floor, but he regained his balance, wiggled up in his chair, and yawned away the last six hours. "What time is it?"

"Eight."

"Eight? We need to dress for the funeral," my father said matter-of-factly.

But whose funeral? "Whose funeral?" I asked.

"Your Uncle Wayne," he answered quick before I could think, his voice flat and painless, unlike the greeting I received when he first got home.

And I started to smile, waited for my father to smile. It was a joke, had to be a joke. But that was something Uncle Wayne would pull and not my father.

"Uncle Wayne's coming to cook on Saturday?" I reminded, thinking I had misheard him. But he wouldn't look at me now. He searched for something in the house, something like he always did.

I smelled the sulfur of the eggs I had eaten rising in my throat.

"What happened?" I managed to say.

My father stood from his chair, stretched, and walked from the room, came back with his dress suit. He laid the pieces carefully on the table. Then he dropped the washrag into the basin, squeezed out the red water, picked up a small mirror, and began washing off the clay from the sunken part in his cheek just above his wiry beard, sunken like a crescent moon, what he could spot in the chipped glass.

"What happened?" I said. "Tell me."

My father spit in the basin, put the rag down, his attention now on his suit.

"Get ready, Mathew." There was an edge to his voice that I knew better than to challenge.

I walked to the kitchen, the metal sink, the eggs stirring in my stomach, but at the doorway I wheeled, came back to my father, and hit him, hit him straight in the chest as hard as I could.

He fell back a little, more startled than when I had woken him.

"What happened?" I demanded, and put my fist up.

He lifted a hand.

"I'm sorry," he said.

"Not good enough. You can't not talk to me." I breathed heavier and faster than I wanted, but I needed the oxygen so I could hit him again. The eggs in my stomach churned as I waited, waited for my father to move his hand.

"I remember when your grandpa explained fences to me," he raised his voice—not angry but enough to make me pause. " 'Why all these fences?' I asked him, and your grandpa told me, 'That's how you'll know whose soil belongs to who.'

"I remember clutching the wire for the first time." He unhooked the waders and pulled his work shirt off, touching the place I had struck in the center of the sternum, a red circle spreading deeper red in the filthy blond-white and gray hairs, the sparkles that spread like night stars to his shoulders and neck.

"The rust came off in my hands. Strand after strand, Mathew . . . five rows of barbed wire." He opened his palms to show me cuts, deep ravines used for clenching steel wire. He looked at my fist still shaking, and pushed it down. Then he breathed easier and the fall and swelling in his chest allowed me to catch my own breath.

"We began using electric fence when I was twelve," he said. "Electric's not as good. Every two weeks the cows had broken a different place. Wayne and I had to fix it—there was only one strand, a thin string, easy enough to fix, but no good." He picked up his coat and dusted it with his full attention, first at the shoulders where they drooped without arms in them, then down the back at the tails where the split had a tear and needed to be sewn.

"Wayne touched the electric wire the first day we turned it on. He jumped back so fast, fell into a row of corn. Your grandfather and I laughed. 'Stupid boy.' I called him that for a week—stupid." Father looked at his shoes; they were caked with mud. He set the coat over his chair, beat the shoes against the chair legs. He leaned over to rub them, flake the rest of the mud away. Then he slipped to the hardwood, fell as if something in him had broken and forced him down, the red mark on his chest, and he stayed hunched like a true pig damp with mud. "There aren't any diamonds in Alabama, Mathew. Why would he want— think— There's no time for being foolish here. Not enough men for it. Not now."

And I opened my palm, looking for a place to hide my mother's earrings, but I had hid them somewhere already—the pot in the cabinet, I remembered. My father looked beaten, fallen into some other world. And now I knew. The far-off rumble, the rain, the diamonds—I knew what had kept my father, what had happened to my uncle.

"I couldn't bring him out of that hole," he said. "I went after him, but I couldn't make him."

I leaned over and lifted my father, gave him room, and we stood like the pictures in the pine box, my father and grandfather, my Uncle Wayne, but without the smiles, without the huge black gum unburned, the 250 acres behind us to prop us up, and I waited, waited for my father to hold me.

Services were held at night before work. After Bossey's elegy, each miner lowered a bag of clay rocks into the shallow pit, something from the earth gathered and given over.

It was a ritual of farewell to follow the deceased, so in his next life everyone could welcome my uncle, welcome what his life had been, and it was a way of keeping the deceased's spirit from leaving too soon, the rocks weighing him down until we could say good-bye. My father did the shoveling. No time to dig Uncle Wayne out of the thirty feet of dried mud and bury him proper. Father wanted to take him to the farm, the same place as my mother and Grandpa Sanford, but Ray's business venture wasn't up and running yet, taking dead bodies into the Southeastern Desert anywhere for a price.

My father sweated clay, wiping the red from his face and beard. And it occurred to me that his life was one long continuance of cleaning away layers of mud and skin. Eventually, he would have no skin and be exposed. But in all that bare red flesh, what would be revealed?

He stopped shoveling and motioned me to the front.

"You put your arm here," he pinched the ball of my shoulder and twisted my arm out. "Take this wreath. Cross it to your wrist, and say, 'My father's brother. My father's brother. Amen.'"

It was a wreath he had kept with him from my mother's funeral—flowers white and blue and too perfect to be genuine. He ripped out the sash that said, *In God's Care*, placed the circle of blue and white in my hands.

I was twelve and the men's coveralls gave their bodies an impassable shadow, spread them into giants. They stood back of us as I stepped up to the pit, the new grave.

"My father's brother," I said, the pit like the black ditches on the moon Uncle Wayne had pointed to at night after the sky's haze had cleared.

The shoveling was almost finished, the rope and pipe sawed off, and I jabbed the thin green spikes of the wreath into the sand and kneeled, slipped one of the blue earrings into my uncle's grave, buried it in the shallow layer.

I looked at my father gazing across the mining field into the last inch of the sun.

"Amen."

"Amen," the miners echoed.

"No men for it," my father said, and I picked up the other shovel to help him.

CHAPTER 28

Thirty-five Miles from Birmingham, February 2044

"Whoops. Damn it, I've got to leave your foot alone.
Let's try. No, I'm sorry. I didn't mean—" and in the dream
Father was laughing. But which dream? The ones that returned again and again—which dream? As I rubbed my
eyes awake, the music continued.

> *I think of you every morning*
> *Dream of you every night*
> *Darling, I'm never lonely*
> *Whenever you are in sight*

The house smelled of south Dothan—Bahia grass and
dry wood. The house Father and I had lived in years ago.
Bahia my father had told me about, that I smelled often in
Jennifer's hair, a sweetness carrying through the air on long,

hot days. The house in Dothan had been built for a farmer, and the smell of grass had grained deep into the wood. But we were near Birmingham now and *Love Connection* had just finished. Jennifer and I had been fighting.

"It's step one, a wide move to the refrigerator—step two—and here!" Jennifer laughed from the kitchen.

"I know this stuff, I just can't get my feet to work right." The other voice was raspy, weak—my father.

"I've got patience, Chris." She shuffled something across the counter. "I usually do this by myself while you and Mat work. But I'm not quite used to this house yet."

"My wife loved to dance," he explained.

"I know. Mat's told me. He has a picture of her."

"I never gave that to him," my father said, "I'm afraid I loved her too much to share," his voice withdrawn, but Jennifer's voice stayed upbeat.

"Remember the wedding when you and I danced?"

"Yes. We didn't fall into a single mining shaft." He chuckled, still so frail, like the radio reception when the sun was too strong and stations as far away as Kentucky came in small, static pieces.

She confided, "That's the last time I danced with anyone."

"Okay, okay," my father cleared his throat, "I think I can still do this."

I cracked the bedroom door, an algebra problem going through my head. It was due Monday—but that was years ago, some Monday when I was younger, when my father danced in the kitchen, and I woke enough to watch him and he never caught me, never knew.

> *I love you and you alone were meant for me*
> *Please give your loving heart to me*
> *And say we'll never part*

Under the kitchen lights, their hands clasped together, wrapped around each other's back— From the microwave, stepping to the refrigerator, oven—

I love you for sentimental reasons
I hope you do believe me

"You do know it!" Jennifer smiled. Faster, faster the footwork working, her dress wrapped in flowers, the dress, its fabric bunched up between his fingers—rich red carnations outlined in dark purple, green leaves falling between the pleats and the square low neck where I could see her skin rise, her heart, her lungs breathing strong. And my father, he looked young again, new again, each step fluid and steady.

I've given you my heart

"Now lead me," she said, spinning under his arm, making a bridge with her hand.

Father's toes turned out, crossing to the table. His small, fat fingers jerked a little with each turn, the clay minerals catching the light. Sparkles, shimmers flaking down the beautiful white wedding dress. His black tuxedo flat, strong—

But it wasn't a wedding dress or a flower dress. She was in the long white shirt, what she put on when she left me in the room, when we talked about babies, what she wanted that I didn't.

Two aluminum pots crashed from the oven top. Jennifer simply kicked them under the table, spun under the bridge as Father pulled his hand away.

"Sorry," he said. "I'm knocking things over. I'm ancient. My hands don't—"

"You're beautiful," Jennifer stopped him. His pajamas were sweaty where her hand had held his back. She undid a knot, a clasp under her thick hair. Then she put a ring on a silver chain and placed it around his neck. "For you, Chris."

He held the silver ring, turning it in the light. "Take care of Mathew."

"Of course I will. But Chris, tell me, why won't you let us take care of you?"

His face sunk into loose skin, heavy clay. "I can't tell you really. I've given—" But my father stopped.

He flicked the silver ring with his finger, let it curl up on the necklace and twist down—back and forth, alchemy in the light.

> *I love you and you alone were meant for me*
> *Please give your loving heart to me*

The box closed in.

CHAPTER 29

Letters, 2041

> CODE RED today. Ozone index reading at 230, accompanied by 40-mile-per-hour winds. Due to the severity of the ozone, do not go outside until further notice. Take precautions. Stay indoors. Ozone accompanied by high winds and blowing sand.
>
> —*WDMZ 1610 AM, 1:05 p.m.*

Chicago, hog butcher of the world—that had been its nickname forever. Like New York was the Big Apple, Chicago was the hog butcher, yet the Big Apple seemed more inviting, a place you could bite into, hold on to, and the taste would always be good. Ever since my uncle had called my father a graceful pig, I never wanted to move to Chicago, near that butcher. Even when I thought maybe, maybe I would go to the Saved World, Chicago didn't appeal to me. But Mrs. Philips had moved to Chicago, gone to live with her sister who lived close to the lake. It's where Jennifer wanted to go, always wanted to, in this massive *city* and not the blue-skied places of the Saved World, the fields I had dreamed of and my father had wanted me to find there.

Jennifer's mother sent letters at least once a month, and at times in bunches, especially near Jennifer's birthday

in April. Mrs. Philips needed her daughter, and it was difficult for Jennifer to think of anything else until the letters
dried up.

At the bottom of the stationery, Mrs. Philips attached a
flicker-photograph. By placing the photograph in a window for the sun to catch or near a lamp, it would start into
motion like a miniature movie, lasting for ten seconds or
longer, depending on the light's strength and how well the
photo responded. Ray had brought out postcards that
worked the same way. On one card, the sun climbed and
set over New York, a whole day of buildings pointing to the
sky, the lights in the squared windows flashing on, off, and
on again compressed into seconds. He also had a postcard
of Fred Astaire and Ginger Rogers, the two spinning down
a staircase. He said anything could be put on a flicker-
photograph. His favorite was of a man playing the piano.
Like Astaire and Rogers, the piano photo was in black and
white, but you never saw the man's face, just his dark
hands going up and down on the keys, hands slipping out
of cuffs and a pale suit. *Performer, 1933* is all it said. Ray
had no idea who it was, and since the flicker-postcards
were silent, we didn't know what music he played—jazz or
blues—Ray just liked the movement of the hands.

Mrs. Philips' letters sometimes came with paper-clipped
money against the flicker-photographs. She had panned
across every room in her apartment until that space, doorways and corners above doorways, had become more familiar than the homes Jen and I constantly moved in and
out of. She made it so that we could walk in anytime and it
would be as if we had lived there always. And Pearl, the big
tabby cat named after the river in Mississippi that had
dried up and forced the family to come to Alabama, where
Terry died, always Pearl jumping from some bureau or
desk, falling like a full vase; Mrs. Philips' sister, Bobbie,
waving quickly before heading out the door; Mrs. Philips'

legs in the Chicago River, in Lake Michigan. But occasionally the camera angled up until you saw the sky, a sudsy gray in the pale weather, but sometimes the sun was out and splotches of blue shimmered in the light. And photographs of people on sidewalks, the camera mostly focused on legs, that motion of people marching to work, and around one another and some in step, but not quite dancing, and then the other pictures of the sky, and Jennifer's mother's legs like two thin paddles kicking and kicking—*The water is good here,* the letters claimed.

Jennifer always left the most recent letter on the kitchen table, out of the envelope, with the folds opened into a triangle. She did this so I would look, and I did, then placed the folds back together carefully, a placard for her to scoop up as if I hadn't touched anything at all.

Eventually, she sealed them in boxes—the sturdiest boxes, with Jennifer's handwriting on the outside—*From Mom,* each one said—*Perishable,* written underneath—and they smelled of Jennifer's hands and perfume and cat hair and tape and strangely like smoke, and she placed them on the top shelves in closets as far away from the dusty floors as possible.

Her mother began with a date handwritten in small, spare lines—the writing was stingy, just as I remembered Mrs. Philips and the quiet distance she kept, but not the words, which always started, *My Dearest Jen.*

And some words would be marked through, sometimes whole paragraphs cut out, the money gone, the photos missing—whatever Birmingham decided to keep.

My dearest Jen,

I have missed you. I thought of you today like every day—don't doubt that. Do you think you'll come up soon? Let me know. With your birthday almost here, I

decided to bake a cake. Now, don't worry, I'm not going
to try and send it. The desert would melt it into a big
gooey mess.

But I always think of you and cakes ever since you
turned three, when I made that Italian Cream for your
birthday, my grandmother's recipe, which I will gladly
send, if you want—let me know. I spent hours on that
cake, hours. I went out to the store again and again because I forgot one ingredient, then another—you know
how I'm scattered, especially on the holidays. But I finished the cake and set three big candles in the center.
And you looked at it like you didn't know what to do. So
Everett, who I wish could have known you, could have
lived and known his daughter now, so Everett and I sang
and helped you blow out the candles— Well, we blew
out the candles. You watched the smoke as it drifted:
that was amazing to me, how you traced that movement.
Then you reached out to grab it and I pushed your hands
back and removed the candles and hid them and pointed
to the white icing. I said, "Cake?" and you looked at us
one more time, then opened your mouth and dove in—
the hours of making, the recipe, the frosting I had
swirled just so. I gasped and Everett laughed and then I
laughed, but not you. You kept eating and eating with
the icing all over your face. I cleaned it off, but you didn't
want to be clean and jerked your head and cried until I
was done. I know I've told this story many times. But I
made you a cake today, just like that one, while Bobbie

was at work. I wanted to send it to you, but I can't.
Besides, I couldn't get out—————————————————

—————————————————————————————————

—————————————————————————————————

—————————————————————————————————

————————————————————————

The rest of her letter was marked through except for the ending, which said *Love* and *Happy Birthday* and showed the flicker-photograph of the cake lit with candles. I kept trying to count them, but couldn't, though it had to be twenty-seven, and I watched the speckled flames flicker and flicker for ten seconds and glare into the camera lens, the smoke stream up and disappear, and then Mrs. Philips reached over and blew the candles out. She clapped as if someone other than Pearl were there, and as she stepped away to leave the cake in the middle of the table alone, the photo stopped.

We had moved to Whately near the Claiborne Lock and Dam in southern Alabama, and Bossey said we might be here the rest of the month if the flooding up north continued. The river kept swelling, the water coming down and down. As I drove to work that night, I slipped over to the bank and cut the engine. All that water rushed faster than I could breathe and hold in or catch up to. Even if I got out and ran alongside the bank and chased the water, I'd never catch up to it. I knew where that water ended, somewhere before the Gulf Coast. But maybe this water emptied into Mobile Bay; maybe it traveled that far. My breathing slowed, and I headed to the dig where the equipment drowned out the last draws of the current.

When I returned from work, Jennifer was sitting in the

kitchen. Usually, she had books open, studying for her business degree, or had the television on, voices humming with the refrigerator. But this time, there was nothing, not even breakfast, and she took my hand, led me to the bedroom, and made me sit on the edge of the bed.

"Happy birthday," I said, but she said nothing.

She had taken the letters from the closet and lined them up along the tri-folds so the photographs were on the outside of the triangles, setting the pictures on a long coffee table that had come with the house and along the wooden floor and onto the top of her dresser, so that they formed a crescent around the base of the bed. Some of the photographs I recognized, all of them frozen, waiting. Then Jennifer took the shade off the lamp, and from one corner she slowly moved across, setting the pictures to start, each going through its ten-second motion like a burst of firecrackers, so many photographs coming to life, seeming to walk toward one another, backing away, a montage of her mother and Chicago, with its sky moving just enough to be real, white and cold, a cold fog rising from people's faces, the scarves pressed below the eyes, and street signs for State and East Chestnut, Grand, Adams—buildings, just the smudgy outline of their corners, and windows too dark to see into, and waists half-covered in coats, pants, and skirts, and black shoes marching, but where? Where were they going? All in motion, and not one hog butcher among them.

Jennifer placed the lamp in the center and most of the pictures started up again. The pictures she had set in the corners, too remote for the light to touch, remained still, unable to draw enough light to begin the replay, and she sat on the bed next to me with her hands in her lap. And she would not speak and she would not cry.

"Jennifer—" She put her hand over my mouth and kept me from holding her.

"Just look," she said. "Look."

Her mother's legs kicked in and out of the lake, and the white apartment walls panned from a mirror to a painting of flowers, to a vase of carnations, and Pearl jumped from the bureau, and outside the people marched through Chicago, so many people, their motion draining the stillness out of me, this other world, the total silence of it.

CHAPTER 30

Millers Ferry, June 2044

Two feet deeper, but the memories will not vanish. And I'm almost to the clusters; I can feel them grind on the bottom of my boots. Mud is trying to build on my eyes. I turn the nozzle to a trickle, catch my breath, and my light flashes across a large piece of mica, enough to blind me. My father's ghost appears.

"This," his voice reverberates as he leans down and picks up a handful of sand, grassless, "this was black." He nods, certain, pours the grit and sparkles over my palms, opening, light slicing, hurting. I shield my face; sand falls to the ground.

"Your grandfather planted fields. There wasn't any worthless digging, this nothing work, no tunnels in the ground, digging for China. Wayne and I helped him, then played, row after row—we had corn, long rows of corn. Long stalks for running through." He clasps his hands over my sleeve, rubs the dirt into my skin. "There was lots of rain, June droughts, but not a desert," he assures me, "and not just irrigation lines to fit. But plows, pickers, cultivators. You drilled the seeds, spent days unraveling barbed wire, nailing posts, planting. It was the best work for hands." He takes my fingers gingerly and they turn in rhythm, fingers on a piano.

"Come on," he says, the sun slipping under his elbow, and I'm blinded even more.

When I open my eyes, I'm no longer in the shaft, but at the top, with the sun smaller than a half-moon on the horizon, sinking fast—but wait, it's the moon, pale and rising, giving enough light for me to find the earth, my crimson flag 19, the pulley, my father next to me, a dry field in front. The other mining shafts are gone, the stadium lights, Bossey's trailer. It's just my father and me alone in the desert.

His hair is washed, stripped to its white and gray, wrinkles fraying with mica, lulls of wind, his face still red as it was the evening he died, and when he swallows I can taste the clay full in my throat.

"Where are we going?" I ask as we walk into the dry field.

He says nothing, and suddenly, we're transported into a yard with two trees burned, the limbs switching between sky and earth, trying to choose which way to point, which way to divine where spring begins. My waders crease up tiny clay rills that drip on the steps of the elaborate wooden wraparound. My father unlocks the door.

I smell basil, onions, and red peppers cut into slivers, grease fried into the air.

The plates are set, the green dinnerware, the pattern from my parents' wedding, and my father and I sit down.

"Do you want some more squash?" my uncle calls from the kitchen. "Turnips? How about some butter?" Uncle

Wayne brings in a plate of biscuits, tosses one to me. I catch it and he laughs, "Good hands. Good hands, nephew. You've got a future playing football, maybe even basketball. What do you think, Chris?" His eyes light up blue like Father's. But his face is paler, thinner, especially his chin, like a sandbar extending out in a river.

"Don't feed him too much. He'll expect me to do the same next week," Father says, and winks at his brother.

"The boy needs to be fed. Develop some muscle so he can grow big like you and me."

I wipe the clay from my hands with paper towels. I tear a chunk of the biscuit with my nozzle.

"Don't bring that in here. I told you to leave it outside the house." Father grips his fork and knife straight toward the ceiling, grips them strong.

I let the tube drop, look behind me, and watch it snake out the open door, all the way across the dark yard into the eye of the moon. If I follow it back, I wonder, will I be sane again, will I recognize where I am?

Then I become conscious of my hat, its coal dents and metal scratches, as Uncle Wayne reappears with two glasses of tea and slices of lemon. Both Uncle Wayne and Father give me strange looks as I turn the light off, remove the hat.

"Thank you," Father exhales, causing his chest to sink to his stomach.

Uncle Wayne walks around the table, grabs my hat from the floor. "Don't listen to that old man. I wear mine all the time at supper."

He puts the helmet on quick and flicks the beam straight at my father.

"Stop it, Wayne," my father says, and I feel the tension in him building inside me.

Uncle Wayne simply sits down and digs into the serving bowl of okra, face-first. He lifts his head, laughing, buttered okra falling down his chin, a piece rolling from the metal visor. His eyes sparkle; the light flickers on and off—there must be a short in the switch—and I jerk back.

Somehow the hose isn't on the floor. The hose is in my hand, the nozzle switched on.

"Don't do that." Father stands up. His chair legs make a scudding noise as Uncle Wayne looks helplessly at food rushing across the tablecloth—biscuits, green beans, ham—in a stream of water.

"I bring you over here and you act this way?" my father says. He stares me down, and a clay wall, not wooden boards, a clay wall rises up, encircles me, seals me from the dining room, from the house, the moon. The door slams. I swallow the chunk of biscuit I have chewed off; it tastes like chalk and soft metal; the clay wall is dripping.

I am in the mining shaft again, have managed to return. The plate of food, my uncle, the house—all have vanished except for my father's eyes. They are set in the tunnel wall.

"You're just a ghost," I say, his eyes staring at me hard, burning inside the mud, turning it red and black, black into red, his body taking shape.

Am I going crazy? Am I crazy?

And if you want to leave, Bossey had said, and stepped out of the way.

The dizziness in my head opens just enough that I stop shaking.

I turn the nozzle full, put my hand forth, and scrub my father's body from the walls until he fades into streams of water.

CHAPTER 31

The Vote List, 2026

My dearest Jen,

*   I thought of you today, we had—————————*
————which reminded me of the dust, those thick black
storms with the sun making everything red, and at night,
just more and more black, but the—————————
————————————————————

—————————. Oh, they're trying to do something
about it, but when the wind picks up and blows————
————————————————————
————————————————————

*——feel that loneliness like when you strike a match,
as if someone has struck a match deep within, but not
someone in the distance or even a close friend, it is
yourself, your hand striking until you start to burn.*

*When the wind came on, those horrible storms, you
used to get in bed with me and Everett. You did the
same with me and Terry. The storms, that thick dust,
gave you headaches, and I tried to give you medicine,
but it never helped. Only when the storms left. And I
hope————————————————————*
————have————————————————
————————————————————————
*————————————————Mathew is holding
you. I hope your headaches are gone. Still I don't know
why it made me feel so lonely.————just makes me
do that.*

Affectionately,
Mom

Several weeks after Uncle Wayne's death, the Carter
Bros. Fair pulled into a nearby town. The fairs traveled
throughout the Southeastern Desert, stopping for five or
six days before moving on. It was the one time that you saw
workers from the other mining camps.

On Saturday, my father's day off, he woke up from his
chair-sleep and took me. We hadn't talked much since
Uncle Wayne's funeral, and the loud, weird noises,
mechanical music, and flashing and reeling lights of the
small fair helped maintain our determined quiet. It was as

if my father and I had signed a pact: he wouldn't punish me for going through his boxes, especially his pine box, ripping a picture in half, taking my mother's earrings, and I wouldn't confront him about the visas, about my mother. I blamed my father, fairly or unfairly, for Uncle Wayne's death. If my father had only taken all of us out of the desert, had used the visas a year ago, a month ago, then Uncle Wayne would be on a farm again like he wanted. His death sat over us, sealing our pact.

At the Carter Bros. gate you didn't have to pay to get in. Instead, you had to sign your name on what was really a census, but was known as the Vote List.

"The Vote List," my father muttered over and over under his breath with such animosity that I couldn't relax until we had gotten safely inside.

"No one votes here," he claimed, and he was right. After the land was marshaled, we had been appointed a handful of representatives.

"Georgia, Mississippi, and Alabama still have half a state left to govern," my father pointed out. "But Florida," he shook his head, "they have nothing." The entire state had dried up into limestone sinkholes and sand and was vacant except for the coastal miners living there from Orlando across to Tampa and north.

The Carter Bros. Fair was actually sponsored by our appointed representatives. A tall poster always stood at the gate with their paper fingers pointing at the booth where the government official held a notebook, alphabetically listing all the names of the people who lived in the surrounding camps. The poster had a cartoon blurb that said, "In order to get representation, you need to sign up!"

"They just want to know how many of us are left breathing," my father quipped. "When no one's left, they won't even send the circus around."

To ensure that many of us would be left breathing, my

father had invented a scam. Every few years he walked up and notified the government official on duty that he needed to add a new name to the list. Always it was a newborn son. And the official would ask to look at the baby and my father would say, the boy's not here, he's with his mother. Then he would lean in close and reveal to the official, with all sincerity and urgency, "My son's illegitimate. His mother's not even on the vote list. I just want to make sure the boy's represented."

Usually the bureaucrat nodded over my father's plight, whatever bureaucrat it was, and sympathetically let him add the name.

"The boy ought to be represented," the government official allowed, giving me a long pitying look, and I had to bite my tongue. My father demanded the truth from everybody, not just me — "I am the way, the truth, and the light," he said often while sleeping, and I was certain he wasn't talking about God. But if I said something, which I wanted to, my father wouldn't let me go to the fair. The lights and music cranked and churned and shouted — between the mix of words, music, and the sugar smell of hot oil frying chicken and flour, I could almost hear my name, could hear the fair calling, too strong to resist.

One time, after we had slipped inside the gates, I carefully questioned my father, "Why did you do that?"

"Your brother, you mean?"

"That's a lie," I admonished.

My father's face turned somber, the clay in his cheeks taking on a burnt glow. "The government's a bigger liar than I could ever dream of becoming."

"Sorry," I said quickly, withdrawing my accusation. I had done it now. My father would turn us around and force me home.

But instead he placed his hand on the back of my neck. "I'm just sorry they're not real." Then my father reached up, brushed my cowlicks over to one side like he did after cutting my hair with the measuring bowl. "For you. I think you could use some brothers."

"And sisters," I added. "I'd like to have some sisters."

He nodded. "Okay." Later, it occurred to me that my father had never wanted daughters because of Mamma. "So much power in the naming of things," he always said, and he didn't need another reminder, something else in this world to remind him of his loss.

Each summer when we flipped to *Harrison* on the list, typed in black ink was my father's name and mine, and my five younger brothers—Virgil, Jeff, Mike, Joe, and Nicholas—and, as promised, one sister, Jessica—all sturdy names, but children I never had the chance to play with. My father signed for himself and for them (it was legal to sign for your children), and I signed for myself.

"You got that many kids?" a supervisor asked once. He was tall, his head swinging forward and back like a hammer, watching my father sign. My father always drew out the letters of each word as deliberate as he could do it, middle names included. "Why don't they come to the fair?"

"They don't like it," my father said, "except for him," and he jabbed me a little, turned to me. "Why are you the only one who likes it?" he asked.

I'd been trying to think of what to say to the supervisor, how to prove my family did exist, then *he* sprang that question.

"I don't know why I like it," I said, and stepped back.

"Don't know?" My father raised his voice and pulled me toward him. "Don't know?" He glanced over at the official. "I take you to the fair on my night off and you don't know why you want to be here? If you want to leave, just tell me. I can take you home. You ready?"

"No," I said.

"What about your brothers?" The supervisor cut in.

"They all get sick," I said, "on the rides."

"All of them?" The supervisor grabbed up the list and checked the names. Some of the long papers fell out onto the counter.

"Except for Virgil. He was thrown out last year for putting a smoke bomb on the Scrambler," which some kid had actually done.

The supervisor went over the names again. "You ever do anything like that?"

"No." I tried to inch away from my father. "I haven't done anything wrong."

"He's the best one of the group," my father said. "Don't worry, I'll keep an eye on my boy." He nodded and the official slowly nodded. Then the official waved for us to go but looked at me like I'd better be careful, like he was watching.

As soon as we got through the gate, my father said, "The government's not getting rid of us so easy," and he squeezed my shoulder and smiled. "Thanks."

I can't believe you did that, I wanted to say, but couldn't after he said thanks.

"Yes, sir," I told him, and he walked off to get tickets. I wandered from one corner of the fair to the next, trying to calm down, trying to find its boundaries, making sure I didn't touch or mess with any of the rides—I was being watched. And yet I felt like I could do it—burn something, put something awful in the metal gears, tear something up. A belt might work, or shoelaces. I had coins in my pocket to lay out on a track. And I wanted to, but how to get away with it? I walked to every ride and circled, scheming until my father caught up with me.

"What're you doing?" he asked. "The night's half over." He raised his fist, the tickets sticking halfway out. There was no way we could use all of them.

My father stared at me, kept doing it. Then he sighed

and his shoulders fell. "Stop dreaming. Come on." And he started toward the Midway.

I looked down and kicked my ankle with the side of my other foot. "Stupid," I said, but not loud enough for my father to hear. "You're being stupid," and kicked harder. "Wasting time for what?" I promised myself never to do that again.

There was also a place for Uncle Wayne on the list. "You bet I'll add names," he said to my father and winked at me, though he seldom went to the fair with us. "Women like the rides," he noted and took dates from Lula D's. "Besides, it's good for you and Chris to go together. Don't worry, I'll give you lots of cousins. You'll see." And he did.

But we couldn't vote, no matter how many Harrisons the two of them registered. So what was my father's point?

On this night, however, he signed only his name and put the pen down.

"Father," I said, "what about Virgil and Jeff?"

"They're not here anymore, you know that," and he walked off, leaving me with the government official.

I shifted toward him and started to call for him to wait, but the supervisor cleared his throat in an effort to move me along—the line was jammed and crooked all the way to the makeshift parking lot where an old Kmart had been—so I took the pen and scribbled my name.

I lay the pen on the counter, and turned to where my father had vanished, his short back slipping and turning. He had on a solid green button-down that hung loose off his shoulders, cut just above his knees—hunter green, he called it. Whenever we went to the fair, he always loaned me one of his shirts with red stripes. The red stripes reminded me of his hair slicked back with water—my father never used any oil, there was so much clay he couldn't get out. At home he would comb it, but later he would run his fingers through, making furrows, stripes of white and silver, depending on how much mica he had mined that evening. Sometimes when the wind hit his shirt, it would blow clear off his back, and his hair would pick up sparks of dust, creating an illusion that he was moving through ripples of water.

As I stood there, a gust came up strong and I felt my father's shirt blow against my arm. I snatched up the pen and scribbled in my sister, Jessica, and all of my brothers, including Nicholas, who was only one and a half.

Underneath was a space for Uncle Wayne. I tapped the pen, wondering what the government would do. Would my smiling representatives send me to hell for this?

The supervisor cleared his throat a second time and brushed at his thick mustache. "Are you done, boy?"

I looked down and quickly signed for Uncle Wayne, for the names he had added.

"They're just sick," I said.

The government official nodded, his head bobbing like a watch ticking, and I heard him mumble, "Okay, okay," in the same level beat, even if his mouth was shut. He fumbled with his mustache, pulling his thick head to one side like taffy, and the next customer stepped up and took my place.

I caught up with my father buying tickets, and I grabbed the belt loop of his jeans. "I signed them all," I told him proudly, thinking he would be happy. We were partners now, just like when we tricked the supervisor years before. But he said nothing, and I didn't mention Uncle Wayne. I kept my finger in his loop, kept a good hold.

All night he took me from games and pavilions to rides. My father liked the ducks. He liked throwing nickels at milk jars. He liked the exhibit of the Pig-Man: "A half-man, half-pig eating machine," the barker advertised. The Pig-Man ate cream pies and chocolate pies all night, covering his face like mud. But I wasn't impressed. Bossey was twice the size of the Pig-Man and could outeat him—with better manners, I was certain. I did feel a little sorry for the Pig-Man, however, and the Snake-Lady with a python heavy on her neck—neither looked at the audience for long. They carried a vacant expression as if they were bored with us and had lost the desire to be noticed. Quietly, they became dead trees, or a picture, or a TV show, something flat and lifeless, full of color, but vacant.

My father liked to play the milk jugs and watch the Pig-Man but didn't like the rides, except for the carousel.

"They make me dizzy," he claimed.

So I gave my tickets to the man at the bumper cars, the teapots, the spider, and the spinning strawberries, and strapped myself in, waiting for the man to pull back the long switch and start the machine rumbling. From inside each capsule, I saw the lights of the Ferris wheel, taller than anything, a circle like a can lid grinding round and round that the other kids in school rode, that the miners took their wives and dates on. Then my ride would spin away and face me to my father for a second, his eyes fluttering to the lights, the haphazard strands of people walking. My father never glanced up to see if I could see him, and after all the twirling rides of sitting alone, I pulled out the half photo of Mamma and watched her, watched my father until they faded together. Then I shut my eyes and placed my parents on the Ferris wheel, fingers interlaced, moving closer and closer together for a reunion kiss, the photo I had torn magically resewn.

Afterward, my father played one last game of shooting ducks, something he enjoyed most, and we walked to the carousel with the last of our tickets.

I had decided that as soon as we mounted the plastic horses, buckled ourselves in side by side, that's when I would confront him, would say something about the picture and the earring in my pocket, about the visas. I was still mad, even if I regretted ripping the picture, wishing now I could truly have the photo complete again. As soon as we settled in on the horses, I would say something, and he couldn't get away. He couldn't just walk off.

The man took my tickets, and I waited, but my father stepped aside.

I stopped.

"Aren't you coming?"

"Not tonight. I don't want to." My father had looked unhappy the entire evening, except for when shooting down the ducks.

"But I want you to," I said.

"Not tonight," he told me firmly.

He was in a pig mood and wouldn't budge, so reluctantly I nodded and trekked to the horses. There was a blue one with a long red plume shooting straight up, its neck, eyes, and legs already in stride. As I climbed onto the plastic saddle, I felt as if I were already in the middle of a real gallop.

I fastened myself in and looked at my father. I would have to tell him now. But he wasn't looking at me. He was watching the people around him, his hands set firm on the railing, gripping it strong and letting go. His knuckles turned white, then flesh, back to white, then flesh again. It looked painful, I thought, my father hunched over, staring down, his red face bruised by the dark. But I would have to tell him now, before the carousel began spinning.

"I opened your pine box," I yelled, and he glanced up. "I know what's in your pine box," I said.

He said nothing, but I knew that he had heard me.

My father glanced at his hands, the splotches and mica in them. Then he looked back up as if he had been trapped forever at the railing and still couldn't break free. "I should've taken your uncle out of that hole," he said. "I should've told you about the picture of your mother—"

"Why didn't you?"

"I should've done it."

"But you didn't. Why?" I twisted the reins, the blood in my fingers turning purple.

The operator pulled on the switch. The horse began to rise.

"Their lives ended with me," my father said. "I couldn't save them." And suddenly the carousel took off spinning round and round.

The blue horse galloped, and together we eclipsed the Ferris wheel wheeling to the sky. A few seconds later, we came back to my father, growing more and more tired at the railing. His whole body had sunk in around his shoulders. He wouldn't look at me now, was avoiding me. By the end, the instruments inside the machine had trickled to a murmur and my horse was out of breath. By the end, my father looked completely lost, and I decided to say nothing else, nothing about the visas, about my mother, about how much I missed Uncle Wayne. It would do no good. I handed the man the unused tickets, went around one more time, spinning and spinning, such happy music I wished I could give to my father.

CHAPTER 32

Selma, March 2044

Jennifer would not let go of me. The ground lights rolled back and forth, the wind strong. Like my uncle's funeral, my father's funeral was held at night. But my father hadn't died in a mining hole. He died in a house just north of Selma, on our retreat from Birmingham to Mobile. Every day there was mud and rain, flash floods in the desert. Our retreat had stalled out. Tonight, however, was okay, cold but okay to travel, the uncertain weather resting up to catch us later once our convoy was snaking to Mobile to begin again.

The ground lights rolled back and forth and Ray brought my father out in a silver casket to a flat stretch in the desert, a place between Highways 22 and 37, our caravan of trucks and equipment huddled around like prairie wagons circling. After Bossey's prayer, the workers placed small bags of clay rocks next to my father's arms and hands to keep his spirit from floating away too soon. My father was dressed in his tux, hair slicked silver into shadows, the scars on his throat like long worms, a reflection of the raspy scars inside. "Amen," we all said, and the workers went to their trucks for one last swallow of beer, a taste of food before the caravan restarted its journey south.

"Are you going to be all right?" Bossey came up and asked, his eyes focusing hard, expecting an answer.

Jennifer wouldn't let go of me. She nodded. "I'll be with him, Bossey. Don't worry," and I wanted to ease my muscles, my shoulders, wanted to give in to her holding.

"If you need the week off, take it. Or two weeks. We'll get to Mobile by morning unless a storm comes on, and you know the routine from there—a couple of days just to set up camp, check out the houses. With the weather changing like it is, we can't work anyway."

I said nothing, could only hear my father's voice: *Just take the week off*, his voice thirsty and rough, needing to relax, a wet rag across his face, nothing to do for him now.

Bossey reached over and hugged me like he always hugged me, choking and strong. "I told Mr. Chris I would look after you, Mat. It was my promise, and I intend to keep it."

Promise, my father said. And if I answered, I would become as thin as his voice, sparkles in the dust, the wind shambling and fading.

"Are you sure you're all right?" he asked.

Jennifer nodded and Bossey walked to the casket, shuffling back and forth on his walrus legs to where a small group of miners lingered.

Ray sat on the hood of his Suburban, watching the sky rise, then shift with stars; it was clear, an actual cool breeze blowing from the west.

"Amazing," he said, and scribbled on an old map, taking a swallow of scotch Bossey had left behind. "Amazing."

"Come on, Ray," Bossey called for him. "We've got to get moving."

"Just a second," he said, and hopped down to stretch his wiry frame.

He walked the same path Bossey had swept open with his boots, walked it until he reached Jennifer and me. "So when do you want to take him home? New Brockton, right? Are we going now?" Ray glanced at the coffin and back.

"I need some time," I said. "I need to drive a little bit."

"Sure." Ray took his fertilizer cap off, fitted it snugly on his bald head again. He did this two more times, struggling to slow himself, struggling to be respectful. His body was all jittery. "I'll stay here as long as the sky doesn't wash me out." He grinned. "Can you find your way back?"

"I'm just taking one of the highways here," I explained.

"Where to?"

"Just to drive, but I'll be in by morning. You can wait?"

"Yeah, I can wait. Bossey's hitching my trailer onto his, so my things will get to Mobile just fine. Besides, you're not traveling too far with your truck loaded down."

Jennifer and I had packed all of our boxes, the ACs, and the generator into the truck bed and tied a green canvas on top.

"It's not a problem," Jennifer said, wrapping her arms tighter around me, her black hair draping over my shoulder like a shawl. "If you want to drive, let's go. But if you need to do this by yourself—"

I shook my head.

"Good. I want to be with you. And I can take the truck, catch up with the others when we get to Selma. You can travel on with Ray."

"It's a deal, then." Ray nodded. "See you in a little while," and he walked to the casket, shut the lid over my father's face, the scars on his neck like worms shut into the dark.

"On three," Ray said, tilting the scotch, and the group of miners wheeled the casket to the Suburban, slipped my father's body in. "I've got a long night coming."

As the sun scaled higher, we drifted past Columbus, Georgia, a good number of the buildings crumbled down, except for a few that stood like monuments, their windows hollowed out for the wind to whistle through, for the sand to wear down in waves and gashes. Wires dragged from limbless poles, and much of the streets and houses stood covered, covered halfway under the intense desert, an archeological site in reverse, not in the process of discovery but concealment.

A sign said 220 miles to Savannah Beach. Jennifer and I hadn't been to the beach since our wedding and I sped up, wishing I had Ray's energy, reaching for the Atlantic Ocean I had never seen. Later, Ray revealed that the Atlantic had invaded coastal and central Georgia, washing to the old Interstate 75; 220 miles, the sign promised, but Savannah was under water, a submerged city.

"We don't have enough fuel," Jennifer said as she took her eyelashes off in the mirror. She undid her bra, took it out from one of the sleeves of the dark dress.

"How much further are you planning on going anyway?"

When I didn't answer, she touched my neck, rubbed a ball of clay in her fingers. "I love you. I know you miss your father. I miss him, too." She lifted her hand to shield the sun. Then she turned up the radio, squishing the clay like chewing gum into the knob. A station out of Atlanta popped in and out, advertising chicken and cars, but no music.

"The sun's too strong," she sighed, and flipped the radio off, but I was surprised we could pick up anything from Atlanta. Then she inched next to me.

"Mathew," Jennifer whispered, and somewhere in the road, somewhere braced in the glass, my father's voice called my name, but not for help, not for a washcloth to peel away the skin, layer after layer of mud, and family caught between this world and the next stalled out—he called to bring me closer to him.

"Your eyes," and now it was Jennifer's voice, no longer my father's. "I know your eyes are brown, so this will probably sound silly, but they remind me of blue diamonds." It was the first time she had told me this. "The kind your uncle talked about, that you told me about, the earring that was your mother's. It's the same blue as yours. In the light, a certain way—specks of blue—cut into your irises like glass." She leaned up and kissed me, an imprint in the clay, wet and healing. "Your father had such blue eyes. He was beautiful." She touched my ears, rubbing strips of red clay loose.

"I have something for you." She snapped a new bracelet onto my wrist. It was turquoise and silver. "I picked this up for your father after I made him dance with me the other night. That night you and I argued over children, remember? I wanted him to give me lessons, and I had planned to give him this in return." She rubbed the clay back into my skin, jiggled my arm to see if the bracelet would sparkle.

"I woke up and saw you," I said, and felt like I was six, I was seven, my lungs constricting, and I wished that my shirt was buttoned all the way to keep the desert sand out. I never told my father I saw him dancing alone in the kitchen. Those evenings just before school, waiting for him to get ready for work, wanting to tell him, wanting him to show me the steps that he took and where they led.

I looked at the bracelet, the circled metal, silver and aqua intertwining.

"What did you think?"

"You were great. The two of you like Fred Astaire and Ginger Rogers." Uncle Wayne would agree. "I didn't want you to stop." I shifted in the seat, more comfortable under the steering wheel. I could move now, breathe like their steps in the kitchen that night, one, then two, the simple box until the corners vanished.

The sun reflected off the silver, cut into my eyes while she kissed my neck slowly, undid the buttons on my shirt, pressed her palm against my ribs.

"Pull off the road, Mathew," Jennifer whispered, and the sun continued to burn hot.

CHAPTER 33

Claiborne Lock and Dam, 2041

> This is a contaminated site.
> RESTRICTED.
> Do not swim in the river.
> Do not drink untreated water.
> Do not bathe in the river.
> Take precautions.
> CONTAMINATED SITE.
>
> —*Road sign posted on Highway 17, April 19, 2041*

We camped at places near the old lock-and-dam sys-tem because initially the dams worked—not to generate much electricity, but to keep enough of the river back to form lakes. We stayed at each lake until it drained low enough that we had to move on to the next—but each year, more and more of the dams broke apart during the February floods. Bossey said the river was becoming like its old self, like how it was before the electric companies and Corps of Engineers got involved. Above the abandoned state capital in Montgomery, you could raft on the Coosa, what was known as the Devil's Staircase. Rapids continued all the way to Rome, Georgia, but we weren't allowed to travel that far into the Newer South. And with the rivers also came history.

My father pointed to Selma's Edmund Pettus Bridge whenever we came through, broken and impassible. "Dr.

Martin Luther King led a freedom march across that bridge in 1965 to get African-Americans voting rights. They marched to Montgomery."

"What happened?" I asked him.

"He made Alabama change for a moment."

In the camps, everyone was blanketed in clay and marl and dust so thoroughly, red-brown was the most noticeable color on clothes and skin. Washing turned people pale or black and every hue in between, but only until they stepped outside into the hard weather.

"Did they tell you that in school?" he asked, and I shook my head. "They don't like to talk about that part of history. Sometimes people choose to have amnesia. To look at someone as if he or she is less than you, anyone—" My father stared at the Selma bridge, its frayed wires and pavement. "Don't ever do that."

"What about now?"

"Everyone's too busy trying to survive. We depend on each other. All those war books you love," my father said, "many of the battles in Alabama were over race, not Queen and Country." He hadn't forgotten that, would never forget that, and I pulled into my shirt.

"Don't bury yourself in your clothes," he said. "Don't be self-conscious." He pulled my sleeve up, one arm, then the other, both of us wrapped in dust and mud, but underneath I could see a difference. "When you go north, some people may call you river trash," he said. It was a name some of the government agents called us. "No matter what they say to you, even if they're hostile, don't hide yourself. Promise me."

"Yes, sir," I said, yet I wondered what I would do if I felt unsafe.

"And don't look at anyone, treat anyone like you're better, for any reason."

"Yes, sir."

My father nodded, satisfied. "Good," he said, and we drove on.

Bossey knew the history of the lock and dams, of steamboats like the *Orline St. John* that caught fire and sank, because his family many generations back had worked on steamboats as slaves and laborers and captains. He also knew about the battles on the Alabama and the Coosa. I tried to get close when Bossey talked about de Soto and later the Creek Wars and when General Wilson took Selma and Montgomery. My father wanted to listen to these stories, too, and when Bossey finished, my father added, "There's nothing of value to fight over now," and Bossey agreed. *And nothing exciting*, I thought, but never spoke up. And when I remembered the picture of my mother, I wondered what stories she might have told, what history, what dreams I would never uncover in what Bossey said and my uncle said, in stolen library books, that even if my father knew, he would never tell me. I wondered.

The Alabama River in the south was sluggish, the only excitement coming at the dams, the sound of rushing water dropping over concrete. The government cautioned us that all the sewage dumped from Birmingham was dangerous for swimming, but no one seemed to get sick. At least not right away. A few kids dived off the highest points and were killed because of rocks or shallow water. We placed stones on top of one another underneath the bluffs as memorials to them, but by the following year, the memorials had been carried downriver or buried.

The ones who made it had an invincibility to them that we envied. The rest of us took ropes tied to dead trees or steel rods shooting up from the broken concrete and swung down into the water and shouted the government warnings into the night air. "*Do Not! Do Not!*" we said, and splashed each other without dying.

We followed the rivers, our life consumed in their

fluctuations as much as the desert consumed us, and sometimes Jennifer and I sat on the dams or the banks or the
broken inlets to the rusted paper mills. Jennifer always
dipped her feet in, let the current eddy around her legs,
and we watched the water curl and drift and skate as if it
would never stop, just as we had done at Mexico Beach for
our honeymoon. I always thought of blood, its movement,
how the river was like that, especially when the waters were
high, how the fast current seemed like it would never end,
and yet it would, it could happen.

"Do you think the river goes all the way to Chicago?"
Jennifer asked. It was her birthday. She had set up her
mother's flicker-photographs and sent them into motion,
and afterward we drove to the Claiborne Dam because she
wanted to and waded out to a sandbank.

"Just the Appalachian. Up north to Georgia."

"Yeah, but the water from Chicago has to get down
here eventually. Maybe underground."

"I don't think so," I said. "Hog butcher."

"What?"

"Chicago is the hog butcher of the world."

"That's not how my mom talks about it." Jennifer
shrugged, and more of her black hair fell across her shoulders. She had on a T-shirt and jeans, the cuffs rolled up but
still getting wet. "All those passages marked out in her letters, I wonder what she's telling me. What do you think?"
and she stared until she had my full attention because we
had never talked about the letters. She left them out on the
table, and I had read them and fixed them so careful and
all those times, I thought I had fixed them back perfectly
unmoved.

"Hog butcher," I said. "It's hog-butchering stuff. What
the government wants to keep from us. You know, a thun-
derstorm," I giggled, "or a power outage—God forbid if

the Saved World had a power outage—we shouldn't know about that. They treat us like children."

"Prisoners," she corrected.

I nodded. "I used to think it was all bad stuff, like my father told me. The pictures your mom sends—it doesn't look all bad. So maybe they're keeping away small things. I'm sure they've had disasters, but your mom keeps sending letters. She's still doing it. The Saved World hasn't killed her yet."

"Don't say that." Jennifer punched me in the shoulder. "I don't want anything to happen to my mom."

"Okay, okay, I won't jinx her."

"What are they keeping, Mathew? Sometimes I think the government just doesn't want us to know anything. But I need to know. I wish I could see her." Jennifer eased her elbows into the sand and mud. She wiggled her feet, and I pushed one foot down with my foot. "How about you? You said you think Chicago is harmless."

"I didn't say it was harmless," and I could feel the fight, that same fight pulling us like the water pulling. I tried to focus on the rush, the crashing it was making at the dam a little further away. The water edged to the top and slipped and slipped like it was spilling from a jar.

"It's better than here. All of Mom's letters say that."

"What if she's lying?"

"My mom isn't lying." She punched me in the shoulder again, and this punch left a sting.

"Watch out—" I started to tease, then Jennifer sat up, stiffened her back, and pulled her legs from the water. I dropped my raised hands; they felt suddenly numb. I didn't know what to do with them. "I don't know. All my life, I've never been able to figure out what that place is. Used to, I felt like I had to understand it, but now I just feel indifferent."

"Indifferent enough to leave?" she asked.

"I don't care about it—what's real in the Saved World? What's unreal? What's saved? If it's all a lie, I don't care."

"But I miss my mom. I want to talk to her about what she's written and what's been marked through that I can't read. I want to know all of it. Even if it *is* scary. Even if the worst has happened, is still happening."

"What would be the worst?"

"That the world is dying," Jennifer said, and looked at the dam, the black water spilling. "That your father is right."

"It is dying, just more slowly than he says." I watched her, hoping that the tension in her shoulders would relax, some place that I could touch and draw her in.

"You're just guessing," she said.

"I'm sorry. I'm not sure I've ever cared about the Saved World except that it's what my father wants. His wishes. And my uncle—I could have gone with my uncle, but when he died, what reason was left to go?"

"Me," she said, still watching the dam. "One day you'll have to make a decision, Mathew, for me."

CHAPTER 34

Indigo Creek, March 2044

February 8

Dear Jennifer,

    As I write these lines, I want you to know that I'm okay. Around me————————————————
————————————————————————
————————————————————————
————————————————————————
————————————————. But that is all I can tell you. It's all I know myself. We've been told to stay inside, the same as when we were in Louisiana and Alabama.————————————————————

—————————————————————

—————————————————————

——————— *and I worry about seeing you, Jen. Will I
ever? Bobbie says I have to have faith, the belief that
you're all right, that you will make it here safely, eventually. I know I don't need to worry.*

   I love you. In the next few days we should———

—————————————————————

———————————————————. *I'll mail this letter
then. Below is a picture so you won't forget me—I know
you won't forget me—I'm worrying again. I'm afraid I'm
aging badly. Mail me back so I know that you got my letter, okay?*

   Affectionately,

   Mom

Ray and I had driven for hours, the road slipping in
and out of sand and gravel wakes. Late February and
March was the one time of year when the highways of
Alabama reconstituted themselves. He hadn't said anything to me either, nothing about my father's death, nothing about the fact that I had shown up in Selma a day late.
In the background Johnny Cash sang, his voice rough and
steady. "A Boy Named Sue" had already come on at least
twice. Each time I heard "Ring of Fire," I thought of my
honeymoon years ago—Jennifer and me hurrying to the
Gulf—and outside of Columbus yesterday when we
pulled over.

   How can desire exist in this place? I could still smell
her hair, thick and black, the smell of cooking grease and

shampoo, her neck, its long curve to her shoulder, the feel of her skin, clothes empty on the floorboard, shapeless in the cornfield, absent now, but what had been here. My arms wanted to reach around her, shield the desert back, but she was on her way to Mobile, and Ray and I were near New Brockton, my grandfather's farm.

The flat desert looked peaceful, especially through the tinted glass of the Suburban, which washed everything violet and yellow. We had passed one convoy of miners and a convoy of dump trucks loaded down with clay rocks that kept spilling over the tailgate like the first heaviest drops of rain. Every so often we came by an abandoned house or a carless diner offering burger and ice-cream deals, or scratched-out signs. We came across fences, too, a few feet standing before stooping to the ground, grass or weeds sprouting toward the sun, hoping the ozone would heal itself. But the land was not as wrecked as the city of Columbus. In fact, every so often it looked as if life might start again, might actually take root.

Ray slowed down. "The Joshua Marion Folsom Memorial Bridge," he announced, tapping the windshield at a small steel bridge that crossed the Pea River. "We're here, Mat." There was a sign for New Brockton six miles away, Enterprise just a little further.

"Any of this familiar?"

The bridge was squared and steeled like a shoe box high enough to hold us. Around it, sand: so in that sense, yes, familiar like everything else. But no, nothing stood out, not Mixsons Crossroads that we just passed through, or the names of other small towns—Clintonville, Tabernacle— leading to New Brockton.

"My family left the area before I was ten months, before I could walk," I told him.

Not even one birthday, was how Uncle Wayne had put it, shaking his head. And the deed, which my father kept under his bed, was my only physical connection to this place, the 250 acres of my grandfather's farm. One plot line ran along the Pea River where it met with Indigo Creek; a pecan grove and pine woods marked the west and north boundaries respectively. I unfolded the heavy paper, careful not to crumble it. I had guarded it in my hand the entire journey, and my sweat had left an imprint in the shape of a crescent.

"We're going to have to follow the riverbank, try to find this Indigo," Ray said. During the summer and fall we actually drove in the riverbeds, but now there was a rill of water, a small fluid stripe inside the hull of what used to be the Pea River. The hull was mucked and dangerous, too soft to hold us. "Give me a land number again."

I had several to choose from, but he needed just one. "Lot 185," I read out loud, and Ray punched it into a keypad. Next he punched in *Coffee County courthouse, Alabama,* and we waited. The keypad was a surveying tool that tracked down old public records, and after a few seconds, the satellite transmission answered, longitude and latitude numbers lighting up red on the display: 85.940, 31.437. Underneath was a small map of New Brockton, and the coordinates of our current position—85.924, 31.448—in white. All morning I had watched the white numbers flicker like seconds ticking from a watch, wondering how long it would be until we had a match.

Ray veered onto the bank above the long sink of the river. "I think it's only four or five miles," he estimated, and put the Suburban in four-wheel drive. The terrain from here on out would be bumpy and winding.

"I'm sorry," I told him.

"For what?"

"Not talking. Being late."

"A whole day late," he scolded, and laughed. "I almost sent a tractor after you."

"Without a driver?"

"Of course. How else would you know it was from me?"

"That would do it," I said. "Tina still says a ghost tractor wrecked her store."

"Everyone tells me that, too. And I tell them, yeah, that was something." Then he turned the radio down.

"So where did you go?" In the background, Johnny Cash sang, *I feel the rain a fallin'; it's swirlin' toward the river's end, still I haven't seen the sun since you left with him*, the guitar weaving in and out like a second drum.

"This is going to sound crazy, but Columbus."

"Georgia?"

I nodded. Jennifer had said to pull over, so I did. For months we hadn't been able to bring our bodies close enough to make love, and it was my fault, my mind on my father's illness. If Jennifer were here, I could keep the distance from rebuilding, keep her from slipping back into the desert.

"So did you get it out of your system?"

"What do you mean?"

"Your father."

"His funeral," I said. "Maybe that last day, being there and seeing him die." I looked toward the truck bed, the silver casket, the simple wooden cross my father wanted as a marker on top rocking back and forth, shovels and tanks of propane gas, all of it rattling under the hum of the motor. I wanted to open the lid and examine his face one more time, examine him resting, the scars on his neck, what killed him.

"You never get over a parent's death," Ray allowed, but his tone had shifted, was introspective. His father and brother had been killed when everyone tried to leave Alabama. But he always said that when his mother left, it was like a death, too. During one of our burial trips into northern Florida, Ray told me that she never gave him the opportunity to go along. "Never even mentioned it. That last day she talked to me like nothing had changed, like she'd be there when I got back from school and we'd eat together before she had to work. It never bothered me that she was a prostitute," he said like he did that first time in the school hallway. When he was in his room sleeping and she was in the next, he layered pillows over himself until he almost heard nothing. "Like being in a tomb," he promised, "and safe." But behind the blank stare and assurance was always something hushed and concealed.

Before Christmas he received a postcard from Nebraska saying that she was all right, and one the next year from Oregon, then no more. "Like circles in water. The pebble in the center sunken and vanished until eventually the circles are rubbed out, too." He told me that as far as he was concerned, she was as good as dead, and after she left was when he decided the desert was his home. "The desert has always accepted who I am. It wants to engulf everything. There's no betrayal—you know what to expect from the desert. And I had to accept it. Not outrun it or outmaneuver it." I wondered what the desert was to my father, this dry land that had taken most of his family—not acceptance, I was sure of that.

"I couldn't leave my father before he died. I don't know if I can leave him even now," I admitted.

"What, you thinking of leaving for the Saved World?"

I shook my head. "Jennifer," I explained. "She wants children—"

"And she doesn't want them here," Ray finished the sentence with a decisive *here*. "I don't blame her, Mat. I wouldn't raise kids in this place." The sun sharpened through the haze, and he squinted his eyes at the ground.

"I'm not leaving."

"Neither am I. I guess that makes us fools." Ray

laughed, pushing his glasses up and pulling the green brim
of his cap down more tightly. "And I've seen the Saved
World. When you go into Birmingham, the sky turns blue
so quick—it's weird how it goes from white to a pure blue
in seconds, and you see grass, at first patches, then fields of
it." As I listened to him talk on about the Saved World, I
knew it was all lies. Ray was lying just like Ms. Jones had
lied to us at school, and I felt uneasy.

"But I don't want to leave this place," he said, "even if I
don't understand it sometimes. Why are we so damn stubborn, Mathew? I mean, look at what we call paradise."

The land was hilly on the bank, packed down, but flat
everywhere else, all sand, dead trees, dead farmhouses and
barns.

Whenever we followed a riverbed, we never ventured
too far from the bank, afraid that we would get lost, that the
flat surface might trick us, a hole in the earth washed out, a
lime sink we couldn't detect. Today the ozone had started
to build a white mist to keep the hues in the sky locked out,
and it was only a quarter till two, a half of a day still left.

Ray slipped me a piece of folded paper.

"Open it. I want you to read what it says."

It was an old map of Alabama. Coffee County was circled and underneath the legend were some words scribbled in Ray's handwriting.

> The stars do live even here,
> Too impossible to find.
> But tonight at least,
> With the funeral over,
> These stars in the desert
> For us to admire.

"I wrote that at Mr. Chris' funeral."

When I didn't answer, he continued, "After Bossey's prayer. All those stars out, clear sky. Do you remember the last time we've had a sky that clear? I don't. It was something."

He was right. I hadn't noticed the stars in months. But as his words burrowed in, half memory becoming memory, I realized that I hadn't truly noticed the stars since Uncle Wayne revealed the sky from his porches, the large wraparounds decaying. Those stars, I remembered, from years and years back, tangled in my uncle's voice, his hands and toothpicks and stories—they were the most brilliant. I read the poem again, looked at the circle over Coffee County, the lead indention so deep, it could never be rubbed out.

"When did you start writing poetry?"

"I'm always doing something. I scribble a lot when I sit around for too long. I've got notebooks of stuff—stacks and stacks of journals. Ideas mostly. But sometimes I get inspired."

"That's why you stay here—inspiration."

"Part of it," Ray conceded. "But what about you? What keeps you?"

"I don't know," I said. But it was a lie. The people I loved sooner or later died around me—their death, my endurance—that's what marked and kept me. I just couldn't tell Ray this.

He waited a little longer, took the map, folded it, and placed it on the dash. "I thought you might want the poem."

"I do," I said, but my words sputtered, and I was afraid he would think I didn't mean it.

"It reminds me of my father," I added, but I was still thinking of my uncle and his porches, the stars, and Fred Astaire and Ginger Rogers somewhere on the moon.

What reminded me of my father was no longer his

dancing, but days ago, all of us near Birmingham, outside of the huge scrap heap, a yellow dog, worn bones and patches of fur, twisting on its arm, its fangs poised to bite any trespasser. So many workers had defected, and not just from our mining camp, slipping past the checkpoints. I had asked my father to go, but he wouldn't. Stubborn, like Ray had said. But why? There was nothing here. And hadn't that been Ray's answer? All this death, that dog ready to bite me even though it would never live again, my father staring down at his boots.

"Mr. Chris would be glad you're taking him home."

I had gotten too quiet, and these trips turned unbearable without conversation.

"My father told me where he wanted to be buried when I was twelve. He made death a part of everything. Told me over and over," I explained, "but he didn't want me to take him." I shook my head. "My father's always wanted me to live in the Saved World."

"With Jennifer in Chicago—a perfect fit," Ray tried to push the conversation, his focus on the riverbank, avoiding the broken trees and carved-up dunes and rocks.

"Is something a matter?" he asked when I didn't respond.

"I'm just thinking that Jennifer will leave me."

Ray laughed, a booming laugh that made me jump. "I said that Jennifer wants to live in Chicago. But she loves you. She's not going to leave."

"There's nothing for her here."

"You're here."

"It's not what she wants."

"Well, I haven't seen it. Jennifer still acts crazy about you, always talking about how much you love her hair and you won't let her cut even an inch." Ray put his fingers in my hair and pulled at it and I pushed him away. "I haven't noticed a difference."

Now that my father was dead, she would expect me to go. *Nothing here*, she would say, *Nothing here for either of us.*

"She won't leave," Ray insisted.

"I hope you're right," and I glanced down at the coordinates flickering, the numbers edging closer.

"Is it really blue?" I asked.

"What do you mean?"

"The Saved World— My father didn't believe the Saved World was blue or beautiful."

Ray looked at me, then back to the bank. "He never left the desert, Mat. He wouldn't know."

"Are you lying?"

"Why would I lie?" Ray charged.

"You have to—just like Bossey."

"I can do whatever I want."

"Then tell me about the Saved World. Tell me what's real."

He paused as the truck jerked and squeaked and shifted, then kept going. "Why do you want to know so bad?"

"You just said you wouldn't raise children in the desert, but you would in the Saved World. Jennifer wants children."

"Look, I'm never going to have kids. I don't want kids—"

"I'm not asking for you. My father said you had to enter that world the right way. If I decide to go with Jennifer, I want it to be right. You can help me."

Ray wouldn't answer, and it was just the radio, Johnny Cash's deep voice pushing forward—that's all I heard.

"I can't tell you anything else," Ray finally said. He sounded defeated. "You just have to trust what I've told you."

"I don't." And suddenly the front end of the Suburban nose-dived. The casket, all the equipment in back, slammed to the front, knocking our seats but not breaking them, not breaking us against the dash. Then the pointed tip of a shovel clipped my ear and cracked the windshield into a wall of tiny lines, a net.

There was a second, a long second, when I didn't move, when I didn't have any power. I waited for the earth to fall and fall, just give in, the glass to scatter up and over me.

But just as fast, we stopped hard, gripped in a slant, and the shovel broke through, sending the glass net down in pieces. The pieces fell but seemed to float, to never touch bottom, and if I reached through, I would touch the same nothingness, the sides of a tunnel with no lights, no possibility of reversing the spiraling sand, reversing gravity, not even the air to lift me.

"Shit," Ray said. "Are you okay?" And my thoughts pulled back inside the cab.

He cranked his window open and leaned out. "We're stuck in a damn washout," he reported with disgust.

"It's all right," I told him. "We'll get out of it."

"No, we're stuck good. It's my fault. I should have seen it."

The smell of gasoline and antifreeze drifted into the truck, and I felt the pressure of the casket—if the seats broke, the casket would pin us. In front, chips of glass dropped over the hood in sharp, tiny splashes.

"Damn," Ray said. "Damn," he repeated, his wiry body jumbled around the steering column, his seat belt keeping him in place. He bulldozed his shoulder into the door, but it wouldn't give. "Nothing's working. Damn this shit—"

"Just a second," I said, and took hold of the latch on my side. I used all the maneuvers I had with the gray Chevy's door so difficult to open until I heard a familiar click, the door popping free, and we both inched our way out like crawling bugs.

Ray turned and felt under the seat for something—a bulky emergency radio that the government agents used. He flipped it on and raised the volume.

"Marco. Come in, man. I need your help. Over." He started pacing the riverbed, his boots sinking down in the muck.

"Marco," he said, and a voice crackled over the receiver in reply. I watched him, my best friend, his cap and head hunched down, his thin body focused on the radio, determined to have his way. Then I looked at the Death Machine. It stood at a 60-, 70-degree angle, the grill smacked completely in the earth, broken glass everywhere, glittering in the water like silvered fish that appeared with the March floods and vanished before April Fools' when I was younger. The Suburban was bogged in, especially on the driver's side, part of the front wheels sunken, and part of Ray's door. Beyond the washout was a plateau of flatland that once had been a farm, had held crops. I wondered how close we were to Grandpa Sanford's 250 acres. And I looked for barbed wires, electric fence, for a house, a landmark of any kind, something from my dreams, but I saw only a few burnt trees, tall and limbless, the devil's spears, harpooning the earth. I thought of Grandpa Sanford's tractor stuck in Tina's grocery. And here we were stuck again. Ray had said it was his fault, but it was mine, too, for asking about the Saved World, for distracting him. I still wanted Ray to answer me, but I couldn't bring that up now.

"Marco's coming," he reported, and mumbled the time on his watch. "Probably going to take him until night, though."

"What if he can't find us?"

"He just has to track down our signal. The batteries are

good in the receiver, and the roads are fair. Besides, this has happened before. Not when you've traveled shotgun, but I've broken down a few times, trust me. Nothing quite this bad, I have to admit." Ray shook his head at the mess. "But Marco can get us out—

"My legs," he said, his thoughts always shifting, as jittery as his body, "I can't stop them from shaking." He wrapped his hands over his thighs, then grabbed his calves through the thin khakis. "Are you sure you're okay?"

"My neck hurts a little," I said. "The shovel nicked my ear. It hurts, but no blood. And I feel like I got punched in the gut."

Ray nodded. "Yeah, I got that ache in my stomach, too. And that shovel—it could've sliced our heads off."

I touched my earlobe where the metal had whirred by.

"So why didn't you call Bossey? I would have called Bossey first thing."

" 'Cause he won't be happy. Marco's helped me out before. I pay him. Bossey doesn't like using government equipment except for mining and emergencies. My business isn't an emergency to him." He added, "I don't feel like getting scolded." Then Ray yawned and stretched his arms. "Does any of this look familiar?"

"We're near the farm. The coordinates had almost made a match. But the landscape . . . I can't tell."

"If we find your family's burial plot, we can dig while we're waiting."

I nodded.

"Damn," Ray said, and I thought he was talking about the truck, our predicament. "Mother Nature doesn't waste time, does she?" But it was the desert. No matter how familiar you were with its pale, bronze horizon, at times the endlessness of it made you breathless.

"You're right," I said. "She doesn't. She's taken it all."

"If a storm comes up, this brook will swell and my

truck'll be ruined." Ray had leather seats, carpet on the floor. I doubted the engine would recover.

He stared at the sky, using his hand as a shield, and I did, too—all white haze.

"There's nothing we can do about it," I said.

"Yeah, I know," Ray sighed, then chuckled. He dusted some mud off his pants. His voice had become wispy, reminding me of Bossey's voice, of small tatters of cloud floating away until vanishing completely.

At least it was March and not sweltering. But the sun's rays were just as deadly, nothing in the atmosphere to protect us.

"So where do we take your father?" Ray asked.

And I wasn't sure. I had no recollections of the family cemetery or how to begin. I strained my eyes—in front of us, debris and white mist fell closer to the earth like a fog.

"Come on," Ray said, handing me a pair of sunglasses. "Let's walk around."

It wasn't long before we hit a small creek, another small rill of water feeding into the Pea River, which we assumed was Indigo. We had been walking on Grandpa Sanford's land the whole time. And down the rill we went for a while, until we found a fence line: three strands showing, buried, then not buried, caught in waves of dust, but never the five full strands my father told about. And an electric fence wire curled around a post—we found that, too. Eventually there was a house and a barn, both fallen, the roofs atop the pile like long war tents. But no headstones for a family burial. The sun wasn't giving up either, beading on us and beading on the land. And the land didn't change, just shifted the top layer of dust when the wind blew, revealing nothing.

I spotted two dead trunks in the yard—two oaks burnt,

as if set on fire, the branches like dried-up roots ready to scratch out the sky's eyesight. One branch crooked down, two ropes twisting tight into the wood, the end planks sheered off. I went over to the trunks, dug around them with my hands until I found a board, a long thin plank nailed with other boards just below, into a string of ribs. It was the hard back of a swing.

"Ray," I said, calling. He was walking around the house, admiring the structure.

"Here," I said. "Let's dig here."

CHAPTER 35

Porch Stories, 2026

"And some nights," Uncle Wayne said, flicking another toothpick off the porch—it looked like a splinter to me, a sliver from the house for the wind to catch and slip into the pitch, "they would come home and sit on the swing. One of those old box swings under a huge pair of oaks outside my window. Your Grandpa Sanford had put the swing up to watch the sunset, glass of tea in his hand, relax.

"I watched your parents from my room, your mother always in a dress when they went out to the Armory dances, your father in his tux, striped pants, hair slicked back. Her hair would rise up and down and the dress would rise, too—slow, perfect motion—and there would be crickets chirring, your father trying to make jokes, trying to impress her.

"I had broken that girl's arm, you know. Your grandfather wouldn't allow me to leave home for eight weeks.

Eight weeks is too much to ride out, Mathew—I hope you never get grounded like that." Uncle Wayne shook his head and scratched the back of it, all that tangled blond hair.

"So after cooking, I watched Chris and your mother at night until the swing slowed further, your father's foot shuffling over the ground, kicking it lightly. Pretty soon they stopped talking, started to kiss, and that's when I stopped watching, went back to my vanity mirror to watch myself. It was like a prison sentence," Uncle Wayne said, and then he said, "Huh," just the echo of the word without much weight to it, but still with a final push.

"Sometimes, I saw the reflection of the moon through the window, and I pretended to bite it, peel it from the sky and stuff it under my long chin with my tongue, hold it there and taste it. It tasted more like moss than cheese." He nodded with a devilish grin. "Then I'd hear your parents laugh, their laughter like boomerangs coming in and out of my cell, and the crickets. The crickets chirring loud. That's when I opened my mouth, let the moon go."

CHAPTER 36

Indigo Creek, March 2044

Ray and I picked at the ground and shoveled a few yards back of the withered oaks to avoid the petrified roots. First we dug through layers of sand, then black dirt, red clay, and rock, and ultimately it occurred to me what I had spent my entire life doing: preparing for this, all those deep shafts into the earth for useless clay rocks, preparing me to dig my father's grave.

Fortunately it was March, not as hot or humid as summer, but the wind meant more sand blew down our necks, and as much as we covered our bodies, I felt water blisters breaking open, saw them on Ray's skin. Above us, the haze had fallen completely, formed a white sheet over the earth to burn our lungs, the taste in our mouths acid and charring, which the water eased but couldn't remove.

But it was over, the rectangular pit dug, our bodies

sweaty, exhausted, both canteens empty. We crawled out, pulled up the stakes and rope, started back for the truck, leaving the shovels and pickaxes for when we returned with my father.

Behind the white ozone, I made out the sun slipping furtively closer to the earth. With night, the haze would lift slightly, and knowing this made the weather feel cooler already.

I inhaled deep, too deep, and instantly my lungs burned as if a match had been lit. I thought of my father's throat, his inability to talk for days at a time, the therapies of steam and mouthwashes to cleanse the harsh burns, warm teas and the slow, slow healing that followed.

"Are you all right?" Ray slapped my back too hard at first, then more gently.

"I just need some water."

"There's some in the truck," he said, and lifted his glasses. He wiped sweat from his puffy eyes. "We shouldn't have stayed in this weather so long."

"I'm all right," I assured him, my voice fading out. Then I used his shoulder to pull myself up and untangle the cramps in my belly.

"It's not much further," he said. "I need to call Marco anyway, remind him about the bridge. He should be near us by now."

Ray was good with distances and time. He knew how to work the two together until they met up like they should, never getting himself turned in the wrong direction.

He dipped his finger along a half-buried wire and started along its path, our boots cuffing the sand, slinging it back. I kept my shirt over my mouth and tried not to inhale much—that was the best way to deal with the burning, the seizures, and soon we reached the hull of the Pea River, could make out the truck still wedged in its nosedive, the fog lifting and diffusing.

"Look, Mat." Ray pointed to his side of the bank. "What is it, you think?"

I turned, at first only able to make out the up-and-down sanded hills. Then I saw what he saw—a group of rocks, four or five large rocks stacked atop one another like wood for a fire, and out from them a thin stream of water curled down into the Pea River, eroding a narrow gully deeper and deeper.

"It must be a spring," he said, and stepped quickly up the bank.

A few steps in front, he brushed his fingers across the liquid, fishtailed his hand in. "It's freezing. Maybe from the storms?" He shook his head, doubtful. "No, it's too cold. Has to be a spring. I thought they had all dried up, but look—" He pointed at the trickle as if he were a boy again, discovering something for the first time. Then he stared into the rocks, the miniature cave hollowed out, black inside, big enough for one hand. The cave seemed to pull in the surrounding air, inviting us to see what other treasures lay hidden.

Ray pushed his glasses firmly up the bridge of his nose, kneeled at the entrance. He took his cap off, filled it full, and sloshed it over his head with a loud yelp. "You've got to try this." His voice was shivering.

Then he took both hands and cupped the water, raised it to his mouth. "A spring," he said. "Definitely a spring." As the cup tilted, the water began to pour and that's when it happened—a flash of gold, a flash of black intertwined like the blunt handle of a shovel striking up instead of down. Ray jumped, and I did, too, the mouth of the snake sinking into his hand full at the knuckles, missing his face, sinking its fangs, then just as quick, reeling inside the cave.

Ray grabbed his wrist and squeezed. "Mat," he said. His legs buckled and he sank, then vomited.

I watched the entrance of the cave. Water moccasin,

rattler, copperhead, timber—my father had taught me their names on his fingers, then Poof struck them out at me, laughing, monsters for a child to dream of. He told me about their poison, the distinct shape of their heads, their attack, their slipping bodies rising from the earth, deadly, so deadly and extinct in our unsalvageable world. Yes, diamondbacks lived out West in dens and in the Newer South above us still lush with rain, but there was no food for them here, the rains often no good to drink, the sun too vigorous, the ozone trapping the earth and strangling. Once, I had uprooted the curved ribs of a snake in the desert, ribs crushed under a wheel, and I lifted its viper head, touching the holes where fangs had been slotted, afraid the crumbling skeleton would grow flesh and strike.

"Help me, Mat," Ray said, but I was in the wrong world—Daydreamer Mathew lost in tunnels, the empty ribs of a snake. I pulled at the bones and they broke into ash—I hurried over to where Ray had called me, following my hand along his arm.

His hand had swollen red and angry-blue, a ridge surrounding the puncture marks. Underneath where he had his wrist clenched, a red and purple streak worked up his arm like a new vein extending to his elbow.

"It can't get to your heart," I said, repeating the words from the first-aid book my father had given me after I burned myself on a stove. Each time I got hurt, he demanded I read new pages from the book as if it were the Bible. Sometimes I had to repeat the words back to him, and I remembered them like I remembered the government laws. *If you can't prevent injuries, at least you'll know what to do*, he declared. And quickly, I untied my boot string.

The book stated: *If you are unable to get medical assistance, treat a snakebite in the following steps.* The steps were always in bold and numbered in red.

I wound the rope just above Ray's elbow, wound and wound it, sealing his body from his arm. Then I fumbled in my pocket for a knife.

"What're you doing?" Ray asked.

"I have to get the venom out."

With a sterile razor blade, slice just through the skin and the bite mark.

I pulled the blade open and rubbed it on my sleeve.

"I can't feel my hand except for this burning, Mat. God, it's burning." He sucked in a long breath, exhaling in jagged spurts, his chest buckling over his stomach like a chair opening, then bolting, smoothing out a heavy line of sweat in the middle.

If the incision is too deep, if an artery or vein is cut—

I angled the knife down, put my full weight on his shoulder. "Don't look," I warned, and slashed the knife in. Liquid clear and white and red-blue began to boil to the top, and I drew the venom through my teeth, spit the bloody fluid out, and drew up more blood with venom and spit back at the earth and more again.

Finally, I took my shirt and wrapped his hand, wrapped it loosely under his thumb, below the knuckles, until covered.

"Ray," I said, and put his arm to the side of his heart, for the book had cautioned, *Too high and the venom will drain into the body, too low and you risk losing the limb.* There were other remedies if the heart failed, and I started to recite them as I undid the buttons on his wet shirt.

Clear the air passage.

Tilt the head.

Place your hands together and press, count one, two—

He was breathing just fine. "How are you?" I asked. "Is it still burning?" But Ray didn't answer. He had passed out.

A rattle hummed near the entrance, faint, then louder— the snake was coiling up, getting ready for another strike.

"Hang on," I told him, and pulled my best friend from the rocks. Slowly—for it seemed to happen this way, though in truth it must have happened very fast—but slowly, I thought, in all my efforts, his body was drifting from mine like my father had drifted when I touched his shoulder, when I found my father sitting in his chair in the house in Selma. Ray didn't respond.

The sun's white glow continued to evaporate the smog, but there was nothing in the desert to help Ray. He had finally caught some bad luck.

I had asked him after the accident, "Why didn't you call Bossey?"

"Don't want to get scolded," he said without hesitation, but Bossey would know what to do, and I ran for the Suburban, for the emergency radio.

Halfway, I fell down in the mud. The water glittered with silver fish. In spring when I was seven and nine, they packed the runnels and kills all at once with bodies transparent except for streaky, thin bones, eyes, and at the center a heart that pumped so quick when you took hold of them in your palm that you felt your own life drain from you, but no one had seen these small fish in years. As I rolled and lifted, they squirmed through my fingers until my balance was good enough, and I hurried ahead.

The emergency radio was on the dash. I took it and adjusted the knob to 21.

"Bossey, it's Mat. I'm in trouble."

A low static rumbled from the speaker, expanding the miles further apart.

"Bossey," I said, and this time the static gapped and splintered.

"What's wrong, Mathew? Where are you?"

"Ray's been bitten."

"Bitten?" Bossey's voice was hollow.

"A snake," I said. "A diamondback. And I can't drive

him. We're stuck in a washout. We need Carson as soon as you can get him here. Can you get him here?"

Bossey wanted a city name, a highway, some location to fix on, but I had to catch my breath. The venom tasted loose in my mouth, tingling as I spit again and again at the ground.

I raised my head and saw a man walking. He was far down the river, just a blur, a black shadow like the sun's eclipse. I strained my eyes, and he vanished.

When I looked back, he was closer, kneeling beside Ray, and I let the phone drop.

"Hey," I shouted. "Hey, what're you doing?" I wanted to frighten the man, shoo him like I would a vulture, but he wouldn't turn, wouldn't acknowledge me.

My boots splashed into the mud. "Leave him alone," I said, and I was near them now—a couple of steps, just a couple more—he looked up.

It was my father, his blue eyes, his face red, his mouth shut tight. The skin of his neck and arms glittered with mica, slipped in and out of my mind like smoke, like wings, yet his eyes remained constant, that blue I had always known, transfixed, full of disappointment.

I stopped running.

"What did *I* do?" I bullied like my father bullied.

The ghost extended his hand to Ray's chest to heal him or keep him from rising, then thinned into smoke and sand, into nothing.

"What did *I* do?" I yelled louder, turning and turning until I was dizzy, like riding the spider, the carousel, the corralled fairs that showed up each May and June when I was eleven and twelve. The ghost would come back, this time next to me. But the dizziness unraveled one line, then another and another line of my balance, until just as Ray had fallen, I collapsed in the runnel with the spring fish, facing the sun, facing the truck where my father's body sat locked and secured, heavy bags on his arms and hands to keep him from leaving.

The fish squirmed over my arms and legs, but I couldn't walk there now. I heard Bossey's voice from the radio, but I couldn't get up.

"You're dead," I pronounced into the haze lifting, the sun pointing elsewhere, the truck crashed in its slant. The mark in my forehead, the mark like my father's, the split halves sunk deeper as if the sun had pressed its finger and burned into my skull.

"Where are you?" Bossey's voice echoed off the bank, the charred trees, and I shut my eyes, tried to remember that I was at my grandfather's farm, the farm where I was born, where my father delivered me, where my mother died, where my parents courted, where my grandfather played his records, where my Uncle Wayne watched all of it and told me all of it. I was home. I was home.

It was after midnight when Bossey showed up.

He found me behind the Suburban, a good distance up the riverbed, with flares to keep my father's ghost away, my body aching from sitting for hours in a ball, my knees pulled up to shield the March night that had quickly turned cold.

Bossey shut the engine and left the headlights peering down the thin river.

"Carson's got him," he said first thing, his voice raspy, no longer distant. "I think Ray'll be fine. Even his hand. I don't think Carson will have to amputate."

I relaxed a bit, though still uneasy. The biggest man in Alabama had finally showed up, and it was going to be all right.

Bossey shifted back and forth in the same place, foot to foot, hesitating.

"Marco went back, too," he informed me.

After the ghost had vanished, settled back into my father's body, Marco turned along the bank and found us. We sat Ray in his truck, and Marco left the flares, an agreement between us that I would kill the rattler while he drove to meet Bossey and Carson.

"Now tell me what needs to be done, Mathew," Bossey said, but he was watching the Suburban. His eyes had a curious look about them, as if he were witnessing a spectacle. Then he turned away, grabbed a jacket stuffed into the dashboard, and tossed it over. "What's left, Mathew?" He wanted an answer.

"Ray's truck," I told him, drawing my arms quickly through the sleeves. "And my father—we need to bury my father. Ray and I've already dug the spot." I coughed, it was so cold, but warm now—warmer and warmer inside the jacket.

"If it still runs, I want you to take the Suburban—"

"I want to ride with you," I interrupted fast, and gritted my teeth to stop them from chattering.

He nodded. "Are you ready to do this? Are you all right?"

"Yes," I said. I could go to the Suburban with Bossey.

Bossey lowered his head and beat his arm against his wool coat to drum out the wind that had gathered stronger and stronger—the wool had been made from three jackets knifed apart and sewn together just to fit his thick body.

"Then let's do it and get back to Mobile. I found a house for you and Jennifer. A one-story ranch set up pretty well—big enough for a generator to handle."

"Thanks," I said, and tried to give Bossey some reassurance by standing without doubling over, without letting the dizzy spells send me down again, but my words trembled, and Bossey grabbed my arm.

"I'm all right," I promised, my voice failing. Soon I

wouldn't be able to talk, and I felt that ache my father had carried in his throat, so difficult to breathe.

At least Bossey was here. I was glad for that, had wanted Jennifer to be with him. She was still on her way to the new mining site, and I hadn't killed the snake—I didn't tell Bossey, and I couldn't tell him about seeing my father's ghost either. It was the venom, I decided, the venom had mixed with my blood, causing the hallucination, the body like a vulture hovering over Ray. Through the entire evening, I was afraid that my father would reappear, his phantom— Not now, not with Bossey here.

I wanted him to hug me, the biggest man in Alabama, grab my neck until it hurt and a red streak was left burning. I wanted him to greet me like he always did, but Bossey had been worried for too many hours, his promise to my father already in jeopardy. I could see it in his face, those intense eyes.

I held on to him as we walked ahead in the truck lights. *I'm all right*, I said over and over to myself until the echoes and words had no origin, no ending, just a circular breathing that gradually worked its way into my lungs. I could go to my father's casket now, lift him, take the silver casket to the oak trees and bury my father as he had wished.

CHAPTER 37

Millers Ferry, June 2044

Once you've been mining long enough, you can measure the distance you've traveled to the center of the earth by the light's cut at the top of the hole—I'm at thirty-seven feet, the sludge pipe sucking the bottom dirt, sinking me deeper. Jennifer is gone to Birmingham now. It's past 2:30 a.m., and I shut the hose to trickling, reach my hands into the wall's honeycomb. Cool, sparkling—the rocks and mud squish inside my fingers. I pull them from the ground as my grandfather and father had pulled the crown roots of the corn the same way. I can feel this like I can feel my father's hands reach out from the mud wall, sand going through them, a field of cotton and corn behind him. He's telling me how he and Uncle Wayne bottom-plowed the dirt, but they never wanted to bring the clay to the top. "Clay rocks are good for nothing but money. And not much of that." I reach for green leaves, the sound of Jennifer's bus hurrying through—the flicker dies.

CHAPTER 38

The Dreams

The fourth dream scares me. There is barbed wire—
the dancer, jawline arching up, alone in the field—heel,
toe, heel, kick. He dances as if there are two bodies.
    The wire starts at the ankle,

> *Tenderly*
> *I love you for*

wrapping quick to the waist, the grass and crops are dead,
sand has taken over, rusting over the eyes,

> *Dream of you every night*
> *The evening breeze*
> *The evening*
> *Say we'll never part—*

the grass is dead, I'm watching his feet—the wire pulls the body across the field, his arms are locked and he is bleeding, but he won't talk, he won't yell, each pull of the wire tearing new skin, feet kicking,

> *Tenderly*
> *You and you alone were meant*

the dancer trying to stand up.

CHAPTER 39

Fatama, June 2044

Dear Mom,

I won't forget you. And your picture—you are not aging badly. Don't ever think that. In fact, I believe you look younger and younger since leaving the desert.

They've taken out too many pieces of your letter for me to understand what has happened in Chicago. But I have received it, so whatever happened must not be too bad—or I hope, at least, now it's cleared up. Your letter is three weeks old. Usually they get here faster. I'm afraid I'm worried about you, too. I want to talk and not *miss any of the conversation, not a single word deleted by the check-inspectors—if I were there, you could tell me everything.*

We're close to Mobile, again, and Mathew's father has died. I think he wanted, that he was ready to die. Mat has become even more distant, what I wrote about. He doesn't treat me badly, but he seems lost. If I could just get him to use his visa and emigrate. I will keep trying, Mamma, but I think, I think I may come without him. Don't be surprised to see me without him. The spring here has been so much rain and still nothing will grow. Nothing.

With love,

Jen

Last week we moved to Fatama, a small trailer several streets over from Main. It was my birthday, and Ray drove home with me. Jennifer had the cake on the table—double-layer red velvet with cream-cheese icing knifed into swirls—my favorite, with too many candles.

Jennifer had bought the cream cheese and buttermilk and eggs from a black marketer. "Still fresh," the man promised her. And Ray and I kept next to the refrigerator, watching Jennifer lay strips of chicken out in a pan of oil, their pink skins curling up white, noodles boiling, and dried bell peppers, green and red, from Tina's grocery, crushed into flakes, and the scent of good things elevated me from the hard night's work, where Bossey had said congratulations on reaching thirty.

In the curl of steam, Ray told me, "Happy birthday,

Mat. Happy thirtieth, old man. Thanks for saving my life—" He told me thanks for his life every time I saw him now. And in the curl of steam, I watched Jennifer work, her body like glass, a replacement of the body I had held in Columbus months ago, the sweat coming off her hair, the narrow strands at her neck coming from the tight bun unraveling.

Jennifer tossed a metal lid into the sink, then a spatula and knife, walked away from the stove to wash her hands. She rushed them under a towel, and looked up, all of her movements with such purpose.

"Happy birthday." She managed a smile, but it faded, the chicken grease rising thick in the air. In a few days, Jennifer would be gone for Chicago.

Our trailer was boxed like a railcar, divided into five tiny rooms, the walls stapled with wood paneling that had turned wavy from years of heat. Only a thin walkway separated the kitchen from the dining-living area. The floor lamps, the lone bulb in the kitchen darkened abruptly, then sparkled back up. In every house we lived in, whenever Jennifer cooked like this, the lights flickered, the generator outside struggling to keep pace. And as Ray talked about the irrigation lines, how fast the Alabama River was turning to mud, Jennifer whisked the food by us, three huge dishes up her arm, cumin and pepper steaming in our eyes.

All the food reminded me so much of my uncle. He always made a big deal out of birthdays—cakes, cupcakes, decorated cookies, everything made of sugar. "I miss him," I whispered, but Ray hadn't heard me. He was already with Jennifer in the other room, the two of them waving me in.

I put my hand up to let them know I was coming, but as I walked to the table, my breathing climbed and faded heavier and heavier in the June heat. Even with the air conditioners, you could never keep out the heat. The lights began to flutter.

"You going to make it, old man?" Ray kept on as I grabbed the edge of the table to steady myself, the candles burning dizzy, swaying up and down, up and down spiraling, drawing blackness, a flood of water from everywhere in the room, flooding out the light.

It's too dark, I tried to tell them, but the water twisted and untwisted, not letting me speak. I breathed in hard, and this time the blackness unshuttered, the light at the center growing full again.

It's over, I promised myself, *it's okay*. But since that day in New Brockton, I had these spells often, the venom still in me, and quickly I sat down.

I blew out the candles, every last one, flattening the light into smoke, yet Jennifer wouldn't talk, and after food and cake and too much wine, Ray began to ramble.

"I'm not kidding about the restaurant, Jen. Mat and I have tons of antiques we've refinished. Enough to decorate a huge place, give it an old-fashioned charm. Come on, Jennifer, what do you think?" Between last night and now, Ray had come up with an idea, had planned out every detail. It made me wonder about his journals, how many stacks he had in boxes, how many were lying around his house. I imagined him writing and writing for hours. When did he have time to rest? The devil doesn't need rest, I told myself. That was the answer.

"They'll love it in Birmingham. People will show up in droves. Especially with your cooking, Jennifer. And you can run it. You've got the business degree. Mat and I promise to stay out of your way. We just need a name, a good restaurant name." Ray touched his mouth with a napkin.

I had to smile. Forget about the checkpoints, our constant migrations, the fact that we would have to find a huge place every time we moved, the awful roads, the heat—

with Ray, anything was possible. I searched his hand for a twinge of pain, but his motion was unaffected, the scar of the snakebite, the two purple dots, the cut I had made—all of it fully healed. Before long, the small dots would dissolve into his skin perfectly.

"I don't want to manage a restaurant."

"Oh, come on. You'll be terrific. A meal like this tonight—"

"I want to have children," Jennifer said, and pushed her fork down. It fell from the table to the cracked green tile.

She didn't bother to pick it up, and she wasn't looking at Ray either—her attention was solely on me.

Ray turned to me also, and together they had me boxed in.

I chewed on a mouthful of cake, glancing up, then down, letting the roar of the ACs rise overhead and fill the room. Maybe in that noise, maybe there I could escape.

"She's always wanted children," I answered quietly.

Ray nodded. "Yeah, I know. But what about the restaurant? What do you think?"

"I still want children," Jennifer said. Then she pulled her bra out from one of the sleeves, like magicians at the fair that would be here soon, magicians with their quick hands pulling rabbits from the Saved World for us to applaud, then watch disappear.

She balled the black lace up, tossed it into the kitchen.

From outside, a strong gust rumbled the trailer. The lights flickered. The winds had been aggressive all June, and at times in the middle of the day I sat up in bed, coming out of a dream, thinking that we were no longer in the desert—we were on a boat in the middle of an ocean, the wind rocking us, no coastline in sight, just deep salted water we couldn't taste and an unrelenting sky.

"What about *Spaghetti at Last*. I like that name. What do you think, Jennifer?"

She curled one palm inside the other and eased her thumbs under her chin. Her dark eyes refused to move, the bones in her face blading sharper at her mouth, refusing to give.

"We could just name it *Ray's*." He spun his butter knife in his plate, a compass turning, turning.

"All right, we'll have a child."

"Not here. I want you to come with me to Chicago, Mathew."

Across the table my father's spirit lifted his head, his eyes opening, and in his wide neck I saw the scars that the desert had spent years engraving. The sparkles on his hands had grown into black cancers, and they bloomed open as he reached across. I pulled my hands away, pulled them under the table, and the lights jumped. He disappeared, but traces of mud and smoke remained. I put my hand out and brushed the debris from the table.

Jennifer stood up, her chair tipping to the floor. "I said I want you to come with me, Mathew."

I watched her eyes, watched them wait and wait on me, not wanting to give up.

When I didn't respond, she bolted to the kitchen, the flow of her black skirt, a pattern of lilacs, a skirt she loved, its flow slapped the table and my arm.

"Drink. Come on—drink." Ray filled my glass with wine, his voice loud and boisterous. "We get him drunk, he'll get you pregnant," he yelled into the kitchen, pleased with himself, as if nothing had just happened. "And I'll get my restaurant."

I heard the faucet shoot full blast and dishes jangle out of place and fall, the lights dimming and fluttering in obedience.

"Come on, drink," Ray cajoled again, so I lifted my glass as he wanted, but Jennifer's skirt had left a mark. I rubbed my arm while I watched him guzzle his wine. His hand, the knuckles, the rake of bones—he was going to be okay, as if nothing had ever happened—no snake, no phantoms, his new truck running better than the last. He was almost fully bald and his thin body had whittled more and more down to a toothpick, his clothes so baggy that they engulfed him like the skin of a raisin. But he would be all right. He would never wither fully. Something in this burning, dying place kept him going.

"Thirty years old. Unbelievable," he said, as if doing it for the first time, as if my age was a triumph. "You've finally joined the club." And he poured himself the last from the bottle.

Ray shook it with alarm. "Is there any in the kitchen? Do you have more wine?"

"No. You've drunk it all."

A silly grin took over. "Well, we have to get some. I've got ten bottles from the 1990s at my new place— You have any idea how much that stuff's worth? Let's head over there. Since I forgot your present, at least I can get us some wine. It's only a few miles. What do you think?"

"Not now," I said. "It's really time for you to go home."

He sighed. "Home? You're not coming?"

I shook my head.

Ray wanted to keep talking, and he would go nonstop until the next shift if I let him, but he would never tell me the truth about the Saved World, not that it mattered. The Saved World wasn't going to save me. It was just another ghost.

"I was trying to give Jennifer something to do," he whispered. "The restaurant idea."

I lowered my glass, poured most of my wine into his. "Thanks. You're my best friend. But trust me, if there's one thing Jen doesn't want, it's pity."

"It isn't pity. It's a good idea," Ray insisted. "Besides, I owe you. You saved my life." He lifted his elbows off the table, raising his hand to show me the proof, and as he did, he slipped from his chair.

I grabbed his shoulder and Ray grabbed my arm, both of us desperate to keep him from falling. In the struggle, we managed somehow to wrestle like we used to wrestle at recess—"King of the Mountain," "For Queen and Country"—until we had him upright.

He regained his balance, and I leaned away, exhausted as if my years had aged back inside me all at once, as if I had aged that quick.

"I'm worried about you losing Jennifer," he said, catching his breath. "I remember what you told me in New Brockton. Is she really going to Chicago? I've been thinking a lot about that." His face slumped, his whole body pruned down in his seat.

"Don't worry," I told him, but when he refused to budge, I lifted my voice, "Drink up. I promise I'm all right." I pulled at the rim of his fertilizer cap. "Come on, partner." Then I pulled his green cap off completely.

He reached for it, but I pulled away, half wishing that he might fall so I could grab for his shoulder, wrestle him, reverse time a few moments until he was in a happier mood. He snatched the hat back, touched the bald spot on his head as if I had offended him, and placed the cap over it.

"Are you sure you're okay?" he said.

"I'm sure."

"Good. I'm not worried about you, then," he chuckled, and the silly grin returned just like that.

"Don't be."

"You saved my life—"

"I know," I interrupted—I didn't want him going the other extreme and getting worked up. "I'm glad you're okay," I said steadily.

"Me, too," and he tapped the purple dots on his hand, lifted his glass higher and higher, as if it could keep going, could carry us both and sail through the roof, locate those stars from my father's funeral that Ray had written about and I could no longer find.

When Ray left, Jennifer returned for the birthday cake and the rest of the dishes. She pushed her chair in, scrubbed down the plastic tablecloth, tailing the wet rag directly in front of me like a fish no longer interested in a baited hook. Jennifer wouldn't talk, and the mud and glitter from my father's hands had vanished, too.

A few moments later, I heard her bare feet in the kitchen—Jennifer rarely wore shoes in the house, especially when cooking. She explained that she felt freer, could move faster—even dance. I listened to her feet creaking on the tile, listened for steps that were recognizable, one, then two, as Jennifer shifted weight from one leg to the other, a rhythm of their own, the dishes routinely clanging from their muddle in the sink. The spigot was going full blast. We didn't have a dishwasher, and Jennifer had gone through every utensil in the drawer, every pot and pan.

I should help my uncle, I thought, looking around for my father, exhausted from his work, napping.

They're not here, I reminded myself.

Then I heard a loud thump. I heard Jennifer yell, and I walked in to find her gathering rings of canned onions and squash from the floor. Carefully, I placed my hands on her back where her blouse and skirt opened.

"Sorry," she said, and let my hands stay. "I'll have to buy more tomorrow. Can you grab me a towel?"

I spotted one inside the refrigerator handle and pulled

it loose, turned the spigot down. The water tank would be empty before she finished, at this rate, and I didn't want to make a special trip to the barrel house just to fill it.

"Jennifer—" I started, then stopped. I wanted to tell her about my father's ghost, how he followed me now, was always here. But how? And how to keep her from leaving? Having a child in the desert was against his wishes. My own wishes were too haunted to ever become real—my father, my uncle, and my mother, even myself when I was younger, myself just days ago, in March, now June, the months themselves—all of us alive and dead—ghosts for the wind to carry and lose, carry and lose in the desert. My hallucinations were the last imprint of that life, leaving, returning, never to fade from me completely. How to tell her?

"I don't want you to go to Chicago" was all I said.

Jennifer didn't answer, just kept at the seeds and broth. She mopped at the dingy floor for what seemed a long time. Then she brought the whole mess to the counter and put it aside.

She walked up, touched my face. "Your eyes look older. This last year . . . you've become so much older, Mathew. Even if you wanted to have children, I wouldn't stay. I would raise them in Chicago. I want you to know that."

Jennifer moved her hand, stared at the kitchen bulb, then out the window at a street lamp glimmering. It was hooked to our generator with a long piece of electric wire Bossey couldn't use, and because of its size, the lamp died out more quickly than the other lights.

Tenderly
The evening breeze
Tenderly

The music was in the walls of every house and trailer we moved into, lingering whenever a gust forced its way into the tongue-and-grooved boards, the tin siding, fleshing out traces of saxophone and guitar, clarinet, the voices I listened to as a child. Since my father's death, I hadn't opened Grandpa Sanford's record player. It sat in a box with his albums, waiting for the turntable arm to be lifted, the clumsy knobs switched on. But even with the loud ACs, the drip, drip of the faucet, I could hear that music.

"Jennifer," I tried again.

Her attention stayed with the lamp.

"Why won't you go to Chicago?" Her voice was even, no longer demanding. "What keeps you here, Mathew? Why can't it be me who keeps you?" Jennifer turned, placing her arms over my shoulders, and threaded her hands around the back of my neck, the white blouse drenched in sweat and kitchen water. "Why can't it be me who keeps you?"

And now her dark eyes refused to let me shift out of their gaze, just like at the table. We hadn't been this close in weeks, months, since March, since driving toward the Atlantic Ocean, not since we pulled over in Columbus. I loosened the knot and let her hair fall thick over my hands.

"I'm scared," I admitted, and the trembling began to build inside—the ghosts, the music, and the dreams, all of it, all of them shaking and shaking me. "You should go see your mother."

"Without you?" she asked. "Why?" Jennifer's voice lengthened and eddied as she brought my head down to her shoulder—her perfume was lilacs, and warm skin, a passage back to my own skin, soothing. "What is it? Why won't you tell me? There's something in you, you won't tell, you've never revealed. Why won't you, Mathew?"

And each piece, each word, flooded with water, twisted and untwisted further into quiet. She left my hands on her shoulder blades—the monarch wings my father promised existed, opening over me, protecting, the gold and black glittering, fluttering like my father had said— and I heard Nat King Cole and Billie and Ella, heard them in the wind rising and falling, mixing into one voice through the earth, through me and Jennifer, no lights, no darkness, completely, nothing here now, completely.

CHAPTER 40

Porch Stories, 2026

"The foxtrot, mambo, and waltzes—your father was a strong dancer. He and your mother had them down—step one, step two, three, four, and swirl." Uncle Wayne stared at his hands, then reached for mine. "Come on. Let's see what you can do. Dance, Mathew. Come on. Dance."

CHAPTER 41

Selma, March 2044

> Dust storm approaching from north Florida. Strong thunderstorms possible. Winds high, 90 miles per hour possible. School, government, and mining operations canceled. Do not travel south. Prepare to evacuate if necessary. Do not go outside. Listen to this station for further updates.
>
> *—WDMZ 1610 AM, 11:05 a.m.*

I pushed open the door, my arms full with groceries that Tina had given me. She was handing out bags from the back of her trailer for all the workers. Years earlier I had been part of the driverless tractor that wrecked her shop, and for months I was afraid to go with my father to buy groceries. Tina had a temper. But eventually he dragged me along and Tina said nothing, just stared at my arm in its cast as if I had been rightly punished. When I saw her now, she asked, "How's Harrison doing?" and "Do you still have that tractor?" Whenever she mentioned the tractor, she grinned.

It was March, and we were stranded just north of Selma, bogged down in rain for three days. Mobile wasn't that far, but the roads were impossible to see clear.

Father sat in his favorite chair, sleeping, facing the window. He had the drapes open to the rain and white-gray light, his mottled hands gripping the armrests like a bird viewing the world from a coop. And beside him on the floor were a stack of books that looked as if at any moment they might tumble.

I placed the bags next to the oven, unloaded sugar, glass jars, and canned vegetables—

"It's not so cold," he said, his voice chalky, unable to swallow.

"Do you need something to drink?" I asked, afraid that I had woken him, and I looked around for Jennifer. She was usually home.

"Wayne," he said, "I couldn't save him." Lately, my father didn't answer me directly—he talked to someone else while he talked to me, someone at the window, by his chair.

"Not that day, you couldn't," I told him.

"You still blame me?" my father asked.

I paused and looked at him, but I could only make out the back of his chair rocking slightly, ticking like a watch, his arms firm on the armrests, a red flannel blanket lumped on the floor at his feet, and the books. When I was younger, the chair had been a strong rust color, yet through the years, it had turned a dismal brown from the packing and unpacking, from the sun and my father's piggish body. More and more the sun had tattered it, bowed the frame, pulling the strings loose, my father sinking into a deep sleep, further and further deeply in.

"Where's Jennifer?" I asked, opening the refrigerator, setting the reconstituted milk on the top shelf. It was an old refrigerator that shook and hummed, cool like the March weather. I didn't want to talk about Uncle Wayne.

"You do blame me," my father said.

"We all had permissions to transfer—we could have left anytime. We could've left before that storm."

"Your Uncle Wayne knew about those transfers. He knew."

"That's a lie." I shut the refrigerator too hard. The door crept open, and I shut it again. "He looked for diamonds so we could get out of here."

"No, he knew," Father insisted. "I loved Wayne—he was my brother, but he was a little crazy. Those diamonds."

"Shut up," I said. "He just wanted to get me out of here."

"That's what I've been trying to do, son. It doesn't seem to matter."

"But he wouldn't go without you, Father. You were the reason he stayed." I stiffened my arms, leaned on the counter—it was covered with sand, and the grit rolled under my palms.

"He was crazy."

"Shut up." I didn't want him talking about Uncle Wayne.

"Shut up, shut up—that's all you can tell me? Your uncle knew about the visas." The chair rocked faster.

"He didn't," I said. "I don't believe you."

"You'd believe Uncle Wayne?"

"Of course I would."

"Over me?"

"Over you any day." And I needed to stop. My father could get too upset, his mind dizzy, the blood in him too strong.

"Did Jennifer tell you where she was going?" I asked. "Did she say anything to you?"

"Your uncle's a dead man and he was crazy," my father said. "A crazy fool—looking for diamonds—killing himself."

Uncle Wayne had pointed to the stars, to one that turned pink that he told me turned blue, and I had dreamed of it and seen it.

"They're real." I hit my fist on the counter.

"Then you're crazy, too," he said. And my father—his

voice began to crack and wheeze, his breath shortened and sputtered—he was having another fit.

When I reached the chair, his hands were at his neck, up and down, his fingers scratching out deep rows from chin to collarbone, deep rows redder and redder.

"Stop," I said, and grabbed his wrists. He had been scratching at his throat for months, inflaming his skin, but not this hard. In a few places, specks of blood spread from the small cuts, and he was fighting, was trying to get his hands back to his neck.

"Let me alone," he ordered.

"You'll hurt yourself."

"It doesn't hurt," he insisted, the ruts glowing pink and red. "I'm your father."

"No, you'll get hurt," and his strength weakened a little. I could smell the sulfur leaving his skin.

"Mathew," my father barked—his voice, his words shaking uneasily, "just leave me alone. Leave me alone, son."

Then the strength in his hands passed, and his head slipped to the side.

I watched his breathing draw in and out, long deep breaths, calmly now and measured, the ruts in his neck quivering. I went to the kitchen for a washrag, soap, and water—rubbing alcohol would burn, might wake him. He needed medicine for his heart, too, but I couldn't give it to him now—and I took some bandages.

"You need to be more careful," I told him, but my father sat at the far end of the room and stayed quiet, facing the window, his chair no longer rocking. I could hear him snoring—lightly at first, then his breathing stopped and gurgled, started over.

"You need to be calm, Dad," I said. "You need to stay calm." But I was whispering, whispering so I wouldn't wake him. What good was it to tell him?

I walked around the counter and sat on a stool to watch my father, the back of his brown chair. Clouds and sun had mixed into bright haze, and from that drizzle, drops brushed against the window, pushed the blurring light through glass, making everything almost silent.

CHAPTER 42

The Dreams

I look up and before me are cornfields, hills that plunge and rise unending. And I'm not wearing shoes, no boots, just toes digging at the earth—the cuffs of my jeans are rolled. I stand, digging up the earth for a long time. I listen to the wind sway in and pull back, bring the new leaves, the sound of corn being shucked along. It's a language I want to decipher, and at some juncture I decide to cross the one fence—its five strands rusted through, my father not anywhere to grab hold, yet I make it over untouched. I wait for the wind one more time to call me forward, then I'm inside.

The leaves slap my knees, my face, my hands, but I am high-stepping and stepping far—the wind rushes from the edge of the field, and I race it as long as I can until it overtakes my steps, and I must slow down to breathe, kick deep in the black dirt. And I know. I know I'll never find a way out of here, but I don't want to.

I sit down, look through the stalks, such crooked ribs blotting out the distance in every direction.

I hear a new hum, but not the wind, the sputter of a plane, a loud boom of it low in the sky. I catch a glimpse of the silver wing, which isn't silver, is red with a black cross, a biplane—the Baron straight from my books swerving overhead. And he is sputtering. A rain of gas slinks across the tassels. I count the seconds all the way to five, then far off—the explosion.

I wait for a zephyr to bring me the smell of smoke. Instead, a tunnel opens at the roots, a loud hum burrowing into my stomach, and I jump in.

CHAPTER 43

Millers Ferry, June 2044

The wind brushes overhead with my father's hands, hard and whistling, driving a plume of dust down the tunnel.

I'm thirty-seven feet, and I fleck the dirt off, pull the top of my shirt over my lips and nose until I'm able to gulp in a patch of cold air. That's when the siren sounds.

"Dust storm," I hear people yelling across the mining field. The voices ricochet off the devil lights, snare their own echoes, weave and split like atoms that the wind chases and tries to extinguish.

And I almost have another bushel of rocks when my light catches a new sparkle, the voices, these pieces of sound falling, gathering like mica, becoming two hands in the mud that wave me closer. I touch the fingers—they're slippery, then dry, they push past my arms, head, and neck, and I know these hands, their smell of good food from the kitchen—"Uncle," I say, and smile—his body wraps around mine.

"Dust storm, Mathew. We didn't get much of a warning," Bossey shouts into the hole, and I look up—flag 19—its red edges flutter, then disappear. The other miners yell, more and more of them, their voices like particles of sound into mica, falling and falling, the siren wailing, the pulleys creaking faster.

"Hold on, Bossey," I tell him. "Just a second."

His boots stop and turn. "Up, Mathew. Did you hear me? Water's out. We only have a few minutes."

"Second—" The word rises and echoes, circles with the dust.

The mottled hands in the clay wall are at my hands again. They squeeze my fingers, push through the mud, and I drop the pan I'm holding. "Diamond," a voice whispers, I whisper, the miners yell, the mica converging, reshaping.

The hose dies, and the wind howls a thick kettle of dust pouring, pouring down over Alabama for good. The shaft has turned icy like nights in winter, and underneath the waders, my shirt turns chilly and wet.

"Up, damn it," Bossey keeps saying—he's having trouble breathing again, and I can barely hear him. He sounds more like the echo of a person than anything.

"But it's a diamond." I'm sure of it. My uncle's hands open a small gash in the wall, and I see his diamond, the tail of a rattler swimming away.

Arms and wrists here—the first words from my training. I know what to do. I dig, dig through the new opening. There is music echoing, the cave widening—Ella, Benny Goodman, Nat King Cole, their hands together, dancing—

How can I tell you what is in my heart?
How can I measure each and every part?

"Up!"

Such elegant voices, the wind circling my feet with its howling, ready to move in steps one and two—

Jennifer's bracelet appears on my wrist. "Come to Chicago," she says, and fades from me.

The bracelet tears into silver and turquoise, spills over the diamond that is just a little further, and beyond that, a dry field, a tractor plow. But my shirt stops rubbing against my back. I can't dig anymore through the mud, the mica, but almost, almost—the diamond within reach, its radiance enormous, burning.

> *How can I tell you how much I love you?*
> *How can I measure just how much I do?*

"Wake up, boy—wake up." Someone is nudging me with fingers dull like hammers. My uncle's legs clamp tighter—a sweep of dust whirls into a storm, the jewel almost in my hand. Its light cuts through my fingers, bones, and joints, spreads into leaves, small stalks of corn, the wind making diamonds of blue sky, pieces of iris shedding new fingers and hands, so many hands to touch, to follow, and several yards ahead, no longer miles, is the field, the gem, palms dancing with palms, Ella, Billie—*Ah, you're playing Billie*—I stretch through the mud and reach—

"I have it!" My uncle's blue diamond. I'm at the cave's end, and I pull my legs across the black dirt until I'm running through stalks, upturning roots and flattening the stalks down.

"Father?" I say, "Grandpa Sanford?" whom I have never known, but the tractor plow is closer, a tiger's tail for catching.

And I want to show Bossey and Jennifer my uncle's

diamond, show them that he wasn't crazy, but the wind sweeps and the jewel falls. I dive for it, my arms, elbows bending, sinking completely beneath the sand—then my boots seal in thick, black mud, and the cave, the mouth of a viper swallows me up, again. The viper closes its mouth hard and bites.

"Chicago." Jennifer touches my face in this new darkness, sketches a line down my cheekbone, the red taillights of a bus vanish.

My breathing stops, sputters. I punch the mud but can't move in the snake's belly. There's too much dust and mud becoming vinegar in my throat.

"Up, Mathew. We don't have time," the wind scorns, no longer Bossey's voice, and another rope hits the nozzle, turns into barbed wire, pricks my skin, drops from my waist into rust. I see the cave entrance—smaller, but big enough for me to crawl through, crawl under the checkpoints at Birmingham, a yellow dog spinning with its fangs poised ready to growl as the wind trembles the ribs, ribs pressed into mud, the field at the end, sparks of mica, my father at the tractor.

"Father," but I'm out of breath, and the dog is behind me, chasing, running as fast as it can.

"Wake up, boy. Wake up."

Overhead, a last thin stretch of light, dirt falling and falling through the shaft, an endless gravity carrying until its echo vanishes, too—

How far would I travel
To be where you are?
How far is the journey
From here to a star?

And if I ever lost you
How much would I cry?
How deep is the ocean?
How high is the sky?

CHAPTER 44

Honeymoon, 2035

By morning we were at the beach. To be August, to be this close to autumn, the weather was clear, actually manageable in the day. In some spots, the ozone had lifted, sewn itself back into the sky, showing off patches and streaks of blue.

I parked the truck at the edge of the giant water, and Jennifer leaned out the passenger window.

"You're too far in," she said.

The small waves collapsed at the tires, the wind sweeping out from the Gulf, catching her black hair, flopping and twisting it into braids.

In the distance, I spotted the abandoned hotels and wondered if they had fallen to the tenth or fifth floor, imploded, their glass views of the ocean shattered, or had they been left undamaged by the sun. In the distance, hotels like small hills, and in front of us the ocean going on and on like the desert without boundaries.

I shifted the truck into reverse, the gears grinding.

"I'll beat you to the water," Jennifer announced, and swung her door wide.

Before I could answer or do anything, she was gone. I snagged on my seat belt, knocked my elbow clumsily against the door handle. Outside, the wind rushed up to net me, keep me, until finally I was able to dip my toes in the brown water.

"I beat you," she said, taunting, "I beat you." I grabbed her by the waist, but she pulled loose and ran back to the truck. I collapsed in the wet sand, the air thick with salt. I had never breathed air so salty. Cool water slipped over my body, slid back, tugging, wanting to roll me out into the deeper gulf.

"Get up," she said. "Come on, get up." She was walking back to me now, and above us, patches of blue building and building.

We staked the tent further up the beach, in case the tides came crashing, because we had been told that the tides came crashing and drowning. If we drove along the shore, eventually we would meet up with miners and their camps. They drained the ocean for minerals, drilled for oil. Bossey told me that over half the mining operations in the Southeastern Desert were along the Gulf of Mexico. But Jennifer and I had driven to what had been a tourist stop, empty now, what once had been Mexico Beach.

"I can't get anything on the radio," Jennifer said, and slammed the Chevy door that Ray and I had tried to fix. Then she joined me in front of the tent, where it opened out to the ocean.

"It's beautiful," she said, tucking her foot behind my ankle. The sky was faintly blue, the sun staying far enough back—it was one of those rare moments in the desert when you could get comfortable, imagine beauty, however dangerously, in the sun. "Do you think we'll find dolphins?"

"I don't know." But I remembered what the miners had sworn to be true—dolphins would abandon the ocean 30, 40 miles out, the waters the hole in the ozone layer had not yet scorched, and swim toward the dead surf of northern Florida, especially in August. Jennifer and I had hoped to catch a glimpse of them on our honeymoon.

"Maybe if we go far enough out," I suggested, uncrossing my foot from hers, and the sand peppered down her leg. The ocean had inched toward us, but other than a few lolling waves, it remained flat, unbroken.

Jennifer gave me a sly smile. "I bet they'll get very curious." And she pulled my arm, pulled until we were both standing, walking, disappearing into the surf.

The water at Mobile Bay was warm and muddy, river water filling the ocean. I hadn't expected it to be different here. But these waters had traveled from the Arctic or the Antarctic, somewhere other than the desert, somewhere with a true winter. I didn't expect the heavy salt in my mouth either or my eyes to burn. Soon we were up to our chins, standing on our toes, and I arched my body into the cold sea, leaned against the waves, and relaxed.

"You're supposed to be looking for dolphins," Jennifer reminded, and I opened my eyes.

Nothing. Nothing other than listless waves, no fins, no bodies rising and falling like the huge whales we had watched on videos at school. I secretly hoped a whale would come up right next to us, tear through the ocean, and harpoon the sky, drench us with rain before crashing back down.

"Maybe we can stay here?" Jennifer balanced her legs on my hips.

"Maybe we should," I said, and she lowered to kiss me.

"I'll never leave you if we stay here," she promised. "I couldn't leave with my mother. She begged and begged, but I couldn't."

"What will we do for a house?"

"We have a truck and a tent. That's a start," she said.

"And food?"

"I don't need food." She kissed me again.

I had to pull away to catch my breath. "I can't exist without you," I told her, whispering, and slipped my fingers through her hair, and the salt began to build in my eyes.

I closed them so they wouldn't burn and dipped my face in the cool water. The wind stopped and became a slow echo, water filling a pitcher, the spiral in my ears, and I wondered, *How can desire exist in this place?* like I always wondered with Jennifer.

When I came up, she was laughing. "You're not looking at me? What is it? Are you trying to hide?" She pulled my shirt up and off, tossed it toward the sun.

"Hey." I reached back, but her legs gripped my waist tighter, the shirt floating helplessly until it began to sink.

I turned around—she had taken her blouse off, too, hurled it even further, and shouted my words, "I can't exist without you," outroaring the waves, overwhelming the horizon.

Jennifer splashed her head down.

"We're free, Mathew. We're free here."

I placed my hands on her belly and worked them up to her breasts, her cold skin not smooth like skin anymore, but still what I needed to touch, to keep. The sky still held patches of blue, vulnerable blue, and the cold rushes of water came over and over.

"We're free, Mathew."

Her face floated in the salt and her hair fanned out in the lazy clip, clip of waves.

And I didn't want to go home. I could stay here with Jennifer on our honeymoon, without food and shelter, forever, for as long as she wanted.

"Why is it you don't talk about your mother?" Jennifer asked after dinner. She had thrown the red shirt back on, bundled her knees. "What happened to her? Did she leave the desert like my mom did?"

We had just finished the fresh purple hulls and chicken livers Ray had snuck out of Birmingham for us. The fire we had made was dying back, and the wind off the ocean swirled, drawing air in from the coast.

"She died when I was born," I said.

Jennifer turned from where she had been watching the coals. "I'm sorry, Mathew."

"It's all right." Whenever Jennifer wanted to talk about my mother, I couldn't. She never pressed me—even now, I knew she would let it go, but I needed to tell her.

"It happened when everyone was leaving Alabama," I said as my Uncle Wayne had said. "There had been a drought for three years, wells were gone, dust storms, and the army's attempt at Fort Rucker to seed the sky had failed. The sky had split open and wasn't going to heal. Then a dust storm came that lasted twenty days, and when it finally died down, everyone panicked.

"Unfortunately, Mamma was pregnant with me. And it was June. It was very hot and her water broke. This happened at the farmhouse in New Brockton—my grandfather's farm. My father called the hospital, but it was empty. He called every doctor in the phone book. No answer. It was just my Uncle Wayne, my father, Mamma, and now this baby wanting to be born. So she pushed and shouted and pushed until finally I dropped, fell right into my father's hands—sixteen hours of labor, according to my Uncle Wayne—and my mother, she was exhausted. She kept bleeding. My father and uncle snapped the cord with a knife, wiped up the blood, and cooled her face with rags of water while I screamed—red, purple, and yellow, my body switching colors they were unable to soothe. My father rocked and talked and said 'Hush' and 'Hush,' but nothing worked.

"They tried to wake Mamma, but she kept hemorrhaging and bleeding. She wouldn't stop bleeding, and finally my father gave me to my uncle. Then my father leaned over the bed and held her, begged her to wake up.

"If a doctor had been there, she would've lived. If I hadn't been born. It's not my fault, my uncle said. It's the government's, the sun's fault—"

"It's true," Jennifer said. "You were going to be born no matter what people did, what the sun did. Just like me."

"I'm just not sure my father has forgiven me for it."

"Mr. Chris loves you."

"But he keeps himself separate from me, Jen."

"He loves you," Jennifer insisted. "He just wants us to go north, to get out of the desert."

I watched the fire, watched the flames lick the wood, sparks flopping upward in the same pattern of river water. "Uncle Wayne's told me stories about my mother, but that's all I know, except whenever I glimpse my father dancing and he takes the invisible air as if he's taking her. He can't leave the dancing alone."

The wood settled into the orange coals, and the sparks twisted into river water, the flow turning black, then ashen.

At the end of the week, we ran out of food, out of drinking water, and we had to go home.

We waited on the beach to see if the dolphins might come, but they didn't make it, didn't flicker to the surface like the sun flickering on the desert, they didn't curl up and down like mining pulleys, horses running full steam and breathless. The waves just brushed and brushed over our toes quietly until night.

CHAPTER 45

Millers Ferry, June 2044

"Jennifer." I keep calling for Jennifer, but the echo breaks and breaks until it vanishes. "Father," a wall of sand falling, caving in. Second one, second two—*Remember, Mathew, to wait five seconds. It's only clumps of mud, just wipe them away—wrist, arm*—the mud collapses into black—"Hold me, hold me," I say over and over, and where is the diamond, my uncle's blue diamond.

Coming out of the hole—one foot on the tunnel's wall, then the other. Easily I lift myself with the rope.

But how did I come free of the mud? the choking sand? the sun? with everyone crying, "Get out. Get out, Mat. It's a dust storm." I didn't listen. There was a diamond in the hole, a diamond to take.

How did I come free? Just now, that moment, my

hands reaching into the mud wall for a diamond my uncle had sworn was here, while above, voices echoed and circled with the dust until the dust became thick, black like Sumner's Hill. I couldn't breathe, and the sparkles, the miner's light—all of it blurred into dust into mud.

For a long time, longer than several days, a week perhaps—have I been trapped that long?—all I could smell were heavy layers of soil, wet, heavy with metal, a circling, circling dust. Then my feet were reborn, began to climb, my hands pulled at the rope—I had somehow managed to lasso the sun—I had become that sturdy, that strong.

And now my feet lift and lift. I pull and pull at the rope effortlessly until I'm out. The hard-hat light has no use with the sunlight and delicate clouds in a blue sky—a blue I have rarely seen except for moments in late summer, my father's hidden pictures, those backdrops on Jennifer's television, at school, what I've dreamed of.

And I inhale and exhale without the sun hurting, scorching. The wind snakes across my body with the bottom sulfur of the ocean as if the Gulf is close again, that time when we traveled to the Gulf of Mexico. The gravity of the waves keeps pulling and pulling from down in the tunnel, where I have just come from—the rope has fallen from the sun into that ocean, but it's only a faint noise. I cannot see the brown water spreading out like a fan into its own desert, Jennifer swimming, shouting.

In front of me is a field of long grass—seeding Bahia. The land isn't as flat, there's a roll to it that catches on itself and falls down in uneven waves. It's impossible to find an end, so I rub some of the clay from my eyes, remove my hat, and click off the helpless light. I spot a tractor with a plow. An old Deere tractor, green, yellow, and rusting. A man is driving the tractor, digging up the land. And it seems far away from me, but I can run to it. I can get there.

"Grandpa Sanford—" It's my grandfather, I'm sure of it. But the man is more shadow than anything—a swirl of dust and black from his boots to his face.

I run. The tractor and plow stop. The diesel smoke rises, then sinks and wools over my eyes. The engine chugs, but the large back wheels don't move. Green and rusting—it's the old tractor my father took with us from mining camp to mining camp until I wrecked it in Dothan. It lasted a month longer and then was useless to drive. The seat with its cushion torn out, the perch where the man had been sitting, is empty. Behind the plow—a ribbon of turned land, clumped Bahia roots, and black dirt. But where is the driver?

And I'm tempted to get up in the bird's-eye seat—that's what my father called it. But the engine is running, and that scares me a little—I don't know how to drive a tractor.

I sit down, flatten my back to the big wheel—the mud on it soaks into my shirt, and I sift my hands through the Bahia, the black seeds shaking off. There's one hill that looks like a whaleback, and the wind comes up, flurries, pushes the hair down on the whaleback.

The wheel jerks forward, and I roll out of the way.

The man is driving again, digging up the land. How did I miss him?

"Hey," I shout, and run after the tractor, but the man keeps going—the flannel coat, the rough hands, a thick blond-silver beard—it's my father.

"You almost ran over me," I say, but he doesn't answer. My legs are getting tired, my side aches. "Dad," I shout and shout. The tractor won't stop.

Then the long stalks of Bahia catch, twist my feet—I stumble and fall down, trying to suck in the air as the tractor hums, slips further and further, hums like Louis Armstrong, like Nat King Cole, their voices cut and split along the wind.

I sit up and the tractor is a green-and-yellow streak now, far down on the whaleback, and in front of me, right in front, my father extends his hand. His tuxedo is pressed, black and white cut perfect to the waist.

He's going to show me how to dance. That's what he's going to do. And both our hands shimmer, our arms, those flecks of clay, our smiles the same as if we are brothers again.

"You almost ran over me." I'm not going to let it rest. And he waves his fingers for me to come forward, but I hold up. I'm not sure I trust him. Is this a ghost? Is this my father?

He stamps his foot. "Mathew," he demands, his voice raspy like an old bull, too familiar to ignore. I walk ahead and place one hand to his back and he places one hand to mine.

"Good," he says, waiting, and then we start.

It is a simple box, the same that I've watched him dance with Jennifer, that I've watched him dance alone.

"Set the rhythm," he instructs. "If you're leading, you have to set the rhythm."

I think of the kitchen, the flashes of mica. Above us, the sun is stronger than any bulbed lamp. His hair is smooth and sparkly, his elbow crooked into form.

"I've got it," I tell him after a while, and shift my bare feet without stepping on his waxed shoes. We're in the Bahia, the smell of freshly turned dirt around us, Bahia swaying, and then my father stops. He looks behind me and I turn. My Uncle Wayne is walking toward us, with my mother in a blue dress of satin, the one from the picture, her black hair, her high cheekbones the same as my cheekbones, our brown eyes—but I don't know what to say to her. What do I say?

Do I tell my mother about Jennifer, who I can no longer find? Tell about the mining, the diamonds? I look for the half picture of Mamma I keep with me, but it's gone somewhere back in the tunnel's dust.

My uncle sits down, my father next to him, and the old record player is in front, the black album spinning and spinning and scratching out violins, piano, a guitar—and underneath those scratches, Nat King Cole's low, sweet voice—

Tenderly

The evening breeze

Tenderly

I need to apologize for coming here so late. But she doesn't want that, I can tell. But what do I say? She steps and I step and she takes my hand.

Mathew, when will you come along?

The bus will be here soon. I keep thinking you'll return from the mining site, go with me, but everything's packed, the trailer is empty. A secret here—before our wedding, I almost decided to go, that it would be best to leave before we married, before we started. But I stayed because I love you, and no matter what the desert did, I told myself, I'd stay.

Even last week when you said I should go, should go to my mother, and I could tell that you wanted me to, even then I wasn't sure I could. It was a start—those words of yours, a gift. Then a few days later I found a line in a poem from one of your father's books. Another secret—while you work, I open his boxes and open his books, trying to find something in the pages, some unlocking to explain who I am in this place. I opened a small book of poems by Naomi Shihab Nye and read this line, "I want, I need immediate bloom." My whole body stopped because it understood what my mind had been unwilling to acknowledge. I wrote the passage down, and as I watched my handwriting unfold with her words, I felt certain I must go, that I could.

When we first married, when the warnings came and we had to stay inside, together we pushed the desert out. You held me, pulled my clothes away, and I pulled yours, our skin a barrier against the sand, but now I dread those days inside together, listening to you pace the trailer up and down, mimicking the wind. And when you do come to bed, I hold you but you won't hold or speak—do you realize how lost you are? One day while you slept, I traced my hand over your body, traced you from finger to foot, and started to cry—the drops fell on your body and still you didn't get up.

Please get up, daydreamer. Get up. I'm going to Chicago, but you can come to me.

There is one more thing to tell you. After you said I could go, that you wanted me to, I had a dream that the wind and sand couldn't shut out or swallow up. I want you to remember it—

Two birds slipped into the desert, our desert, a red and a blue, and don't ask how they got here, it was where they found themselves flying and flying. I hoped that if they flew fast enough, they would find rest, water, or at least hoped that the flight itself, the speed of their wings could undo the desert, its sand and drought, as if flight had that power, that magic, as if flight was suste-nance in itself, holding them, their hollow wings above the sand. Then suddenly the bluebird disappeared and the redbird circled, then fell . . .

For a while, I thought the dream meant I couldn't

leave you, Mat, but now I worry that it means you'll forget me. In some ways I think you already have—you've forgotten something of my presence, of how to hold me. If I could only get you to turn. But don't forget me. Don't forget that I'm waiting for you. Take the visa from your grandfather's box. Come to Chicago.

I have to leave now, but you must know, and this is the hardest thing to write, to write and not be able to say to you, to tell you and hold you after. Mat, I'm pregnant. There. My last secret, my last one. I have to finish this letter now. Please come north. I'll be waiting.

With love,

Jen

Sources and Permissions

About the Author

James Braziel has published short stories in *Berkeley Fiction Review*, *Chattahoochee Review*, and *Clackamas Literary Review*, among other journals. *Weathervane*, a chapbook of his poetry, was published in 2003 and nominated for a Pushcart Prize. He has also been the recipient of an Individual Artist Grant from the Georgia Council for the Arts. He currently teaches creative writing at the University of Cincinnati. *Birmingham, 35 Miles* is his first novel.